THE REVELATION OF GABRIEL ADAM

THE
REVELATION
OF
GABRIEL ADAM

S.L. DUNCAN

MEDALLION
P R E S S

Medallion Press, Inc.
Printed in USA

For Liam

Above all else, have faith in yourself.

Published 2014 by Medallion Press, Inc.

The MEDALLION PRESS LOGO
is a registered trademark of Medallion Press, Inc.

Typeset in Adobe Garamond Pro
Printed in the United States of America
ISBN 978-1-60542-737-9
10 9 8 7 6 5 4 3 2 1
First Edition

Acknowledgments

So much of getting this story from an idea in my head to the book in your hands was made possible because of the efforts of some very special people, and I am eternally indebted to them all. First, thank you to my agent, the brilliant John Rudolph, whose insight and counsel made this book better in every way and to my wonderful editor Emily Steele for sharing my passion for the story. Thank you to all the talented, brilliant book lovers at Medallion Press for being champions of *The Revelation of Gabriel Adam*. And special thanks to Lorie Jones for her sharp eye and attention to detail.

To my family—thank you for your encouragement.

Thanks to my friend Peter Rankine for his honesty in the early readings and to author Mindy McGinnis for her eleventh hour insight.

And lastly, but most importantly, I am forever grateful for my wife, Kate, who endured me through this whole adventure.

CHAPTER ONE

Pastor McPherson crept through the cornfield, his boots heavy and caked in mud. At last he was close enough to feel the warmth of the bonfire's heat in the air. A glance over his shoulder told him how far he'd come without being seen. In the far distance at the edge of the field, he could just make out a twinkle of porch lanterns.

For a moment he allowed himself to catch his breath. Letting a knee sink into the wet soil, he planted his fire extinguisher into the ground and leaned on the handle as if it were a cane. His tar-riddled lungs had struggled to keep up, not helped by the ever-present tightness that constrained his chest, but he'd done well to remain silent. Little currents of pain carried a familiar objection from the muscles in his lower back. *You're too old*, they said, and he agreed.

Stalking through the field bordered on ridiculous, perhaps even dangerous given his age, but there was no way in hell he'd let those damned teenagers get away again. Too many times they'd trespassed onto his land and trashed the field, running down his crop with their new trucks, only to leave behind enough drained beer cans to fill an empty grave. All while their witless parents turned a blind eye.

Not tonight, he thought.

In the front pocket of his shirt, one of the clear plastic corners of a sandwich bag had inched out, exposing its weather-sealed contents. Inside, a 35mm pocket camera blinked its tiny green light, ready for use. Fresh batteries. New film. This time, he came prepared.

This time, their parents will know.

McPherson kept to the darkened rows of corn, well out of reach from the bonfire's glow that shimmered behind swaying tassels and flag-shaped leaves.

Ahead, figures and shadows haunted the field at the light's edge.

Behaving like degenerates, he thought and stared into the darkness. The field was quiet. Unusually so. Typically by now, he'd hear the spoiled brats laughing and dancing, poisoning their minds to the incessant beat of some talentless pop sensation blaring from the speakers of their car radios, but as he listened, only a stillness lingered ahead.

The pastor checked his hearing aid. A high-pitched squeal told him it was functioning properly.

Something didn't feel right. Nor did it look right, either. The light fluttering through the corn was bluish white instead of the orange hue he'd seen so many times cast by the teens' bonfires. Also, the air smelled wrong—crisp and sweet from the crop, unlike the noxious stench that should be choking his lungs by now. Even stranger, there wasn't a hint of smoke.

Fueled by the uncertainty, his imagination ran wild with new possibilities of the light's source. He dipped his fingers down into the soaked earth and wondered what could possibly burn in such wet conditions. *Perhaps a lightning strike.* A spatter of rain began to fall, yet the field ahead glowed brighter.

As he got back on his feet and hobbled deeper into the corn, the intensity of light built until it became like looking into the sun. McPherson shielded his eyes and inched closer, hesitating just behind the last row. There he saw it, exposed by the radiance, a shallow crater surrounded by a grand circumference of flattened cornstalks.

Fear held still every bone, every muscle.

At the center of the clearing, shadows poured from a single burning bush like blood from a wound. They moved with purpose, slithering across the ground as if alive. Buried within the crackle of fire and the rustling of corn came a sound like a hiss through the chatter of teeth.

A sound from something animal. Something predatory.

McPherson's mind raced for an explanation, but when none was given, intuition urged him to go, to leave and find a way back to the farmhouse as quickly as possible. The fire extinguisher fell from his hands and rolled away, already forgotten.

He turned from the light and saw nothing but endless rows of corn and darkness. The drizzle had turned into a downpour, and the porch lamps he needed to guide him home had disappeared behind sheets of falling rain. Without them, his bearings were lost.

But it is so beautiful, whispered a voice in his head.

McPherson's anxiety calmed at its sound.

Come. Stay only a little longer.

Blue flames danced amongst the branches and leaves of

the bush, yet the fire did not consume them. Instead, the bush remained whole, unharmed. Lured back, the pastor found the spectacle impossible to resist. He drifted to the clearing's edge and wondered, as he looked upon the kaleidoscope of light, if perhaps this was some reward for his faith. Thoughts of fame and fortune filled his mind. Removing the camera from the plastic sandwich bag, McPherson took aim through the lens and moved closer to the bush for a better shot.

The instant he stepped beyond the last row of corn and into the clearing, the world seemed to stop. Sounds of the field vanished inside a groaning rumble in the earth. Rain refused to fall, the droplets of water sparkling like jewels in midair. Leaves no longer moved. In the microsecond it took for him to realize his mistake, something lashed out from the crater and spewed forth a stream of energy into the clouds above.

The shock wave bent corn away from its epicentre and vaporised rain as it expanded.

McPherson was thrown from his feet, and his shoulder struck the ground first and dislocated. He rolled, hearing a popping and then crunching sound echo in his bones. Before he could acknowledge the pain, an inhale to the clearing's center, as inescapable as gravity, pulled him toward the flame. Wind rushed by as he grasped for stalks with his good arm, fingers scraping through mud and root, desperate for purchase—anything to stop from being dragged into the fire.

As his feet entered the crater, a vortex ignited around the bush and spiralled upwards like a tornado.

Regrets from a sinful life filled his mind. *The money, the deception. The lust for innocents.*

Muscles seized; joints locked. Indentions made by invisible hands appeared on the skin of his wrists, the marks of three fingers reddening under their grasp. His captor held him, prying his arms open, joining his feet together until McPherson's body took the shape of a cross.

Debris cut through the air, tearing through his clothes.

To his horror, a shape formed inside the vortex and split off like a branch growing from the trunk of a tree. The limb, wreathed in fire, rocked hypnotically as if guided by a snake charmer's flute, slithering through the air closer and closer.

Unable to look away, McPherson locked on the reaching fire. "Our Father, who art in heaven," he prayed, "hallowed be Thy name . . ."

The end of the branch neared his face and burned against his exposed cheek.

"Thy kingdom come, Thy will be done, on Earth as it is in . . ." His mouth moved to finish the prayer, but the words caught in his throat, clenched shut by the unseen captor. He could feel the vise tighten around his neck like a noose, its physical presence undeniable. To breathe became a struggle for air, his lungs starved for oxygen.

Five digits formed, clawlike, in the arm of flame as voices drifted on the winds. McPherson couldn't understand the meaning of the ancient and foreign words, but they hinted at a great rage.

The shadows that bled from the bush had found his body. They crept up his legs, his torso, to his mouth and nose. Under his clothes, muscles grew. Skin tightened, stretched by the expanding flesh, and threatened to rip apart like the seams of a garment. Ligaments severed. Bones snapped.

He felt compelled to scream out, to beg for his life, to apologize for all the horrible things he'd done, but no words met his lips.

A new presence flowed into his thoughts. The light of his world diminished, and as it faded, he found acceptance. His soul quieted, and in that instant, he knew his final moment was upon him.

But before the abyss consumed him, something quite unexpected happened. In the last remaining shard of life before death, Pastor McPherson heard a voice. Its clarity cut through the falling curtain of his mind and spoke one single word. A name.

Gabriel.

CHAPTER TWO

Gabe checked his watch once more and cast another glance to the five-ton church bell. At the top of the hour, the monstrosity's bone-rattling chime would ignite a migraine as bad as any he'd ever experienced. He imagined that somewhere inside the iron resonator, a clapper hung, aimed at the flared rim of the bell's lip.

Waiting to strike, he thought and pulled his jacket tight. Though the sleeping bell looked docile enough, the memory of the first time he got caught on the tower was still fresh in his mind. It took him two days to get over the migraine, and he heard the cursed thing pounding in his head for a week after that.

Wooden beams in the cathedral's belfry creaked as the December wind cut through the observation deck of the east tower. Gabe adjusted the range of his Nikon ED50 telescope and blew into his gloves for warmth as he looked out over New York City.

"Gabe? Downstairs. Now, please."

His father's voice, layered in an English accent, echoed through the marble and granite walls of the cathedral until it escaped through the hatch under the belfry. Gabe wanted to slam it closed. For weeks they'd lived at their temporary home in the cathedral's residence, and yet the man still shouted at the top of his lungs whenever some stupid chore went neglected.

He knows where I am. He can come and get me if it's so important.

On the eyepiece of the telescope, snowflakes no bigger than grains of sand accumulated around the rubber guard. He blew them off and wiped the glass with the soft palm of his glove, careful not to scratch the lens.

"Gabriel Adam," his father shouted again.

Gabe shook his head and laughed. *Sgt Adam reporting for duty*, he thought. There was plenty to be done inside the cathedral. Christmas decorations of every kind filled the church wall to wall. They needed to be boxed and stored. One of the least appealing ways to spend an afternoon, especially when that afternoon fell on a holiday. He thought about his latest report card—perfect marks.

"Don't I deserve a little time off?" he asked the belfry hatch.

Transferring schools during his senior year had been hard enough. Nobody wanted to get to know the new kid with high school nearing its end. And nobody was studying, either. Most of his class had decided to end the year on whatever achievements they'd already earned, their spots already promised at universities.

Gabe would have, too, had his transcript not resembled a jigsaw puzzle. He'd lost count of the number of schools he'd attended over the years as he chased his father's career around the country from church to church. Because of that, universities weren't exactly beating down his door.

He looked out over the city—at the streets full of busy people—and thought of the things he might want to be in life. Nothing out of the ordinary, really. Become a doctor, perhaps. Or a lawyer. Something that would allow him to take root somewhere and build a life that didn't involve traipsing across the United States. All these dreams began with the same first step—get into a good school. One with dorms and a rich student life. Freedom, girls, and parties—the whole experience. Achieving that meant Scholarship, because not getting a scholarship meant Student Loans. And student loans meant Local Community College, or in his mind, the Living with Dad School of Suck.

While in New York City, he'd made some headway with the local schools. New York University in particular, thanks to a recommendation letter from Professor John Carlyle, an old friend of his father who lived in Britain. Gabe had never met him but figured him for one of those bookish pipe-and-jacket types, smoking behind a desk at his prestigious English university. Not that it mattered. He didn't care if the man thought he was the Queen of England, so long as he had influence over the NYU admissions office.

A gust of wind blew a strand of black hair into his eyes and brought him back to the present. He combed it with his fingers in a futile attempt to tame the mop and then readjusted the focus of the Nikon. The tower served as the ideal vantage point to look for New York's rarest animal, the red-tailed hawk. According to his field guide, Central Park and the surrounding buildings were the birds' adopted home.

The park. What little he could see through the buildings ahead looked enormous, stretching clear across the city.

A flash of brown streaking against the snow-dusted trees caught his eye. He grabbed the viewfinder and pointed the telescope across the park, focusing in on the target. Gabe dared not breathe. There it was—a red-tailed hawk circling just above the canopy. With a sudden dive, it disappeared into the park.

Gabe tried to hold back his excitement so he could steady the shaking viewfinder and scan the telescope across the tree line.

After a moment, the hawk soared into the sky and in its talons, something half its size with a wire tail dangling below.

A rat, he realized and shuddered. *A really big rat.*

The alarm on his digital watch chirped three times, beginning a countdown on its timer. *Careless*, Gabe cursed. For the moment, the bell was quiet, but it wouldn't be for long.

He moved quickly, hoping to avoid another migraine. A nylon bag for the telescope lay open with its accessory containers strewn across the tower floor. One of a thousand lectures from his father about the importance of tidiness came to mind.

He hated it when his father was right.

As seconds ticked away, Gabe picked up all the loose items and shoved them into pouches on the bag. He then removed the telescope from its tripod and broke it down, but the thickness of the gloves made the effort clumsy. With some struggle, he managed to get it into its sheath.

Gabe checked his watch again. *Just over a minute.*

The eyepiece required special attention. He fumbled with the unzipped end of the bag, trying to separate the telescope viewfinder with his cumbersome gloves. Finally, the piece unscrewed. He reached for its small, padded holder but was stopped cold by the sound of glass on concrete. The lens bounced once on its edge, then rolled across the floor like a dropped coin, gaining momentum toward a small drain that allowed rainwater to flow onto the roof below—its opening just big enough to swallow one very expensive part of the Nikon.

Gabe dove at the piece and caught it right before it disappeared. Relief then turned to panic as another sound, this one similar to a piano wire snapping, came from the yoke above the bell's crown. Accumulated snow and ice fell from the crown, disappearing through the open hatch below. Noises from the clinking gears in the belfry sung in rhythm as cords and cables pulled tight.

The sleeping giant had awakened.

Gabe ripped a glove off with his teeth and crammed the eyepiece into its proper container. With the shoulder strap of the gear bag cinched tight to his body, he ran to the hatch and squeezed through, closing it behind him. He began to climb down the ladder, careful not to slip on the icy rungs.

As the digital timer on his watch beeped wildly, the tower came alive with a chorus of moving arms and clinking levers. Cables traveled through the innards of the giant machine, louder and louder until finally there was only one nearly inaudible sound: the hush of a five-ton metal bell swinging through the air.

He hooked his arms through the rungs and held tight, his

teeth still clenched on the glove. The clapper punched the lip of the bell's mouth and sent a sonic boom echoing down the chasm of the tower with a concussion that nearly shook him to the ground.

It struck again. Ice fell from the slits above. With every strike, his brain swelled and contracted. An acute pain pulsed from the back of his skull, creeping forward through his head.

Finally, the assault stopped, though phantom bells still rang in his ears. Gabe opened his eyes to a swirl of vertigo. His stomach turned, a sickness spreading through his body. He loosened his grip on the ladder and slowly made his way to the floor.

According to the bell, the time was four o'clock. His head thumped like the inside of a drum. While the room spun, a feeling of nausea grew in his gut. Gabe braced against the wall, hoping he wouldn't fall over. A sharpening pain at the back of his skull began in tiny bursts. Being out of commission for another two days with an unbearable migraine was not an experience he wished to revisit. Deep breaths helped steady the sick feeling, but he feared the damage was done.

From his pocket he pulled out a pill the size of a grape and tossed it into his mouth. He hesitated, reluctant, and then bit down, crunching it open. The bitter taste soured on his tongue, and he gagged, fighting the chalky substance down his throat.

With any luck, the medication would force the migraine into retreat.

When the room stopped spinning, he set off for the sanctuary, hoping his father's lecture would be more tolerable than the headache.

CHAPTER THREE

The interior of the cathedral loomed with a design that paid homage to gothic masonry used in Europe's medieval churches. At least, that's what Gabe's father had told him in their first days at the church. Walls built from large block stone descended from vaulted ceilings to meet hardwood floors. Antique light fixtures kept the hallways lit, though their illumination provided little warmth to make the décor feel hospitable. Silver tinsel and red holiday bows adorned their iron housings but only looked desperate amongst the gloom.

A quick succession of hallways led to the dimly lit foyer and the back entrance to the sanctuary used by staff. The effect of the lighting suggested that a certain degree of seriousness was required to enter. Gabe often teased his dad that his sermons were solemn enough. "Mood lighting isn't necessary," he'd say.

He stood in front of the closed door to the sanctuary, reluctant to enter. With every step on the hardwood, the loud patter of his shoes had announced his arrival. His father had undoubtedly used the time to strategize another lecture on responsibility.

Gabe took a breath and opened the door.

His father, Joseph, stood atop a stepladder, taking down a string of tinsel draped over a large suspended gold cross that hung above the pulpit. He wore a black Anglican clerical shirt with a white neckband and blue jeans, awkwardly mismatched, in Gabe's opinion, with hospital-white sneakers. Thick hair cascaded around a thin face. Though he was fifty-two, there was hardly any indication of gray.

"I hope it isn't too inconvenient for you to join us," his father said in a Manchester accent diluted by his years of living in America. He finished coiling the roll of tinsel and handed it down to his intern, Richard, who stretched up like a baby bird in a nest waiting to be fed by its mother.

"Inconvenient?" Gabe said. "It's Christmas break. The operative word there being *break*."

Richard packed the tinsel into the box below the ladder. His scowl suggested he was disappointed by Gabe's intrusion. Richard came from a nearby school of divinity to learn the practicalities of the seminary and help out with odd jobs over the holiday. Gabe had decided that he seemed nice enough, but they had little in common. Richard always wanted to engage in theological discussions, which Gabe found to be a complete bore. After countless attempts at these conversations, Richard had begun to act as though Gabe were a pest, interfering with time spent with Gabe's father.

On the plus side, the intern managed to divide his father's attention, a benefit during times of housecleaning and other officially boring cathedral business. For that, Gabe was thankful, though he couldn't see a way out of tonight's project.

Countless bows, tinsel, and poinsettias decorated the sanctuary. Some simple math told him getting everything down and stowed could take all night, but he resisted the instinct to debate his father about evening plans. He walked past rows of wooden pews and plopped down on the last one closest to the stage, usually reserved for deacons.

"By the way, if you keep screaming like a banshee you're going to blow it for Sunday service. You'll lose your voice, and, *heaven forbid*, souls might be lost," Gabe said with a laugh. "You knew where I was. All you had to do was come to the tower." He motioned to Richard. "Or send him. I'm only up there, like, every day after school."

His father furrowed his brow, unaffected by Gabe's attempt at charm.

Richard placed a ribbon into the cardboard box and bowed out of the conversation, as he did every time a confrontation was about to occur. "I'll go see if we have any extra boxes in the back, Father," he said.

The way he said "Father" always made Gabe cringe. It was almost like a challenge, as if he was trying to stake claim to the word.

"I accept that you are prone to being messy and unorganized, Gabe. Your room is a testament to that. But you live *here*, too," his father said and pointed to the cathedral's painted ceiling. "You can help with managing the common areas as well, especially when we're shorthanded for the holiday. I need your participation, not your petulance or wit. Would you care for another apology for my endless dedication to making your life miserable, or would you for once act like an adult and perhaps accept that you may have to make some sacrifices just a few months longer while my profession provides food for your table and a roof over your head?"

The guilt card. It worked every time. "Fine. Sorry." Gabe found a box and removed a red bow from the pew. Thoughts turned to outstanding university admission letters. "Did the mail run today?"

"No. Not until January 2, I would imagine."

"When do you think I'll hear from NYU?"

"Oh, any day now. Your grades are spot-on. Don't go worrying yourself sick about getting in."

"And you're sure that the admissions board received the recommendation letter from your friend in England?"

"Positive. In fact, Carlyle relayed to me a conversation he had with one of their board members, which if I recall, went quite favorably." His father stopped packing a ribbon and seemed to stare at the box, as if considering something. "Have you had time to catch up on your Bible studies?"

Gabe felt the muscles in his jaw tighten at the mention of his father's extracurricular assignments. "I was a little busy with finals before the break and would rather not do them over the holidays. I've told you this. A thousand times at least."

"These studies are important. You need—"

"I don't see how," Gabe said, and his face flushed. "I don't want to be a minister or some religious historian. I'm sick of everything being so goddamned—" He caught himself as soon as he said it. The word echoed off the pillars and walls.

His dad didn't make a sound. He simply lowered his head and turned his back to him.

Gabe found it hard to swallow. "I'm sorry. It's just that . . ."

"I accept that you are drifting away from the church. You're seventeen. There isn't much I can do about the way you think, though perhaps I bear some responsibility for it. I also accept that you are interested in ideas that fall outside the doctrine of my religion. Nothing I can do about that, either." He looked at Gabe, the lines on his face hardening. "But what *you* will accept is that while you are here, you are still living under *my* roof. You will do as *I* say, without question. Chores and Bible studies included. I want five pages from one of the assignments you are delinquent, typed and placed on my desk by midmorning tomorrow."

"But it's New Year's Eve. I was going to check out Times Square."

"Then you best get started as soon as we finish boxing these decorations," his father said, and the discussion was over.

CHAPTER FOUR

The packed snow crunched with every bitter step Gabe took as he crossed the street. In thicker patches, the ice under his boots would squeak, causing his skin to prickle as if someone had dragged fingernails down a chalkboard, an effect that encouraged the headache at the base of his skull.

Freaking holiday homework. Unbelievable, he thought and adjusted the bulk of his backpack on his shoulders. The straps dug into his neck so heavy, it felt like the tower bell itself had been zipped inside.

He loved his father but hated being a preacher's son—especially a preacher who went to extraordinary lengths to tether him to a religious culture he cared nothing about. The Bible studies were ridiculous and childish—some archaic holdover from his elementary school days. Why his father still insisted on them, he'd never know. Mostly, the subjects covered books from the Old Testament. They were cumbersome to read, difficult to understand, and totally unrealistic in his opinion. As a metaphor? Sure, he got it. But as a definitive holy document? He couldn't see how.

He remembered a recent argument he'd had with his

father after watching a documentary on how the Roman government assembled the Bible.

"How can you think science is wrong about evolution when Darwin's Galapagos study proved it?" Gabe had asked. "You have to admit, that sort of questions the religion's authority to speak about it."

"Darwin's study is only *theory*. All science is."

"Theory based on facts."

"Whose facts? The Bible tells us that God created the world as we find it today. You have to keep faith that some things are true, despite society's attempts to undermine what you believe," his dad said.

It was always the same fallback—*it is written in the Bible.*

"But the books of the Bible were written and chosen by men, not God. Just because some anti-Semitic bishop in the second century decided that Matthew, Mark, Luke, and John were the only Gospels that deserved to be read because of an infatuation with the number four doesn't mean God had anything to do with it. I mean, the guy literally believed four *actual* pillars at the corners of the Earth held up the sky."

"You are referring to Irenaeus of Lyon, and his decree in the year 170. An anti-Semite, I think not. Is it safe to assume you'll also point to Athanasius's 39th Easter Letter as the reason Rome adopted the twenty-seven books of the New Testament as further evidence of the lack of God's involvement?"

"Sure. Why not? It happened, like, three hundred years after Jesus died. On top of that, you've got a pagan emperor and a governor's council deciding which books met Rome's standard to be in the Bible. I don't know much about politics, but isn't that like a state run religion?"

"Is it too much to have faith that God worked *through* these politicians? That his divine hand *guided* these men in their decisions?"

Their debates were always circular—two opposing ideas and no middle ground.

As Gabe descended into the subway station, he considered the widening gap of ideology between himself and his father. Thankfully, he wouldn't have to deal with these theological mind benders much longer. Once he got into college, he planned to take a long break from the church and purge his brain of all the confusion.

A nice college kegger might be just the cure, he thought.

Every time the subway train got up to speed, Gabe felt like a little kid. He still got a cheap thrill out of the ride, even with his lingering headache. He remembered flying into New York for the first time, sitting with his father on the plane as he fondly recalled the London Underground and excitedly talked about living in a place that mirrored London's cultural diversity. It had been a rare moment of informality with his father, one that Gabe wished he shared with him more often, but it seemed as he got closer to graduation, his father's concern about Bible studies and his responsibilities at the cathedral had begun to overwhelm their relationship.

Gabe pushed the thought aside and tried to settle into the

commute by reading an ad above his head, but the pictures and letters refused to focus. He squinted and rubbed his eyes, feeling a sudden rush of dizziness. A tightening sensation at the top of his neck traveled over his skin, intensified by the subdued migraine in the back of his skull. His nausea returned. To combat the motion sickness, Gabe put his head down over his knees, hoping it would soon pass.

He wondered if he'd built a tolerance to the medicine dose. Whenever he took a pill, he felt lethargic, even sick, but this was something different. As if a stereo had turned on in his mind to full blast, he felt a flood of pain surge through his head. He must have moaned, because an old woman sitting across the aisle pulled her bag closer to her body and looked at him as if he were on drugs.

Gabe tried to massage the pain out of his forehead. Pulling his hand back, he could see it glisten with sweat from his brow.

His vision blurred, and for a moment he felt scared he might go blind. Through the fog, he watched people around him carry on like everything was fine. Voices from passengers screamed in his ears, exaggerated but also somehow distant. He felt faint, ready to pass out.

But then something changed. Movements of people in the cabin slowed. The old woman became a statue, and the train hardly moved—everything slowing in time. Gabe felt different, too. Removed from everything, as if he were watching the scene from outside his body. Light dimmed. Sounds carried in waves, echoes. The world came to a stop— all except for one person at the far end, standing where the space seemed to resist the light.

As Gabe looked at the dark figure shrouded in shadow, he felt as though all the hope and warmth of life had been ripped away. The temperature plummeted. His breath drifted from his mouth, but it was ethereal, like a dream. It was the same with the passengers, breath seeping out in their frozen state. His heart beat in rhythm to the slowing sounds of the tracks inching along under the train.

The man wore a business suit beneath a black trench coat. Gabe would have taken him for any other commuter except that under his jacket swirling crimson lines appeared, staining the fabric of his white shirt, as if wounds on the man's chest were opening to let blood.

He approached, moving like a ghost between the passengers. Through Gabe's failing sight, he could see that where facial features should have been, there was nothing but a flesh-toned veil. Then cold, blue eyes formed on his empty-canvas face. An airy noise, like the prolonged gasp from a dying breath, hissed through the train.

He was close, only a few feet away now.

Gabe closed his eyes and felt profound fear, as if his life were in jeopardy. If this was a dream, it had become a nightmare.

Wake up, he thought. *Wake up!*

A warmth bloomed on his arm. It spread to his shoulder and chest, flowing over the rest of his body. Sounds inside the train returned to normal, and the empty despair slipped away from his mind.

He opened his eyes and exhaled. The world was once again right.

"You okay, dear?" The old woman from across the aisle

now sat beside him with her hand on his arm. Her touch soft, comforting.

"Yeah, I'm fine. Thanks," Gabe said.

"You dropped this." She handed him the Bible that had fallen from his bag. "I believe you were having an episode." Her smile eased some of his concern.

Gabe wiped his brow with the sleeve of his coat and zipped the book back into his backpack. Wheels under the compartment squealed, startling his nerves and cutting into his throbbing head. The train came to a stop and announced its arrival.

"I get really bad migraines. Thanks," he said, though he wasn't sure why.

Passengers stood and prepared to get off the train. None of them, he noticed, wore a black suit.

The woman didn't seem satisfied by his explanation but dismissed him with another smile.

He thanked her again and waited at the sliding doors. Questions spun in his thoughts about what he'd just experienced. As the doors opened, he hoisted his backpack and ran for the exit. All he could think about was getting out of that station.

CHAPTER FIVE

abe's nerves were all but fried when he entered the jingling door of The Study Habit Café, a small university coffeehouse. When NYU became a realistic option for college, he found his own little spot near Greenwich Village to get familiar with the area frequented heavily by university students. He came often to study or just to catch up on one of the professional soccer matches that regularly played on the café's single television.

The backpack fell loudly on a tabletop, and Gabe slid onto one of the tall chairs. With his head in his hands, he breathed slowly and deliberately, trying to suppress his anxiety.

"Hey, Gabe. Can I get you—Jesus, you look like hell," said a perky blonde girl holding a tray.

"Thanks, Coren."

She took a large step backwards. "God help me, if you get me sick . . . I'm doing extra shifts to cover my Christmas credit card bill. I can't afford to miss work." She raised the round bar tray to her mouth and nose, taking advantage of whatever viral defenses it offered.

"It's just a migraine. Don't freak out," Gabe said. Her reaction made him laugh. He felt better already.

"Oh, good. I mean, sorry. I'm sure it sucks. Anyway, do you know what you want?"

"Caramel mach would be great. Better make it decaf, please."

"Aren't we suddenly health conscious?" Coren jotted down the order on her notepad, then turned and scurried away, stopping to check on a few more tables.

Gabe couldn't help but admire the view. She managed to keep tan in the dead of winter, a trait that, among others, earned a crush or two from several of her customers, including Gabe. Unfortunately, he had become a confidant for her complaints about that sort of attention, placing him, he figured, in the inescapable Friend Zone. Still, she seemed to enjoy his daily visits.

He pulled a paper napkin from the dispenser on the table and wiped the remaining sweat from his forehead. His heartbeat had returned to a steady rhythm, but whatever happened on the subway begged an explanation. *Nobody has hallucinations during a migraine.* Or had he fallen asleep? Maybe it was a dream. He tried not to think about it.

For once, his studies came as some relief. At least they would help to distract his worries. He hoped to read a few chapters and get something legible onto paper. If he went to his father with nothing, any New Year's Eve celebration was off. And if he used the migraine excuse one more time, it was definitely off. "Too sick for study, too sick for play," he could hear his father quip.

Inside his backpack was a mess of books, pens, and crumpled papers. Some were for school, but the rest belonged to the Official Bible Study Curriculum from Hell. Gabe checked his watch. *Not much time*, he thought.

The possibility of missing tonight's Times Square celebration caused his back and neck to tense. He rubbed the muscles and tried to force them to relax. Advice from his doctor on how to prevent migraines popped into his mind: *Avoid stressful situations whenever you can.*

Tell that to my father.

On a worn scratch sheet was a list of dates and assignments. Beside each date was a check mark or nothing, indicating reading he'd done or reading he needed to do.

The first on the list without a check was Revelation.

Coren returned with his order and set it on the table. Her mouth dropped at the sight of the list. "No way. Are you serious? He's making you do his Bible studies on New Year's Eve?"

"Don't rub it in."

"That's sadistic. What's on the menu tonight? Paul's letters? Genesis?"

"You're going in the wrong direction, actually. I'm thinking Revelation. And by the way, your interest in this stuff is totally bizarre," Gabe said.

"I'm going to major in philosophy. What can I say?" Coren glanced around the café, checked her tables, and then sat down. "You know, I don't think I've ever fully read Revelation."

"Consider yourself lucky. It's weird. Certifiably. *Incoherent* would be a nice way of describing it. The whole thing reads like the author took a bunch of drugs and then turned it out. Apparently, it was a bad trip. Multiheaded monsters, an evil woman standing on a crescent moon, horsemen, and wars between angels and demons—it's wild."

"Um, you know all this, and you're calling *me* weird? What's that saying about pots and kettles?"

"The difference is, I'm forced to learn it. For you, it's like a pastime or something."

"I prefer to think of it as an opportunity to become more cultured and learned. But whatever." Coren looked across the room at someone trying to get her attention. "Hold your thought. We'll continue this momentarily. Need anything else while I'm running around?"

Gabe shook his head. "I'm good."

"Shout if you do."

He thanked her and opened his study manual to begin the assignment.

"Can I get you anything else?" Coren asked again.

"No, sorry. I thought you heard me before." He looked up and saw that she was across the room, talking to another table, yet he could hear her as though she stood right beside him.

Suddenly, all the voices in the café amplified. Ambient noises like cups on plates, spoons on tables, talking, chewing, and slurping collided in his head, and the migraine doubled. Every sound and syllable was like a gunshot, each one stabbing into his mind. A heat seared through the back of his head, radiating from the base of his skull. For a split second, Gabe thought someone had spilled hot coffee on him.

The pain spread through his whole body. His heart felt like it was going to beat through his chest. A dull impact hit his knee and then his face. When he heard the table flip over and the cup and plate shatter, he realized he'd fallen to the floor.

In the background of his mind, Coren's scream faded, along with the rest of the world, into silence. As confusion spilled through Gabe's remaining thoughts, darkness like a black shroud pulled over his eyes.

CHAPTER SIX

abe lay facedown on something hard and warm, his breath fogging the onyx surface of a polished floor. He pushed up to his knees, wiped the drool from his cheek, and tried to recall the last moments. Detached memories drifted loose through his mind; however, there was one clearer than the rest—something about the café.

This place was a cavernous room, like a warehouse, lit only by a single domed light fixture. It hung from a chain that reached into the darkened eternity above. Its light covered a small area around him, not much longer than he was tall, and the warmth from its intensity heated his skin to the point of sweating. Gabe shielded his eyes from the glare and looked into the ocean of black beyond the light's reach.

Nothing.

Nearby, another light activated. The fixture buzzed and hummed to life, and in its illumination he could see a person kneeling alone. Gabe stood and so did the figure. *A mirror.*

He felt drawn to it, but leaving the light meant crossing the darkness. For a reason he could not explain, the idea provoked a sense of fear. Above, the fixture sputtered, its intensity fading, dying.

The warmth cooled around him. Gabe tested the floor beyond the luminance with his foot, yet nothing happened. The fixture seemed to have only seconds before it shut off completely. Building confidence as the space darkened, he stepped from the light.

The fixture behind him vanished.

A black void surrounded Gabe. His heart raced, and something inside him urged him to run toward the mirror and the remaining island of light.

A hissing sound filled the air as he ran. It was behind him, getting closer. Panic filled his veins, weighing him down, his legs sluggish with fear. He could feel a presence at the back of his head, nearly upon him, before he dove at the floor in front of the mirror.

There was silence and warmth once more.

Gabe's body shook. He drew his knees to his chest and held them tightly. "Who's out there? What do you want from me?" he screamed at the darkness. Questions continued to twist in his mind, but thinking was so difficult. His head throbbed as he tried to remember what got him here. It was as if he was in a lucid dream, and he wanted more than anything to wake.

In the mirror he studied his reflection, its familiarity comforting. The image seemed to shimmer and change, as if it were reflecting another scene. Gabe saw sky and stone, a bell. *The cathedral*, he remembered. He touched the glass, and a flash of white bloomed around him, blinding his sight.

He was unable to see, and the skin on his face tingled

with the feeling of a passing breeze, cooling and welcome. When he opened his eyes, the dark room was gone. Now he was back at the tower floor of the cathedral's observation deck, and memories of New York came streaming back.

Sunshine beat down, hot like the summer. Wisps of cloud drifted through the clear sky.

Home, Gabe thought. He stood and stomped on the floor. It was solid, real. The view of Central Park looked familiar, but instead of the bare trees and browned grass of winter, greenery and foliage covered the city.

His heavy clothes and jacket felt stifling in the heat. The sleeves and back of the shirt stuck to his skin, soaked in sweat. It occurred to him that he had yet to live in New York during the summer months.

This is all wrong.

As he tried to understand, the buildings on the horizon darkened. A storm gathered over the skyline. Clouds grew tall, an ominous gray eating away at the blue horizon. Their blanket of shadow slid over the city toward the cathedral. It reminded Gabe of a storm formation shot with trick photography used to speed up time.

Winds shifted, gathering momentum. Thunder clapped in the distance, and the church bell groaned in protest.

In the back of his mind a woman spoke. *You are in danger*, she said.

Gabe decided to seek shelter inside the cathedral below. He had to lean into the wind in a struggle to get to the hatch under the belfry. Once there, he threw his weight into pulling it open, but the door wouldn't budge.

The storm strengthened, its crack of thunder louder, closer.

What looked like snow fell to the tower floor, blown in on the winds. Gabe touched one of the delicate gray flakes sticking to his coat. He felt a slight heat as it disintegrated into a chalky streak.

Ash?

He looked to the sky. Flashes of orange and red flickered from one cloud peak to the next.

The clouds. They're burning.

The city beyond the outer edge of the park caught in an inferno. Flames carried through the smoke rising above the buildings.

Dusk fell over the cathedral as the approaching storm blotted out the sun. Nearby, trees in the park burned as a wall of flame sped toward the tower, like an avalanche of fire.

Screams from the streets below lifted to the tower.

The surface of the observation deck became an oven. Gabe tried to shield his face from the heat with his hands as the storm crashed against the cathedral. Flames licked at the sides, climbing higher with each passing second.

His clothes smoldered. Exposed flesh blistered and flaked away. He could no longer breathe. Pain from the heat engulfed his body, dropping him to his knees.

A familiar hissing sound filled his ears, so loud he thought they might burst. Writhing from the pain, Gabe turned toward the far end of the tower. There stood a man he recognized, his business suit billowing in the wind. Blood stained his white shirt in a pattern, the material turning a wet crimson. His eyes, calculating and the coldest of blue, locked with Gabe's.

"You will be undone, Fortitudo Dei. As will it all," he said. Black smoke then flowed from his clothes and body. In an instant he became dust and disintegrated into the winds.

Gabe felt tears stream down his face, his emotions seized by the fear of dying. The full power and ferocity of the storm hit the top of the tower. Rock and stone sheared away. The belfry crumbled and fell, cutting through the cathedral's structure. Gabe tumbled behind the bell as everything he knew was destroyed.

In that moment, his world ended.

CHAPTER SEVEN

I n the endless darkness of Gabe's mind, a small
ray of light pierced through. *The light at the end
of the tunnel*, he guessed, his thoughts awash in
uncertainty. It cut through, expanding to create a
ray of shining brilliance.

From it, muffled voices spoke.

Gabe felt the longing for his mother, who had died giving
him life. He wondered what she might look like, who she
might be. Since he was a child, he had wished to know her,
and now the excitement of their first words lifted his spirits.

He heard a repetitious chirp, like the sound of birds
calling to each other. Somewhere a male finch courted a
female. Gabe recalled being in a cathedral's bell tower,
listening to their songs in a park.

Concentrating, he made every effort to isolate the sound.
The finch sang louder, its tempo quick.

Too quick. Too precise. He realized the noise was something else, not a bird. The more he thought about the sound,
the clearer and more recognizable it became.

Electronic, a heart monitor.

He couldn't remember ever seeing one in person, but

he knew their beat from any one of a hundred doctor shows he'd seen on TV. This one sounded like it was going crazy—furious and fast.

The sensation of circulating blood returned to his body. A hollow wind, like air filling lungs. Nerves connected, coming alive like a million hot needles on his skin.

Fluorescent light at the end of the tunnel neared, bringing with it new and familiar thoughts.

Cold. The frozen subway. Hot. The burning cathedral. Memories of what felt like another life crashed against the shores of his mind as clear as if they were happening in that moment.

The storm. The bleeding man.

Once more, the pain from the final moment hit him as it had in the tower. It felt real. He struggled against it, resisting its inevitable end.

"He's coming around," someone said.

The tunnel's light expanded, blanketing Gabe's vision, consuming what was left of the darkness. For a moment, he could make out ceiling tiles above him. He opened his eyes wider and then rolled them back into his head only to close them again at the harsh brightness. Something soft lay beneath his body. Fingers found a cotton fabric. *A bed.*

I'm alive, he realized.

"Rate?" a woman asked.

"Pressure one twenty over ninety and falling," a man said. "Rate one ten. He's leveling out, Doctor."

"Gabriel?" his father asked.

The calming sound of his voice pulled Gabe into the world, eyes fluttering open and beginning to focus.

Beside the bed, his father sat in a chair and held his hand.

Gabe looked around the room. *A hospital.* On the other side of the bed stood a doctor with a chart in her hand. She monitored a computer screen next to a young man in nursing scrubs.

"What's happened?" Gabe asked.

"You're in the emergency room. Had a bit of an episode, I'm afraid," his dad said.

Gabe tried to remember the last place he'd been before blacking out, but his thoughts were preoccupied by images from the nightmare.

"Episode?" He rubbed his eyes and recalled a woman on a train. She had used the same word.

"You were at The Study Habit and just . . ." His father seemed unable to find the words. "The doctors think you might have experienced a seizure." He smiled, a poor attempt to mask his concern.

"I'm fine." Gabe sat up a bit and felt a sharp pain. An intravenous line connected to a needle in his arm. He reached to pull it out.

"Leave that in, please, Mr. Adam," the nurse warned.

"A seizure?" It all came back. *Coren. The café*, he remembered and imagined the embarrassing scene left behind.

"The doctors say that evidently most of your symptoms are consistent with epilepsy. They want to keep you under observation and run some neurological and psychological tests when you're up for it."

"I thought I'd died."

"Well, I'm happy to report you didn't."

Gabe looked to his hands and rubbed them as if to make

certain of the reality. "I thought I was going to meet her."

"Meet who?"

"My mother."

His father squeezed Gabe's hands. "I'm sure wherever she is, she's thankful that your introduction will be postponed. Your mother, God rest her soul, would want nothing more than for her son to live a full and fruitful life."

Gabe felt the sadness again and pushed thoughts of his mother from his mind.

Soon the nurse finished making his notes and followed the doctor out of the room, leaving Gabe alone with his father.

His dad watched them go and seemed to make certain they weren't coming back before leaning closer to the bed. "I'm curious. Do you remember anything during your episode? Images? Hallucinations, perhaps? Doctors mentioned that sometimes epileptic seizures can cause vivid experiences, which the victims believe to be quite real. Do you recall anything like that?"

Of course he could remember. Everything. He considered telling him but knew how insane it would sound. He'd committed himself to getting into NYU. Telling anyone about the things he'd seen might earn him a commitment to an entirely different sort of institution.

"No. I had a migraine. After that, it's all just blank." Gabe wanted to forget the whole thing. He rubbed the back of his head. The tingling there had not gone away.

His father's eyes narrowed, but he didn't pursue any more questions.

Gabe felt caught in a lie.

CHAPTER EIGHT

Despite the stop-and-go traffic and the irritating crunch the tires made in the icy slush, Gabe felt his spirits rise just from getting out of the hospital. Being that it was New Year's Eve, the staff seemed eager to free up beds for the inevitable flood of those determined to overexert themselves throughout the night, and his father had been helpful in persuading the doctors for a quick discharge. Somewhere in that transaction had been a loose promise to see a specialist on a later date, but that was another day's problem.

Gabe and his father drove along in the cathedral's car with a radio show broadcasting from Times Square playing over the speakers. The host acted as though there was no other place in the world to celebrate. In the background, cheers and laughter nearly drowned out the man's voice, the excitement permeating through the airwaves as everyone enjoyed the festivities.

Everyone, it seemed, except Gabe. He turned the volume down to a whisper and stared out the window.

Despite the bitter cold and the falling snow, no one seemed discouraged from being out on the town. The sidewalks over-flowed with pedestrians. Many of them looked about his age.

Gabe couldn't help but envy their lives. Their freedom.

"I don't think I'll ever get used to the traffic here. It's bloody ridiculous," his dad said, breaking the silence.

"London's not this bad?" Gabe said, welcoming the distraction of some small talk.

"No. It's not great, say compared to Manchester, but it's not this bad, either. One million cars in the city and finding a parking space is akin to winning the lottery." He laughed. "We'll have to go to England someday. I think you'd enjoy it."

A moment passed, the only sound from the radio and the intermittent swish of the windshield wipers.

"Do you miss it?" Gabe finally asked, uncomfortable with the silence between them.

"What? England? Occasionally, I suppose. Oddly enough, it's proper English breakfasts that I miss most of all. You haven't started a day right until you've had a morning fry-up. Mushrooms, tomatoes, baked beans, along with the usual eggs, toast, and bacon. Make that real bacon. Even after all these years, I've yet to become accustomed to the crispy sort they serve here in the States. But I don't miss the weather there, so I suppose it all evens out. Although . . ." His dad looked up through the windshield at the large flakes falling outside.

Gabe looked out into the night as somber thoughts pressed at the walls of his mind. "I feel lost," he said, almost an afterthought, and then turned to his father. "Like my life is out of my control."

The lines on his father's face contorted, and his brow scrunched together as if his seat had become uncomfortable. "Our lives are never truly beyond our control, Son. Certainly, circumstances may dictate what our choices are, but we make those decisions, and they carry us forward. You aren't lost. You're just a teenager with a big, wide world in front of you. It can be scary. I remember feeling the same when I was your age, stumbling through life, with no direction.

"I think that's why I found the structure of the church so appealing. It offered a foundation from which I could find stability and thus, happiness. My parents didn't mind the decision, either."

"I'm not going into the seminary."

"That's not what I mean. Your path is your path. How you are to walk it is up to you."

Fragmented images tore through Gabe's mind. Everywhere he looked, he could see flame. "What if in the end the things you do make no difference? What if everything is predestined and what happens is going to happen no matter what?"

"God gave us free will, the opportunity to be whom or what we choose to be. Good. Evil. Both. This is the human experience, what this whole life on Earth is all about. I certainly don't regret the choices I've made. I never would have been in a position to adopt you had I not chosen to be a part of the church. Just because you can't see the path ahead doesn't mean it doesn't exist. You'll find yours."

Gabe thought of the nightmare and wondered if he had seen his path, but saying it out loud would only make it more real. More insane. He wanted to forget everything about the night, get it behind him, and feel better. He tried to think of something, anything else that would distract his worries. "Do you think my diagnosis will affect my NYU admission?"

"No, but what is important right now is that you get better.

University concerns will take care of themselves."

A moment of silence lingered between them.

"You wanted to see the ball drop in Times Square, did you not?" his father asked.

"Yeah, but there isn't time. And there's no way we could get there, especially in this traffic."

"Well, we could do the next best thing," he said and turned up the volume on the radio. "Just use your imagination."

Gabe nodded, forcing a smile.

The shouts of laughter and cheers on the radio once again filled the car. As they drove, the radio frequency dropped slightly, making a hissing static sound.

Gabe felt the beating of his heart triple. His mind filled with images of the burning city. The sound of the crowd on the radio warped, their joyous outburst turning shrill. Their laughter became screams of pain.

A cold sweat moved over his skin, and he began to breathe heavily.

"You feeling okay?" his dad asked.

"I did see something when I was having my . . . seizure," Gabe said, his confession just loud enough that the radio couldn't drown him out.

His father slowed the car and glanced back and forth from Gabe to the road. "You can tell me about it."

"I don't know. It was weird. A hallucination or something, like you said." Gabe hesitated and looked at his father, encouraged by his stiff upper lip.

He nodded. "Go on."

"I think I saw the end of the world."

CHAPTER NINE

et against the billowing snow, the exterior of
the cathedral was certainly worthy of admi-
ration. The carved stone façade over the entrance portrayed a scene of angels battling gargoyle
creatures, their forms locked in combat, faces fixed
in anguish.

Twin bell towers provided a symmetrical grandeur to the
building and reached into the night like arms held up to God
in praise. Spotlights angled toward each of their four corners
and illuminated snowflakes that sparkled in their beams, giving the impression that the towers were somehow magical.

Below, a man once known as Pastor McPherson stood
outside, examining every detail, the bitter weather met with
little regard. He was taller now, with broad shoulders and a
barrel chest. Gone from his face were decades of life, replaced
by a youthful and handsome appearance.

The long coat covering his black suit ruffled in the wind.
All his senses focused in perfect synchronicity, hell-bent on
one single objective: *kill the boy*.

Richard lamented being at the cathedral this late. *Especially on New Year's Eve*, he thought. But under the circumstances, agreeing to Father Adam's request was the right move. With any luck, he hoped such favor might play into a more permanent position.

Right now there were parties at school raging into the night—even the seminary students knew how to let loose—but he was not invited to them. Not that he would have gone, anyway. The immaturity his classmates so often displayed would be showcased in every way tonight. *Such behavior is beneath me*, he thought and went to lock the main entrance to the sanctuary that led to the street.

The key to the lock hid somewhere on the overwhelmed key chain. Richard counted at least twenty keys on the ring. One after another he stuck into the lock until finally it turned. The noise it made sounded like the sliding bolt of a rifle being cocked, echoing throughout the sanctuary.

Richard thought of a firing squad. *Exactly what I'll face if I forget to do anything.* He then switched off the power to the main lights. The vaulted ceiling disappeared, swallowed by the night.

He decided to return to the office and wait for Father Adam. In the back of his mind, he felt uneasiness grow as he crossed the sanctuary. The hovering darkness above forced a shiver, and he dared not look again. Going through his mental checklist of chores helped to ease his nerves, but the television in the office would work even better. His step quickened.

There was a noise at the front door. A thump and then a heavier bang, like something or someone outside had fallen against the wood.

His first instinct was to stay quiet, thinking they would likely leave if unacknowledged.

But if it's somebody who needs help . . .

"Hello?" Richard shouted at the door, hoping his voice would carry through its thickness. "We're closed for the evening. Thank you." *Vagrants will move on. If there is an emergency, somebody will shout back or knock harder*, he thought.

The door moaned and creaked, as if the wind was blowing against the entrance. Richard recalled something on the radio earlier in the day about a winter storm and wished he'd paid attention to how bad it was supposed to get.

Air seeped through the hinges on the frame. Candles flickered, their weakened flames threatening total darkness for a moment until they steadied, and light returned to the room.

Then silence.

Against his intuition, Richard considered checking the lock. Then another sound—one that could only be made with a key—the bolt inching out of the socket. *Father Adam and Gabriel are back from the hospital*, he thought. It came as a relief, though not without a hint of embarrassment for his cowardice.

Before he reached the doors to greet them, the hinges cracked. The doors blew open and slammed against the wall.

A man in black appeared from the shadows. Wind slipped by and extinguished all the candles by the entrance. His hands were clasped behind him, and upon entering, he turned and closed the door, sealing the weather outside.

"Pardon the intrusion," the man said. Each syllable carried a meticulous pronunciation cast with an accent that hinted at a formal education. He did not approach Richard but instead walked along the outer walls, keeping several rows of pews between them, like a shark circling its prey. "I am Septis, sent by Mastema. I have come seeking you."

"Excuse me?" Richard tried to gather his wits. "The cathedral is closed until the second of January."

"Ah yes. The cathedral. I love them, you know. Their majesty. Their craftsmanship. A challenge to the very creativity of God himself." Septis removed a cigarette from a case and lit it. The flame from the match highlighted his ice-blue eyes. He closed them and inhaled, holding the smoke in, savoring the taste.

Richard took several steps back, away from Septis. Something in the way he said "God" sparked a feeling of panic.

"That is their true purpose, is it not?" Septis said. "A tribute to man's artistry?" He disappeared behind a large pillar. The shadows surrounding it deepened and bled across the walls and over the pews. They moved with an unnatural flow, extinguishing what remained of the candlelight near the door.

"I sense no power in you yet, boy," his disembodied voice spoke from the opposite end of the sanctuary.

Richard spun, surprised by the direction of the sound.

"Unlearned and unprepared. Pity." This time the voice echoed from the growing shadows in another corner of the sanctuary. Each word lingered in the air, mocking Richard with an arrogance of strength.

He searched for movement in the shadows as they closed in, their undulating darkness surrounding him, cutting off escape. "Who are you?"

"I am deception and war." Septis's voice moved from one side of the room to the other.

The shadows deepened at the entrance, drowning the remainder of light. They flowed like lava over several rows of pews and crawled up walls, with whispers of hissing and chattering.

"I am strife and jealousy," he continued.

"No, please," Richard sputtered over the sounds in the shadows. Tears streamed from his eyes.

"I am wrath and revenge." Septis emerged from the thick darkness as if from behind a curtain, cigarette smoke curling away from his mouth, becoming shadow, as if by magic.

Hundreds of red eyes formed in the blackness that gathered around him. Their snakelike voices drowned out the sounds from the outside world.

Kill him . . .

Eat him . . .

Tear his flesh . . .

Break his bones . . .

He wants Solomon's book . . .

Mustn't let him read it, no . . .

Mustn't let him discover its secret . . .

Richard felt something snap in his mind—a primal, instinctual trigger that told him to run for his life. He turned and fled from the entrance, keys jangling violently in his hands. Adrenaline pumped through his veins, his pulse beating in his ears. His heart thundered against his chest, driving him forward. Yet with all his effort, he knew it would not be enough.

Septis leapt into the air, propelled by an inhuman growl. He covered the entire length of the sanctuary and landed with his black dress shoes on the boy's shoulders, driving him into the floor. His neck broke at impact, killing him before his body even hit the granite.

Intoxicated by the kill, Septis took another exaggerated drag off his cigarette while standing on the boy's back. Spreading his arms out as if receiving prayer, he laughed at the image of the outstretched arms of Christ in the stained glass window above.

Some of the ash fell from the cigarette onto his trophy. Septis bent down and twisted the lifeless head to face him. Bones broke and tendons popped in the corpse's neck. Fixed eyes stared back, lifeless, frozen in horror from their final moment.

Near the altar, an enormous metal cross hung from the ceiling, suspended by heavy steel cord. The shadows noticed it, too, and their hissing became agitated.

Septis stepped off the body and went to the altar, hurling it from his way. He tore the cross from the ceiling, steel cords snapping in half and ripping from the walls, and laid it beside the body. From inside his jacket he pulled out a knife and removed it from its protective sleeve. He kneeled next to the corpse, bending low to press his face to its cheek, then placed the point of the knife on the boy's sternum. He turned the head so that the vacant eyes looked upwards to the colored image in the stained glass window and whispered, "Who will dare deny us now that you are dead, Fortitudo Dei?"

He plunged the blade into the boy's still heart with a sickening crunch of bone splitting in two.

CHAPTER TEN

"Slow down!" Gabe shouted.

His father ignored the protest and accelerated the car.

"You're going to get thrown in jail!"

They sped through the city, negotiating the intersecting streets. Turning a sharp corner, their headlights found the trunk of a yellow cab. His dad jammed his foot on the brakes to avoid collision. The antilock mechanism rocked the car with vibrations.

Gabe grabbed the faux leather handlebar on the dash and braced for impact as the car slowed, just short of the cab.

His father cursed under his breath. The panic in his voice caused his accent to become more pronounced. Sometimes, when he was upset or excited, Gabe couldn't understand him at all.

"What the hell is wrong with you, driving like this?" On the dash, Gabe felt indentions the shape of his fingers in the handle. The feeling of being out of control, especially at the hands of his father of all people, was something foreign, terrifying.

Still, his father ignored him, focused only on the street ahead.

They rode the cab's bumper for a calm minute, boxed in their lane by traffic, before something caught his dad's eye. "What's that?" He leaned into the steering wheel for a better view.

"Never mind. Concentrate on the road."

"There. In the sky."

Gabe relented and peered through the windshield and beyond the buildings in the distance to see an all too familiar orange glow coloring the sky.

"That's the direction of the cathedral," he said and hit the horn, causing the car next to them to stop short as he cut in front. The engine revved, and the front end lifted, pushing Gabe back into his seat. The car lurched forward faster and sped around the cab. "Put on your seat belt," his father said. He seemed desperate.

"Trust me. It's been on since we left the hospital." Gabe tightened the band over his chest, ensuring its tension.

They veered into oncoming traffic to get around another cab, but then his dad jerked the wheel at the sight of flashing headlights and swerved back into their lane. The sound of a horn blared past his window.

"You're going to get us killed," Gabe said.

They turned onto a street filled with traffic, ignoring the red light. Cars slid on the snow and asphalt, brake pads smoking in a near pileup. His father spun the wheel again and righted the car onto the road leading to the cathedral. The sudden change in direction threw Gabe into the passenger door, his shoulder ramming the hard plastic.

"We're almost there. Hold tight." He then gasped and stood on the brakes, hurtling Gabe toward the windshield.

The seat belt locked and snapped him back, his face barely missing the dash. They skidded to a stop just ahead of a gridlock of unmoving vehicles swarmed by hundreds of people.

A hellish light flickered behind the buildings. It illuminated the sky and cast the whole city block into silhouette.

Gabe caught a glimpse of smoke behind a building and instantly recognized the shape of one of the towers. "The cathedral," he said. "It's burning."

"Dear God, no . . ."

Ahead, blue lights spun on the police cars that blocked the intersection.

Flames as tall as buildings, both awesome and terrible, burned into the sky. One of the outer walls buckled out from the sanctuary and crumbled to the ground. Showers of spark and ember flew into the air as the last tower toppled, its bell cutting through the burning brick and mortar.

His father put the car in park and threw open his door. "Stay here. Look after the car."

Gabe ignored his father and followed him toward a police officer pushing back the stream of people trying to get closer to the spectacle.

His dad pointed to the burning church and grabbed his clerical collar to present to the cop. "Please. Let me by. I need to speak with whoever is in charge. This is my cathedral."

The officer stood aside and held out his hand, offering a way past. His eyes looked sad, sympathetic. "Whatever you say, pal. But don't say I didn't warn you. It ain't good."

Smoke and fire whipped about in the swirling air currents, casting shadows onto the ground and adjacent buildings. The

orange-lit cloud and smoke and the ash that merged with snow blowing through the air were indistinguishable.

Gabe stared at the wreckage, staying behind as his father disappeared into the crowd. A feeling, like a growing warmth at the base of his skull, anchored to a spot just above his neck and radiated into his body as if something inside him, like a sixth sense or intuition, was sending a warning.

Firefighters at the edge of the blaze had shifted priorities from saving the church to preventing the fire from spreading. Their tanker trucks fired jets of water onto the ruins from hoisted ladders. Rivers of black water flowed through the streets and gutters.

Feeling scared and alone, Gabe searched for his father in the crowd. Police wrangled with the mob of onlookers, and reporters gathered around the grassy area in front of the cathedral, their interest drawn away from the inferno. Lights from the cameras of a television crew cast beams through the smoke. People pressed against a police barrier, their mass forming a wall that blocked Gabe from seeing what was beyond until one of the firemen parted the mob.

The moment froze in his mind like a photograph—Richard's body, smoking and mutilated, hanging upside down on a cross sticking out of the ground.

CHAPTER ELEVEN

A taxi horn woke Gabe. He sat up, squinting at the morning sunlight, and checked his surroundings, half expecting to see the burning cathedral. The car had been moved since last night, where he had retreated after witnessing the horrible scene with Richard. Gabe tried not to think about it as he lay alone in the backseat with his father's jacket draped over him.

Sleeping in a pretzeled position for so many hours had left his body stiff and sore. The muscles in his legs and back felt taut like pulled ropes, ready to snap. He used the roomy space in the back of the car to stretch in hopes of relieving some of the tension.

Outside, the street looked busy enough with traffic and pedestrians—all going somewhere in a hurry despite it being New Year's Day. Most everybody wore a suit.

The Financial District.

A No Parking sign was visible just outside the passenger window. Soot caked the hood, and ash still dirtied the windshield. Gabe caught a glimpse of himself in the rearview mirror. Hair stuck out like he'd slept in an electric chair. His clothes hung in a mess of wrinkles.

His father exited the bank holding an envelope and got into the car. "I didn't think you'd wake. How are you doing?"

Visions from last night returned, the reality now inseparable from the nightmare. "Fine, I guess. What's that?" Gabe climbed over the center console to get into the passenger seat.

"Documents. Passports. As well as a few other things we needed from a safety-deposit box." He opened the envelope wide and offered a glimpse inside.

Gabe caught a flash of pink and blue from two thick stacks of British pounds. A small fortune by his standards. "Passports? What do we need all this for?"

His father stopped sorting the items in the envelope and took a deep breath, his gaze never leaving his lap. "I know our situation has come as a shock to you. All your questions will be answered in due course, but in the meantime you need to understand that what we do is for the best. We are leaving for England to meet a friend."

"I don't have friends in England. I don't even know anyone there, and you said all your family has passed on."

"Regardless, you do have friends there," he said.

"Okay. Sure. That sounds perfectly reasonable." Gabe said, "Richard was murdered last night, in case you forgot. *Murdered.* He has a family. They need to be contacted, his school—"

"I have a grave suspicion that Richard wasn't the intended victim," his dad interrupted. "This wasn't a random act of violence against the church. Premeditated, by what I gather, and done so, as you apparently witnessed, with an unquestionable lack of humanity." He exhaled, as if the words required effort to say. "The symbolism. It was a sign. Our lives are in danger. Particularly yours. That is why we must leave."

Particularly mine? "What about the police?" Gabe asked.

"They will investigate, but their efforts will be futile. The police can't help us. Nor can they protect us from who did that to the cathedral and Richard."

"What are you talking about? What's going on? Look at me, for God's sake." Gabe watched his father, and for a moment he didn't recognize him. Gone was the stoic man he'd known for so long, and with him, all his rational sensibilities Gabe would have expected during such a tragedy. Instead, he seemed nervous, even frightened.

He kept his gaze on the dash and started the car. "You'll find out soon enough, Gabriel."

Gabe didn't understand, but pressing his father for more information seemed futile.

They pulled away from the curb, presumably heading toward the airport.

England. Strangely, it was New York that now felt foreign. Somebody wanted him dead, and on top of that, he was losing grip on reality with delusions about the end of the world. Delusions that looked as though they were coming true. Admittedly, leaving felt right. A fear had been growing inside him like a cancer since yesterday, and he wanted to get as far away from it as possible. Anywhere would be safer than here.

Gabe had enjoyed being comfortably insignificant all his life, and now his life was important to somebody for the wrong reasons. The look in his father's eyes offered no reassurance. If anything, it told him that this nightmare was going to get worse.

CHAPTER TWELVE

From the large bay windows of the penthouse, Septis watched a trickle of smoke at the far end of the park rise into the afternoon sky. He stood shirtless and held the same knife he had driven into the boy at the cathedral. The dried remnants of the kill dulled the blade's gleam, and as snow fell outside, he traced swirling, elaborate patterns, making shallow cuts in his chest with the sharpened edge. In the distance, the still-smoldering ruins of his work instilled in him a sense of accomplishment. But these feelings were nothing compared with the electric anticipation of what was to come.

Black trails caught the wind and moved across the tops of the far-off neighboring buildings. Septis couldn't help his dissatisfaction from the ease of it all. He had hoped for some sport in his effort; however, the boy proved no harder to dispatch than a fledgling from its nest.

At the street below, people mindlessly moved through their daily lives. *An infestation soon to be removed*, he thought. *Now that Fortitudo Dei is no more.*

A muffled cry caused him to turn from the window. His prisoner lay on her own hardwood floor, probably antique and imported from a European château. *The greed of this species*, he thought and laughed once again at her earlier offer of money to spare her life.

She had been stripped to her black underwear and placed in the center of a circle carved in the floor. Her body showed all the signs of a gluttonous life filled with every luxury one could afford, weak and sedentary, though evidenced by several scars, a surgeon's technique had hidden much and given her back several years.

Such pride. How the humans cherish their capital vices.

Flames on six candles surrounding the floor carving flickered as she struggled against the ropes binding her arms and legs together behind her back. Her mouth was open, biting on a thick cord between her teeth.

Septis smiled again and shook his head, as if scolding a child for an innocent mistake. "But you protest in vain, my dear."

Tears streamed down her face, her eyes locked on the bloody weapon in her captor's hand.

"Can you not see? What you are to receive is a gift. An honor." Septis kneeled beside her and stroked away a tear. "This crude flesh," he said, pulling at the skin on her face, "is but a shell meant for a greater cause. I can renew it. Make it younger, firm, something to envy, desired by all. And you will be *worthy*. You should be pleased that I have judged you so."

The woman jerked her head away, her skin pulling from Septis's fingers.

His eyes narrowed in offense and then he stood. "So be it. Perhaps I should kill you here and find another. Someone more suitable. Yes, I can see now that I have made an error in my judgment." He looked at the blade and then at her with a renewed menace, his gaze as sharp as the knife.

She shook her head, pleading and crying through a muffled scream.

"No?" Again, Septis stooped to her side. He ran his fingers over the exposed flesh of her shoulder and through her hair. "You wish to offer your body to me?"

She hesitated, her breathing fast and in short gasps. Her crying calmed and became a sad moan. She nodded.

"That is pleasing to me, my dear." Septis smiled and thrust the bloodstained blade into her chest.

The woman's eyes widened, and with a guttural cough that spilled blood from her mouth, she silenced. Her head dropped lifeless to her chest.

"My master will be most thankful." He cut the binds to spread her arms and then moved her feet together, the corpse now a cruciform in the middle of the ceremonial circle. With a gentle pull, the knife slipped from the woman. Blood pooled under her body.

Once he was satisfied with her position, Septis kneeled at the feet of the body to meditate just outside the ring. He closed his eyes and began the ritual.

The candles dimmed as he chanted, his arms lifting, outstretched over the body. A darkness fell over the room. Shadows grew bold, reaching into the light. They crawled to Septis, hissing, drawn to his power. They flowed over his body to his arms and swirled like smoke out into the air above the woman, becoming a feminine shape before falling to her body. The shadows moved like liquid, pouring into the gaping wound in the chest.

Flames on the candles flickered out, and the ritual was done. Septis opened his eyes. Quickly, he pushed back and got to one knee and outstretched his arms, palms open. He bowed his head. "My master's queen."

The woman's body lay still.

A moment passed. Septis seemed to waver in his curtsey. "My queen," he said, this time louder. "I am your humble servant."

Again, he waited. After another moment, he lifted his head. The woman showed not a sign of life. Septis looked at the stained knife on the floor beside her. The blood of the Fortitudo Dei was to have been the key to granting the pathway to the one who would open the Hellgate.

He moved to the body. The woman's eyes were as lifeless as they were right after he dispatched her of life. Her mouth hung agape. Septis reached to touch her.

Like a geyser, black shadow, smoke, and blood exploded in a gushing pillar from her chest, crashing into the ceiling above. In its fury, Septis heard a woman's shrill voice, angry and bitter, her scream only a momentary presence before being torn from existence, back to wherever it had come.

Septis retreated, crawling to the bay window until the writhing body of the dead woman calmed, her body broken and torn open, lifeless once more, the shadow and smoke dissipating into the light and air.

A terrifying feeling he had not felt in an age burned to life in his thoughts as the pieces came together. *I've made a mistake*, he thought. Septis turned and looked once more to the stream of smoke rising above the city in the distance. *I've made a terrible mistake.*

CHAPTER THIRTEEN

The gentle whine of the 777's engines worked like a sedative on Gabe's exhaustion, but he resisted sleep. Though he doubted the doctor's diagnosis, he figured the best way to avoid another epileptic "episode" was to keep his mind occupied enough so that his out-of-control subconscious couldn't take over.

Stay awake. That was the plan.

The comfort of the business class seat wasn't helping. Neither was the dim lighting of the cabin. With the exception of a few late-night readers, most of the other passengers were sleeping, including his father beside him. Gabe put on the complimentary headphones. He searched the menu on the video screen for a program that might allow his brain to tune into something mindless and stupid.

After several world news stations and one shopping channel, he gave up. None of them held his attention enough to keep the sounds and images of the inferno from infiltrating every thought. He couldn't decide which was worse—enduring memories from the burning cathedral or the visions of the end of the world.

In an effort to stay awake, he concentrated on the things

he missed from back home—Coren, the city, bird-watching, soccer . . .

He recalled playing right wing for his old high school during their final game of the season before he and his father moved to New York. One of his strikers took a hard tackle twenty-five yards from the opponent's goal, and with the blow of the ref's whistle, Gabe had the perfect free kick for his dead-ball skills. The striker positioned himself just outside the far post of the goal, ready to make an attacking run.

Gabe could still feel the rays of sunshine warming the back of his number seven jersey. A two-man wall set up in front of him to prevent any direct shot. He lined up on the left side of the ball, favoring his right leg, and squared the shot. Raising his hand, the play set in motion.

One of their midfielders cut across the opponent's keeper to block his view.

With a precision kick, the inside of his foot punched through the ball, lifting it into the air. It soared over and around the jumping wall, bending from right to left. As it spun, it dipped into the path of his striker's run, just in time to meet his outstretched leg.

The ball rippled the back of the net.

He smiled, ear to ear, while streamers flew onto the field and the crowd chanted his name.

The smile faded. So did the field and the players.

Damn it, he thought. *I'm dreaming.*

Gabe opened his eyes. He was still in his seat, but the seat was no longer on the plane. It sat in the center of a circular pattern of light. Above, a familiar fixture dangled, bathing him in its heat.

It was the same as before. Surrounding the lit area was the black floor that reached into the endless nothing.

With a clanging mechanical sound, another light hanging from the void above came to life, and, as he expected, a mirror appeared. This time he didn't hesitate. He jumped from the seat and ran toward the second light as the one behind him faded.

As soon as he made it to the safety of the light, another fixture clanged to life and then another and another until there were hundreds, even thousands, of fixtures surrounding him as far as he could see, each illuminating a mirror of its own, and each turned to reflect his image.

Gabe looked into the mirror by his side, careful this time not to touch it. Behind his fading reflection, he could see a scene unfolding, a window to another world, another time.

The view through the glass offered a cliff-top panorama of a city spread out in the valley below. Its architecture was impressive, even by modern standards. Ancient domes and pillars, constructed in stonework, shimmered in the desert sun. Enormous walls enclosed the city and defended its perimeter.

"*Persepolis,*" a woman's disembodied voice whispered in the surrounding darkness. Her intrusion startled Gabe, but she did not incite the same fear as the serpentine hiss he'd heard before. Instead, Gabe felt comforted by the sound.

He turned back to the mirror and watched as the scene changed. Fires bloomed around the city's crumbling walls. An invading army fought to take siege. From below came the echo of war cries and the clashing of swords on shields.

Two men dressed for battle appeared on the cliff, reminding

Gabe of old gladiator movies, and looked out over the crumbling city as soldiers streamed from its gates, burdened with loot and plunder. The first man, a servant, addressed the second, whose gold armor matched blond locks that touched his shoulders. The servant spoke in a foreign language and gave something to his golden captain. His voice did not match the meek attire but dripped with authority, his words hollow and mystic. He stopped speaking and honored his superior by bowing. To Gabe's surprise, the blond commander bowed even lower.

From the conversation, he made out two words: *Megas Alexandros. Alexander the Great*, Gabe guessed.

Alexander looked at the gift in his hand—a ring with a stone set in its shining metal. He enclosed it in his palm and held it high to the burning city and said, "*Lapis, lapsus ex caelis.*"

In the darkness beyond the light, Gabe heard the woman's voice again; this time the words were unclear and strained. They sounded panicked and urgent, pleading, before she faded, her last word calling his name.

"Don't leave," Gabe said. "Please."

The voice, now only a whisper, gasped before the silence took her.

Under his feet Gabe felt a vibration, a rumble deep in the earth, like the tremor of an earthquake. After a moment, it was joined by a hissing sound that drifted by in the dark area beyond his circle of light.

A crashing sound in the distance startled him. It came from the outer rim of mirrors. The fixtures were exploding, their mirrors shattering in a collapsing ring all around, the ground shaking violently. One by one, rows burst into a cascading shower of sparks and crashing glass, and the darkness grew.

Gabe watched all around as the ring shrank smaller and smaller until with a deafening explosion the closest fixtures were extinguished, leaving only his solitary light and the surrounding emptiness. The room became still, the ground calm beneath him.

He dared not move.

For a moment, not a sound could be heard. Above, the remaining light flickered and began to dim.

"No, please," Gabe begged, horrified at the idea of being caught in the dark. There was nowhere left to escape.

Around the edge of fading light the hissing approached and moved around its perimeter like a predator waiting to seize prey.

Gabe glanced at the fixture, its remaining life reduced to only a glowing filament inside its bell shape. Shadows grew, strengthening, as the light disappeared from under his feet. The world grew cold.

"Fortitudo Dei," the hissing voice said from the void, its clarity stealing all hope. "Fortitudo Dei," it said again, this time from behind.

There, a man wearing a black suit and overcoat stood, black hair fluttering in and out of his face. Gabe instantly recognized the bloodstained shirt.

He grabbed Gabe by his throat and lifted him off the floor. "It shall all come to pass," the man smirked, squeezing Gabe's windpipe.

He struggled to get free until a pure energy began to

diffuse from his skin, like sweat made of light. The man in black seemed as bewildered by the glow as Gabe did. It radiated out, encompassing them both, a cloud of power that pulsed in the surrounding air, until finally it detonated like a starburst. The man roared in pain and released his grip, his arm and body disappearing in the blinding white.

Gabe's last thought was of his father.

CHAPTER FOURTEEN

urbulence shook Gabe awake. He looked around the cabin of the plane, relieved to be safe in business class and not a hospital bed. The reading light above burned his eyes, more intense, he thought, than it had been before. It clicked off with the punch of a button. Muscles in his legs and arms burned, as if he'd just played the full ninety minutes of a soccer game.

Beside him, his father slept soundly, oblivious.

A passenger across the aisle opened an air conditioner valve above her seat. It made a hissing sound as air seeped out, just like that sinister noise from his nightmare.

Gabe turned the reading light back on. He somehow felt better being in the light, though it did little to relieve his anxiety. In the back of his mind a migraine was working its way into his skull.

Insanity hurts, he thought.

He took a deep breath, filling his lungs with oxygen, holding it for a few seconds before exhaling in a sigh. In both visions, he had seen his own death.

Everyone's death.

The inside of his shirt stuck to his body, drenched in

a cold sweat. It felt gross. He threw off the complimentary blanket, furious, and stood up.

A bathroom was a few rows ahead. Once inside, Gabe shut the folding door and slid the occupancy sign. The fluorescent light of the mirror reflected someone he didn't recognize. Bloodshot eyes glared back, framed by heavy bags that accentuated hollow cheeks. His hair a greasy mess.

He lathered some soap in his palm and onto his face. The fragrant foam and warm liquid helped. Another handful of water rinsed the remaining lather from his skin, and the rest he ran through his hair, slicking it back. Leaning against the sink, he watched water spiral down the drain, swirling away. He then looked into the mirror, half expecting to see some ancient scene play out.

"What's happening to me?" Gabe asked his reflection. A day ago, his biggest worry in the world had been waiting on NYU to send an acceptance letter. Those concerns felt like years ago—worries from a former life.

He studied the lines in his face and took stock of his life. *Why us? We're nobody special.* It had been unusual growing up, moving from town to town to follow his father's career. Admittedly, there was resentment, and over time he'd given his father more grief than was deserved.

His dad always made certain to choose interesting cities and towns for relocation, promising never to drag them to some backwater outpost in the middle of nowhere. But really, none of these places had ever felt like home. The only constant in his life was his father, and now that also seemed to be changing.

A memory came to him. He must have been eleven or twelve

years old. On his way out of their church to play soccer with some friends at a neighborhood field, he overheard a conversation.

His father sat in his office, talking on the phone. Gabe couldn't recall ever seeing his father so emotional.

Gabe hid behind the door and listened.

"Because of Gabriel?" he asked into the phone. "Or because you didn't have the courage to leave your home? I realize you have responsibilities there. Of course, I'm sure the repurposing of the Nicene Project *is* very important . . ."

He paused, listening to the response, shaking his head.

"No, Aseneth, it *was* my choice. Regardless of what family duty I had, Gabriel's adoption *was* my choice. I *chose* to accept the charge." He paced around his office. "That's not true. I did . . . I do love you. But he is my son now. His place in this world is my responsibility. Above all others."

A silence hung in the air like a storm cloud.

"I'm sorry, but I don't see how it would ever be possible for me to return to Iznik."

Whatever response his dad heard caused him to slouch, his shoulders dropping in defeat.

"Then I suppose it is. He sounds like a good man. You have to let me go now. Marry him and enjoy your life. Good-bye." With that he hung up the phone and fell into his office chair.

Gabe eventually spoke with his father about the woman on the telephone and hearing the story of his adoption. As far back as he could remember, he seemed to have always known about it but never knew his dad had given up a woman for him.

The light in the bathroom became nauseating. The memory reminded Gabe of how much his father always did for him, which made the fact that they were miles above the Atlantic, flying to another country, all without a hint or an explanation why, so unbelievably frustrating. Still, at the same time, it was also reassuring. Regardless of the man's refusal to explain anything, Gabe knew he would not take such extreme measures unless absolutely convinced it was for the best.

Gabe wished *for the best* had meant someplace warm and tropical. Someplace far away from the insanity of New York.

He had a feeling England would be neither.

Gabe returned to his seat, sat back, and pulled the flimsy airline blanket over his legs.

A light clicked on above his father. "Can't sleep?" he asked.

"No. I keep thinking about . . . I need to know what's going on, Dad."

"I promise I will tell you everything once we get to England, but now is not the time."

Gabe sighed, exasperated by his father's cryptic response, and switched on the light above his seat. He turned his back on his father and found escape flipping through one of the several magazines provided by the airline, pictures of patch-work fields and English villages passing by.

"It's been eighteen years since I was home. Can't believe it's been so long."

"So, where are we going? London?"

"Durham. About three hours from London by train. It's a university town just south of Newcastle in the northeastern borderlands. Not a big town, really, but it's quiet and a bit off the beaten path. You'll love the cathedral and castle. They're marvelous."

Gabe turned to see a smile form at the corners of his dad's mouth as he became lost in the thought. "I think you miss it more than you know."

"Maybe I do." He nodded to the magazine. "Those rural pictures remind me a lot of where I grew up. Little farmhouses that look as though they sprouted right out of the land itself, quaint villages, grand cathedrals, and local pubs. I guess you can take the man out of the country but not the country out of the man."

"Could you at least tell me what's in Durham that's so important?"

His father paused, as if considering how to respond. "Well, the short answer is *history*. The history of the region is very important. There is a wall north of Durham called Hadrian's Wall, built when these lands were part of the dying Roman Empire."

"We're traveling all this way for a wall?" Gabe asked.

"Of course not. But our reasons are connected. The Roman Empire placed great value in the lands around Durham as a stronghold to defend their occupied lands from the constant invasion of the northern hordes. It is that reason—that effort to hold that land—that takes us there today. I'll introduce you to someone who is very knowledgeable about this history.

"But none of this is a conversation for now," he continued. "You should try and get some rest. You're going to need it. There is much to see and even more to hear. Try counting sheep," he said with a nod to a picture of a white-speckled field in the magazine.

With that, the light above his father clicked off, and Gabe was alone again.

CHAPTER FIFTEEN

The clattering of pots and pans somewhere in the house woke Gabe from a dreamless sleep to a darkened room.

He felt his wrist for the light button on his digital watch but then remembered, *Missing since The Study Habit*. A scene of the emergency medical technicians cutting it off his arm in the ambulance and shouting, "Stat!" at each other played out in his imagination. He wondered what sort of disruption he'd caused at the café. Coren had screamed. That meant she cared, he supposed. At least enough to be concerned. Did she run to his side and try to comfort him?

The embarrassment struck him again, as the memory strayed. He pictured himself spazzing out on the floor like frying bacon while Coren looked on.

Hell with it, he thought. *Probably never see her again, anyway.*

Silly concerns over his dignity soon quieted in the comfort of the bed. He didn't want to do anything but stay in the warmth of the covers.

The previous night existed in his memory like snapshots from someone else's photo album. Various scenes from airports, train rides, and cabs all fit together enough to reassure him that he'd actually experienced them.

The rest was a little hazy. He remembered arriving in Durham. His father had woken him when the train's interior lights came on. Gabe stumbled off into the snowy night, lumbering like a zombie toward a black cab. A man sitting inside had introduced himself to Gabe, but right now he couldn't remember his face, let alone a name. What did leave an impression was his impressive physique and thick Scottish brogue. He was an older man but looked as though he could start as linebacker for any NFL team.

The ride took them through a maze of streets that curved, inclined, and sloped down so much that Gabe might have gotten carsick had he not been so sleepy. Everything after the taxi was a total blank.

A cord on a lamp beside the bed, barely visible, begged to be pulled. Escape from this comfy trap had to start somewhere. He stretched on his stomach and turned it on.

Once his eyes adjusted, he saw the details of the room. Despite its compact size, the room had been decorated like a giant scrapbook. Artifacts and keepsakes of a well-traveled life were everywhere. A brass tea set, with its tiny cups surrounded by an army of hand-carved figurines, was arranged on the nightstand. Pictures and newspaper articles clung to the walls. A Star of David hung over the doorway. Just below it, a cross had been nailed on the door. Gabe noticed a red flag with a white crescent and star draped over a chest of drawers. *Turkish*, he thought. In the corner of the room was a pile of folded clothes on a small chair, apparently intended for him.

He pushed up on the mattress and immediately smashed

his head into the low, sloped ceiling. Stars flashed in his eyes. He crashed back down onto the bed, his grunting cry muffled by the pillow. For an instant Gabe lay still, terrified another migraine had taken hold until a sharp, throbbing pain set in on the crown of his head.

Somewhere in the innards of the house, he thought he heard laughter.

Gabe rolled out of bed and pulled the sweater over his sore head, thankful for fresh-smelling clothes. While he dressed, he scanned the headlines of some of the framed newspaper clippings that adorned the walls. They were all stories of relief efforts from disasters around the globe. Articles about earthquakes, war, and famine seemed odd for wall decor.

One of the photographs on the wall caught his eye, this one of his father. He looked much younger. Beside him stood a tall woman with long, black hair and green eyes accentuated by heavy eyeliner. Her face was soft and inviting, with full cheeks and dark eyebrows. Her features gave the impression that she might be caring, gentle . . . motherly. Her expression, however, was a contradiction. Angry, with her full lips pursed and eyebrows arched.

Was this Aseneth? He knew so little about her. His dad had always been reluctant to talk when Gabe mentioned her in conversations about women or dating. To this day, he'd never even seen a picture of her.

His father had his arm around her, but they both looked rigid, uncomfortable.

They didn't match, either, with his dad tidy and neat in a well-starched collar, much like the shirts he wore today. The woman's outfit looked more like the clothes of a free spirit. A long, billowy dress in a cultural print flowed down to open-toed sandals.

He made a mental note to ask his father about her next time he got the chance.

In the hallway outside his room, Gabe discovered scents of tobacco and greasy food. The smell would have made him sick on any other occasion, but the rumble in his gut said, *Too hungry to get picky.* If someone served fried tobacco sandwiches, he'd be up for giving them a try.

Carpeted stairs led down through the foyer and to the adjoining kitchen. His father sat at the breakfast table, and a man Gabe recognized as the giant from last night's cab ride tended to the stove. He was even bigger than Gabe remembered with muscled arms the size of a man's leg. A white yarmulke adorned his balding head, and remnants of a recent meal peppered a matching scholarly goatee. The hulk had a weathered appearance, with lines in his face that gave him the scouring look of a man never content. As he cooked, he smoked a pipe that filled the whole bottom floor with a light haze.

"Good afternoon," his dad said.

"What time is it?" Gabe asked.

"Nearly half three. How's your head?" He smiled like he'd been waiting to ask.

Gabe rubbed the newly formed knot. "Super. Thanks for the warning."

The large man approached. "Welcome to my home, Gabriel." He rolled his *r* so hard, Gabe hardly recognized his own name.

"Thank you, sir."

"Professor Carlyle is an old friend of mine from Ellon, up near Aberdeen. He teaches history and religion here at Durham University, and he's the man who's been helping you with your admission to NYU."

"I appreciate that, sir."

The professor laughed. "Bin the formality, eh? Call me Carlyle. Friends do. Unlucky that, about New York University. Turns out, you got in."

Gabe slumped and wondered how his life could possibly get any worse.

"Anyway, you must be hungry. How about a nice fried breakfast?"

"But it's three thirty in the afternoon."

"Every day should start with breakfast, no matter when that day begins," Carlyle growled. "Now, sit. What have you been teaching him, Joseph?"

"You'll find he's of his own mind on most subjects."

Carlyle removed several pieces of bacon from its packaging and put them onto a large iron skillet. They sizzled in the hot grease.

Gabe glanced at the meat and then the yarmulke on Carlyle's head. The giant noticed.

"An old rule for another time meant simply to discourage

spread of disease in a ravaged land." Carlyle flipped the bacon, no longer looking at Gabe. "How's the jet lag?"

"I feel like hell."

Carlyle snorted while tending to the bacon. The slightest indication of a smile shined through his facial hair. "Feel like hell? Now, there's a notion coming from you."

Gabe thought for a second that he had offended Carlyle by his language.

The awkward moment passed, and Carlyle said, "You'll adjust. Your father tells me that you don't exactly follow in his path with regards to religion."

By Carlyle's tone, Gabe couldn't tell if it was a question or a statement. He looked at his father, wondering how in the world such a conversation mattered at a time like this. "Isn't that kind of a private matter?"

"Not anymore," said Carlyle.

"No offense but I think it is." Gabe knew he was being rude, but he couldn't help himself. The frustration over the past twenty-four hours boiled to the surface. "Besides, what does my religious preference, if any, have to do with why somebody tried to kill us in New York, or why the only place to find safety was several thousands of miles away on another continent? Isn't that what you two should be talking about?"

He stared at his father. "You're acting like we're the ones who committed a crime with all this running and hiding. Does somebody want to let me in on what the hell is going on here? Our lives, our world has been destroyed back home, and you find it necessary to enter into a theological debate over my religious beliefs?"

Carlyle laughed as he tossed a tomato half into the skillet. "Your world has been destroyed, you say? Funny you should mention that." The smile vanished and he became still. "Because being wanted by the authorities for burning a church would be a considerably better situation than the one you're currently in. *Considerably*."

Gabe rolled his eyes.

In a flash, Carlyle leapt away from the stove, coming half-way over the kitchen table, his face as red as the tomato. "And believe me, sonny jim, you'll know firsthand if and when your world is destroyed. You'll likely have a front-row seat. There are things that you're about to learn regarding *this world* in which you live in, and more importantly, your part to play in it. You'll need to open yourself up to the possibility that you are, despite appearances, more than some anti-authoritative American muppet of a student and realize that perhaps there is some substance and purpose hidden away under that unkempt exterior of yours."

Gabe had retreated as far into his chair as it would allow.

As the stove regained Carlyle's attention, his intensity switched off like a light, and a broad smile showed through the goatee. He flopped down a plate in front of Gabe and practically threw a fork at him. "Now, eat your breakfast. We'll go up to the castle and have a bit of an orientation to what exactly I do at the university. After that, we can find you a new wardrobe and relocate you to more suitable accommodations. By the way, welcome to Durham, Gabriel."

My God, he's totally crazy, Gabe thought.

CHAPTER SIXTEEN

Gabe stumbled through the thick snow on the ground, following his father and Carlyle around the city center. Several narrow streets wound through the buildings, crisscrossing the River Wear, which coiled around the little city like a snake, constricting all the shops into a dense commercial area that bulged out to form a hill.

Near a pub called The Swan & Three Cygnets, they crossed the Elvet Bridge spanning the river gorge and then climbed North Bailey Street toward the castle and cathedral grounds. Gabe noticed a table full of girls about his age behind the window of a coffee shop.

Students. Attractive ones. The silver lining, he thought.

Up the hill they passed another tavern, The Shakespeare, which Carlyle affectionately pointed out as his "local." He said it was over nine hundred years old and built before construction work began on the castle. Gabe appreciated how the town founders' priorities fell into order.

The Durham Cathedral dwarfed the one in New York by twice its size at least. The hill on which it stood formed a peninsula surrounded by a deep, forested gorge and the river below. They walked by a snow-covered lawn opposite the cathedral and through the arched entrance of the castle gatehouse, a towering structure adorned with crosses, windows, and ornate crests.

The castle itself wasn't what Gabe expected. He had envisioned the theme park version, with flagged towers surrounding a singular, tall building, fit for kings and knights. Instead, it was a series of structures, none of them taller than a few stories, like a military base enclosed by a very large stone wall.

Carlyle led them on a cobblestone path surrounding a grass courtyard embraced by a crescent of buildings. He mentioned that many of the university's classes met in these buildings. The Great Hall looked most impressive with its stone brickwork façade. Directly across from it was the keep sitting atop a stepped hill supported by a large earth-retaining stone wall. The imposing octagonal structure above provided a bookend to the grounds.

"This is Castle College, or University College if you prefer its formal name. Oldest college at Durham University, by the way." Carlyle pointed to a door marked Lowe Library. "Below the Great Hall and down the stairs is the Undercroft. Over there—"

"What's the Undercroft?" Gabe interrupted.

"Oh, well, that'd be the student pub," Carlyle responded. "A bit like a dungeon but with lager and spirits. Course that's hardly torture, is it?"

"Wait. There's a pub just for students *inside* the college?"

"Certainly. Every college here has one. Many of the locals

resent the university types, so on the weekends, students keep to their college pubs rather than mix it up with the townies."

"You'll do well to stay away from it," his father warned. "You're not of age yet, so no need to find any trouble there."

"Don't be daft, Joseph. He's almost eighteen, isn't he?" Carlyle said.

His dad shot him a look that Gabe knew too well.

"Right. What I meant to say, mind you, was being that you're American, as it were, and it would be inappropriate, you understand. Ah, never mind. Follow me." Carlyle led them toward a building adorned with a large black clock, though Gabe's attention was still drawn toward the Undercroft.

"You'll be staying at the dorms there in the Castle Keep, at least temporarily," Carlyle said. "The best view of the town can be seen here, though the accommodations are a little . . . well, tight shall we say."

Making their way to the inside of the keep, Carlyle obtained a set of keys for two rooms as well as two document envelopes from a student running an information desk. He handed them one of each.

"We're not in the same room?" his dad asked.

Gabe couldn't help but grin.

"No, the rooms are far too small. End up killing each other, I suspect, and then what use would you be? The porter's number is in the packet. If you have any problems with the room, he'll sort you out. Also, numbers for local delivery and the like should the cafeteria be closed. Your rooms are fortunately buffered from the rest of the student population, but expect a bit of mischief. You remember those days, eh?"

Carlyle gave Gabe's father a sharp knuckle to the shoulder and let loose a hearty laugh.

"I'm not sure what you mean," he said.

Carlyle frowned. "No, I suppose you wouldn't. Anyway, let me show you to your room, Gabriel."

The interior of the dorm hardly impressed. A bed, a closet, a desk that doubled as a dresser, and a chair for the desk. Desolate but Gabe loved it. *Simplistic necessity*, he thought—exactly how he dreamed. He could almost see the open bags of potato chips and empty soda cans littering the desk, the floor covered in dirty laundry, posters of models and rock bands tacked to the wall. He imagined sitting by the metal desk light, cramming the night before a test, exhausted from partying with friends.

For the first time in a while, Gabe felt his spirits lift as he looked out the windows to the River Wear and the crowded shops of the square below, with its statue of a man on a horse.

Carlyle rummaged around the cabinets and drawers in the restroom, tossing towels out onto the floor. Half his body seemed wedged under the sink, and Gabe wondered if he might get stuck.

"Aha! Found it. I specifically requested a few things be put into your rooms. Essentials mainly—toothbrushes, soap, etcetera. And this." Carlyle held up a pair of hair clippers like the ones used on soldiers before entering the service. Curiously, he plugged the cord into the wall by the entrance.

"What are those for?" Gabe asked.

"Shaving sheep. Are you thick? Cutting your hair, twit."

"We need to shave your head in order to prove who you

are," his father explained.

Gabe smiled, trying to get the joke. "You want to what? Shave my head to *prove who I am*? What are you talking about? Look at my flipping passport."

"It isn't to prove to me but to yourself," Carlyle said, all his humor suddenly gone.

Gabe turned to Carlyle and then to his dad. Neither one smiled.

"Look, I don't know what you two are thinking. I don't even know what I'm doing in this country, but I'm done. Done with both of you and done with all of this. Nobody's shaving my head. I'm out of here." Gabe started toward the door.

"Fair enough," Carlyle conceded. "Have it your way."

"I will. Thanks." Gabe walked past him toward the hallway.

A buzzing swoosh flew past the top of his ear. He nearly fell over in shock. His hand went to his head and found a swath of hair cut away. Tiny hairs prickled his fingers. Long black curls fell to the floor. "What the hell, man? Are you nuts?"

"That's quite an inventive hairstyle you have there," Carlyle taunted. "Don't know if the ladies will fancy it, but I can appreciate the abstract and artistic quality of the look. Very progressive. Or perhaps retro. To be honest, I'm not entirely certain what it is. Though, no doubt, it will be quite fashionable. Aye, perhaps you'll start a trend."

Gabe's dad held his fist to his mouth and bit a knuckle to hold back laughter.

"What are *you* laughing at? You two are out of your minds. Do you know that? Crazy!"

"Well, if you don't like it you might as well let him finish the job," his father said and then turned to Carlyle. "You've never been one for subtlety, have you?"

"What? A nice new haircut for a nice new beginning. I'll have you looking the part of a proper footballer quick like."

CHAPTER SEVENTEEN

In the bowels of a building adjacent to the keep, Gabe stood outside a door at the bottom of a stairway below a long hall turned museum called the Norman Gallery, with arms crossed, seething at Carlyle. His father continued to stare, mesmerized, as he had since the haircut incident. "Take a freaking picture, why don't you?" Gabe snapped.

This was his limit—plane flights, foreign countries, trains, taxis, and a clipper-wielding, maniacal Scotsman. He flushed with anger, and worse, felt naked without the shaggy locks on his head. *He can remember toothpaste, soap, and clippers, but a hat is too much to ask?*

Carlyle unlocked the door and ushered them inside. "This is my little hideaway. One of the privileges for being head of the School of Divinity. It's where I keep my collected artifacts and special literature for exhibits and education. At least that's what I tell the school authorities. Sort of a half-truth, really. But then, so long as I bring in the large donations from my benefactor, they don't ask questions."

Stone arches and pillars supported the low ceiling, giving the space a claustrophobic feel as if the room had once been used as a cellar or a medieval prison. On the far side of the room Gabe noticed a steel vault built into the wall with a massive door that looked suitable enough to be housed in any bank. An LCD screen blinked at its side. Completing the dungeon look, an old iron gate stood between the vault door and the rest of the room. How old, he couldn't tell, but he suspected it had been around as long as the castle itself from all the wear and rust on the bars. Gabe wondered what treasures Carlyle kept that required such security.

Antique furniture, mirrors, and rugs decorated the room. With everything looking so ancient, he expected a musty odor similar to Carlyle's house, but the atmosphere was crisp, filtered by an automated air purifier that hummed overhead.

"Have a seat, Gabriel," Carlyle said. It was more of a demand than a cordial offer. He entered a code into an LCD keypad next to the vault door. "Obviously, you've had a miserable, if not tragic, couple of days. Can't say that the topsy-turvy ebb and flow of your situation is likely to calm to any degree, but there you go."

The large man was trying to ease the situation, but there was about as much comfort in Carlyle's words as there was in the hard chair beneath Gabe.

His father seemed to agree. "There are aspects of your life that have been kept hidden from you in order to protect your life," he said as Carlyle disappeared inside the vault. "This is why we are here in Durham."

"You've kept secrets from me?"

"Yes. Very important ones," his father continued. "Truths, regardless of what you believe about this world or where you place your faith."

"Right! Here it is," Carlyle shouted from inside the vault. "I thought I'd misplaced it. Imagine that, would you? What a disaster that would've been." He laughed and emerged, carrying a scroll sealed with red wax. The seal looked elaborate, but Carlyle moved around too much to get a clear view.

"This is why we shaved your head," his dad offered.

"Now, mind you, these aren't the originals," Carlyle said. "Those are kept inside the Vatican's Secret Archives for protection, but these are certified, sealed copies issued from the Office of the Pope. The most secret of documents." He held the scroll up, and the Pope's seal became evident.

"Fine. I'm impressed, but what does an Anglican priest and a Jewish professor need with a scroll from the Catholic Pope?" Gabe asked.

"Aye, I am Jewish. Different, though, from the modern practice. Specifically, I am an Essene Jew. Let's just say that when matters of the Old Testament are in question, we're the experts. Even for our financiers." He nodded to the seal.

"You have this stuff because of the Vatican?" Gabe asked.

Carlyle nodded again and broke the seal to unroll the papers. "It is the engine behind our little endeavor. You might say what I'm about to tell you comes all the way from the top."

"You won't find this story in the Bible," his father said. "There is a certain protocol and procedure for all things. I've touched on this in a few sermons."

"I think I missed those," Gabe said.

"Undoubtedly. But the fact of the matter is, there are rules to this world. Would you agree?"

"You mean like physics and laws?"

"Exactly. What is true for our world is true for other worlds that intersect with this one. That is, these laws are binding, governed by certain parameters," his dad explained.

"You're not going to tell me about aliens, are you?"

"No, of course not. I'm referring to worlds in a different sense. I'm talking about planes of existence. Dimensions. Realms. Earth being one of them."

"Three realms in total," Carlyle said. "There are accounts of the first war between the two other dimensions, heaven and hell. Some of which can be found in the canon of modern theology. Most, however, can't. More important than the *history* found in these texts is what is noted about the *future*. We possess ancient books documented by the Essenes and their ancestors, books that very few have access to, foretelling the coming signs of the next dimensional war—signs that are happening right now."

Gabe looked at Carlyle and waited for the punch line. None came. Not even the hint of a smile.

"It's the truth, Gabriel," his father said.

Much of the rough, grumbling Scotsman had gone, replaced by someone who appeared almost academic. His eyes shined with an eager intensity. He seemed to be holding back but anxious to speak. "The point we are getting to is one of the ramifications that occurred following the first war—the sealing of heaven and hell from Earth. This separation of the realms meant angels and demons could no longer interfere with the world of man in a physical sense once they had been removed. The gateway between them, you see, was closed forever. With this separation came free will. This is the gift and the burden man now carries in this world, with no physical interference from the other dimensions. That is, with two exceptions."

His dad sat down beside Gabe and pulled out a parchment from the scroll. "For angels and demons—beings from other realms—to enter the world of man, they now have to be bound by his laws, by the laws of the Earth realm. Specifically, and most importantly, the law against immortality."

Carlyle took his cue and unrolled the parchment on the desk in front of Gabe. On the parchment, Gabe could see a series of four symbols, all very similar in design. Encompassed inside each of their perfect circles were small characters that resembled Asian text.

His father's hand settled on one of the symbols. "The converse of being subject to death is being subject to life and its governing rules. Particularly *birth*. Now in order to enter Earth's realm, an angel or demon must be born to it, like man, or they must have remained in this dimension following the separation of the three realms."

Gabe pointed at the symbols. "What are they?"

"Names," his dad said.

Carlyle asked, "What do you know about archangels?"

"Not much. They're the messengers of God."

"Yes," his dad answered. "But once, when our world and the heaven realm were still connected, archangels served as dimensional ambassadors and Watchers over Earth. Powerful beings, they were, and capable of traversing the two dimensions in order that they may keep balance between the realms."

"Each possessed different traits typically associated with

higher beings or gods," Carlyle said. "And each was defined by their abilities, be it the power to heal or the power to give strength, for instance. The only gift the archangels were denied was the power to create."

Gabe looked at the symbols, wondering what each meant.

Carlyle continued, "During the dawn of man, several Watchers, envious of mankind's freedom, fell to Earth, led by an archangel known by early humans as Mastema. They were accused of forsaking their own dimension in favor of earthly pleasures. Pleasures including love."

His father picked up the story. "These fallen assumed the features of men and chose to succumb to carnal desire for women. In those relations with women, the archangels finally obtained the power to create life. Their unholy offspring, denied the grace of the true creator, became demons and caused a splinter between the two realms, thus forming a third dimension that could support their unnatural life.

"That day, balance and unity between the realms was destroyed and the realm of hell burned into existence. Four archangels were sent to seal the Hellgate, which opened and grew, like an epidemic spreading across the Earth, replacing our world with theirs. Inevitably, war ignited and after a prolonged engagement ended in a compromise that sealed the realms."

"Now the only way for a being from another realm to enter Earth is to become human. Have you ever wondered where you get your name, Gabriel?" Carlyle asked.

His dad still pointed to one symbol.

"I assumed I was named after the archangel Gabriel from the Bible," Gabe answered.

Carlyle picked up a large upright mirror from the corner of the room and brought it over to the chair, placing it directly behind Gabe. He then retrieved a small mirror from the table where a candle had used it as a base and put it in Gabe's hand.

Gabe lifted the mirror. On the back of his head a mark in the defined shape of one of the signs in the book was clearly visible. *A tattoo.* A closer look revealed that it wasn't a tattoo but a *birthmark*. Instead of sharp, defined lines as would have been given by an artist's hand, the colors blended, fading into skin, impossible by artificial means.

He stared at it, then looked down to the Watcher symbol on the parchment marked by his father's hand. They were identical. A circle and a pattern of lines that resembled an upside-down *Y*.

"Not named after him," his dad said. "My boy, you *are* the archangel Gabriel."

CHAPTER EIGHTEEN

Having never been in a fistfight, Gabe didn't know what a punch to the face felt like. He imagined the effect of his father's words ringing in his ears was a close approximation.

Is this a joke?

Has my father gone insane?

Is this all some horrible dream?

But the last thought disturbed him the most—*My dad and the Scotsman might be telling the truth.*

He thought of the visions. *Visions of the end of the world and ancient times.* Cruelly, it all fit together, though his mind wouldn't accept it.

"How would . . . I don't . . . ," Gabe said, struggling to talk. His pulse quickened, and a familiar tightening sensation built in the back of his head while he struggled to process his father's words. Frustrated anger tore through his mind. He couldn't help it, but it was the only emotion responding to their news. "I don't believe it. A dimensional war between heaven and hell? Angels and demons born on Earth? That's insane. It's just . . . stupid."

"Is it?" His dad nodded to a painting of Jesus on the wall.

"The concept isn't exactly foreign to matters of faith."

"Faith? You expect me to just believe? That my entire future is some big plot to save the world?"

"Not just you," Carlyle said. "There are others. Four in total, to be precise."

"Sure," Gabe said, his tone sour and sarcastic. "I'm one of four super warriors, or whatever, sent to save the world. And you two—two people in nowhere England—are the ones the Vatican entrusted with keeping this big secret. Excuse me if I seem a little concerned about the state of the church." Gabe flinched even as he said it, but propelled by the anger, he couldn't stop.

"Carlyle and I are not just ordinary people. He is a Qumran Essene and an expert in all things concerning the End of Days. I am an agent of the Vatican, entrusted with your protection and care," his father said.

"You're a freaking *Anglican* priest!"

"Gabriel, there are many things about me you don't know. Don't you understand? This cover, this role as an Anglican priest, was the only way I could keep you as my adopted son and remain a part of the church. There are reasons for everything. But the question you should be answering about yourself isn't *why me*. It's *why not me*. Are we not God's children? Is he not?" His dad pointed to Carlyle.

"The importance of keeping you in the dark and apart from the others was for the purpose of security," Carlyle said. "Your safety has always been at risk. Moving from church to church made you difficult to find. Many voiced opinions that you should have been kept in Vatican City, under the guard of their security force. Alas, obscurity proved to be better than anything contrived by the Vatican."

Gabe's hands felt moist with sweat; his heart skipped inside his chest. Oxygen suddenly seemed lacking in the small room, and he couldn't catch his breath.

Carlyle wouldn't let up. "A war is beginning, boy. Whether or not you choose to believe that right now is irrelevant. Preparation is what is important to the future. With the attack in New York, it has become obvious that the enemy is moving faster than anticipated. They've somehow found a crack in the seal, a way to get to Earth through other means. It is time to unite the four and stop the End of Days."

Gabe stood, shaking his head in denial, and moved to the exit. Anger gave way to a deepening sadness from his father's betrayal of trust.

"Wait. There's more to hear," his father pleaded and held the sleeve of his son's jacket.

Gabe jerked his arm away and walked to the door. Without looking back, he said, "I can't deal with this right now. I need some time alone."

The door to the vault room slammed behind him.

CHAPTER NINETEEN

Snow from the Palace Green kicked into the air with every step Gabe took toward the cathedral. On another day he might laugh at such an ironic choice of retreat, considering what he was running from. But for now, it seemed like the only place that felt familiar, safe.

He could imagine it still, the image of the mark seared into his memory. Everywhere he looked, even in the shapes and drifts of snow, it was there—the circle with a pattern of marks. Did he see what they wanted him to see? Some sort of manipulation or trick? One thing was certain—it felt real.

He rubbed the mark as he walked, feeling heavy, burdened by his father's secret. *My secret.*

Unlike the cathedral in New York, Durham Cathedral had three towers. The view tower, the largest of the three, was open to the public according to posted signs, except for after hours and during inclement weather. Both of which applied at the moment.

Gabe slipped into the cathedral behind several students.

Stained glass windows lit up an enormous cavern of pews. Massive arches in the vaulted ceiling spanned from one stone pillar to the next. Luckily, the stairs to the central tower were near the entrance. A small Closed sign stood next to the door to the tower, but only a velvet rope served as a deterrent. Normally, this would have been enough to persuade him to find another retreat, but he needed someplace familiar to find his bearings on everything. Somewhere high above the insanity.

Gabe sneaked past the sign and climbed the staircase until he came to the door to the observation deck. He opened it, and a frigid wind cut through his clothes.

The memory of Central Park came to mind, and he felt homesick. Odd, he realized, considering how little time he actually spent in New York. Leaning against the stone guardrail, all of Durham extended out into the world, with the castle and the village lit up below. Out of habit he scanned the horizon for the red-tailed hawk, suddenly aware just how far away he was from his life in America.

A thin haze of smoke from the chimneys of the flats covered the town. Below, the Great North Eastern Railway departed the train station, lumbering over the nearby bridge. Life went on, like any other night. He had no idea what time it was, though it felt very late under the dark sky.

His father's words rang in his head, *"You* are *the archangel Gabriel."*

How could he be someone else or *something* else? He had his own history, his own identity—the foundation for which he based everything he did—and now it had been torn out from under him.

Yet something *was* happening to him. That he couldn't deny. The visions. Richard's murder. His home burned to the ground by someone who wanted him dead. He knew somehow all these connected to form a truth. And the only explanation offered, the only one that no matter how fanciful at least made sense, had come from his father and Carlyle. It was enough to give him another migraine. He rubbed his head to warm it. His hands stopped at the base of his skull.

The mark.

It felt like a curse.

An hour later, the only light on the observation deck came from the spotlights illuminating the flags above the cathedral. Gabe watched them flutter in the wind and felt similarly help-less. Somehow it made the tower feel even colder. Long ago, he'd lost sensation on his shaven scalp, now numb from the bitter cold. As he listened to the beat of the whipping flags, he thought he heard the squeaking hinges of a door opening. Gabe turned to see a girl standing in the exit.

"You'll catch your death up here," she said in an English accent and then held out her hand, offering a black wool hat for his frozen head.

He took the hat and looked at her, wondering how much trouble he was in, though she wasn't dressed like one of the cathedral employees. "Is the university always this kind to trespassers?"

"Put it on, genius. Might unfreeze your brain," she said

and walked to the edge of the lookout, the soft light revealing her features. A strand of dark hair escaped from under her hat and danced around the sculpted cheekbones of her Persian face.

His mind stuttered for a moment, lost in her brown eyes. "Thanks."

"My pleasure. Enjoying the view up here, are we?" she asked.

"Ah, well . . . sort of, I guess." He fumbled with the hat and tried to put it on with his clumsy, ice-cold fingers.

"You know, of course, the tower is closed."

"Uh, yeah. I had a lot on my mind. It kind of reminded me of home. Am I in trouble?"

"Depends. You weren't trying to sprout wings and fly away, were you? I know I wanted to." She winked.

The question threw off Gabe's concentration. "I'm sorry; who did you say you were?"

"Micah. Micah Pari. Your father said you might be up here. Though Carlyle convinced him to try the student pubs first—possibly a self-motivated plan of action. And you are Gabriel Adam. We have a lot in common, you and me."

With that she took off her hat. She brushed her hair away from the base of her skull and turned around. A small strip had been neatly shaved to reveal a birthmark symbol, another from the scroll.

"Ta-dah! I'm just like you." She laughed.

CHAPTER TWENTY

"The archangel Micah?" Gabe asked.

"You missed a lot of Sunday school, didn't you? Either that or you didn't pay much attention. The archangel *Michael*. Slightly improved though, I'd say." She did a quick spin.

He had to agree. "Why a girl?"

"Why not a girl?" Micah's eyebrows arched, indignant, not unlike the woman in the picture at Carlyle's house.

"Fair enough. So, I'm assuming you got the whole go-save-the-world speech, too? Tell me you haven't bought into this whole God versus Devil stuff."

Her playful demeanor quickly left. "As a matter of fact, I certainly have 'bought in,' as you say. If you had seen what I'd seen, you'd buy in as well. I promise you, the poor boy murdered at your cathedral in New York believed. So, the quicker you decide not to be a *complete* idiot, the better it will be for everybody."

Gabe regretted the challenge.

"I was told that you don't put much faith in things that aren't tangible," Micah continued. "And yet things that are tangible don't require faith, do they? Quite the conflict you're waging with yourself. If you have faith in anything, have faith in this: it's happening. To you. And to me. This is what we are, and there's nothing that can be done other than accept it."

"Just accept it? Like it's that simple. You sound like Carlyle."

"Good. He's right."

"Right about us being angels on Earth? Soldiers in some supernatural war? What war? Look around you. How can you even know that this war, between heaven and hell nonetheless, is even real? Because I don't see any armies gathering and certainly none with pitchforks and horns or halos and bright shiny white wings."

"Because I've seen our enemy's plan. You've seen it as well. Our world, consumed in fire. I'm suffering from the same visions. You know what is at stake. You're just too scared to admit it. That's understandable. You'll need time. I know I did, but thinking everyone else is mental isn't going to make it easier on you or us."

If Micah was lying or crazy, he couldn't tell, but she sounded rational. Two people suffering the same nightmare amounted to something more than coincidence, no matter how much his mind wanted to deny it. In a strange way, Gabe was glad someone else knew what he was going through. "They're horrible, aren't they? The visions?"

"Yes. I'm having some difficulty with them. I can't predict when they'll come or why. And the violence . . ."

"I know. Did they just start for you as well? On New Year's Eve?" Gabe asked.

She nodded.

"That's really weird. So they just shipped you in, too, after they started?"

"No. I've been in Durham for a while. Not long after I was born, I was sent to live under the care of Carlyle when my parents died. We moved around the United Kingdom and Ireland for several years before ending up here. He's sort of been the only parent I've known. Once he felt I was old enough to understand, he told me everything. But when the visions hit, so did the reality, I guess. I'm only beginning to understand. It can be a lot to digest."

Gabe looked out onto the city, wishing he could get lost in it and disappear. "At least he trusted you enough to tell you."

"I know. It was unfair, but your father did it with your best interest in mind. The point is, you know now. You don't have to accept everything at once. It will come in due time. Preparation, however, is imperative. Something is happening out of turn that none of us understand. We don't have the luxury of waiting until you've been convinced of the truth to start readying ourselves for what's to come. For now, just cooperate. Play along, if that's the way you see it. Eventually, I know you'll come around. In the meantime, you've been enrolled, like me, into Durham University. More specifically, Castle College. We'll be under the tutelage of Professor Carlyle in the Theology and Divinity Program, which will, of course, be your major."

"Sounds like I don't have much choice in the matter."

"You do. There's free will in every choice we make. But you'd do well to start listening to Carlyle. His sole purpose for being on Earth is to help guide you and me through these times. He's not all piss and vinegar—he can be a laugh. Well, not often, but you know.

"Look, it isn't all that bad," Micah continued. "You'll attend class here as a freshman with your core studies first. After class, we'll do extracurricular studies with Carlyle. Think of it as Archangel 101. The important thing is to act like a regular student. Fit in, as it were. Be inconspicuous, and an inconspicuous student is one that acts like the rest of them."

"So, pretend nothing's happened. Do stuff like homework and hang out at the student pub," Gabe said.

"Exactly or participate in sport, if you can find the time. Football is quite popular. Sorry, *soccer* as you Yanks call it. Cricket and rugby as well, though you look a little fragile for a scrum. Durham isn't New York or London by any means, but life is good here. Besides, you're the only other, you know—one of us—I've met. I was beginning to think I was the only one."

Micah smiled at him, and he began to feel better about being here.

"Wait. I thought there were others on the way," Gabe said.

Her brow furrowed. "Unfortunately, it seems they are running quite late."

CHAPTER TWENTY-ONE

Septis stood behind the yellow partitioning tape that separated the sidewalk from the cathedral grounds and watched the scurry of activity in the still-smoking ruins. Firefighters dug through ash and rubble, seeking burning embers to extinguish with their crude devices.

He felt cheated, uncertain as to how the dispatched boy had not been Gabriel, when there had been so little doubt inside the church. Now, instead of glory, the destroyed house of God served only as a reminder of his failure. A hollow feeling festered inside, a fear of what his prey's escape might mean.

If Gabriel could not be found, if somehow he were to unite with the remaining three archangels, then Septis would have much to answer for. While the boy still lived, the Hellgate remained closed. To punish his mistake, Mastema would send another by exploiting the splintered pathway between the dimensions, opened by the humans' negligent stewardship of this realm. Septis knew that little time remained before his life would become forfeit.

He could feel traces of Fortitudo Dei left in the city, the tiny echoes made by the growing power of the boy's abilities.

They were fresh and had been stronger here than in any other place. Yet the boy still lived.

Septis questioned his own capabilities, mainly his ability to track this target. He and Gabriel were connected, each possessing power that mirrored the other's, making Gabriel the only child that Septis could find before the archangels reached their full potential as defenders of this realm. Where Fortitudo Dei brought strength to those around him, emboldening their own power, Septis could weaken his enemies by feeding off their fear and hate, transforming it into physical shadow.

Earth was ripe with such polluted thought. The boy's power had shined like a beacon among it, leading Septis to New York. To the cathedral.

But the boy had slipped from his grasp by the time Septis arrived. In his bloodlust, his raw animalistic rage, he had been careless. The thrill of taking his enemy's life had overpowered him in his greed to be triumphant in the eyes of Mastema. Now their cause lay in jeopardy.

As he watched work continue on the remains of the cathedral, Septis called to his shadows. Unnoticed by the passing humans, they flowed inside his suit and down his legs to his shined shoes, spilling over them and seeping into the ground. Through the dark smoke, he could feel the earth around him.

The shadows moved in the energies of the realm that ran through the world like a connected stream of consciousness, a network made by the interactions of all its living inhabitants. They rode its currents, searching for the boy's light amongst so much darkness. Then he felt it—a place nearby, saturated in the essence of Fortitudo Dei.

Septis turned from the cathedral and moved quickly through the city until, after some time, he came to a small café swarming with the human pests.

He entered, the doorbell chiming as it opened. Gabriel had been here and often. Remnants of his power lingered inside the building like a stench. One tall table in particular reeked more than any other. Septis sat in its high leather chair and surveyed the shop. The essence of Fortitudo Dei had begun to spoil from time. The boy was not here.

"Hello," a blonde waitress said. "I'm Coren. Can I get you anything?"

Septis turned to her and smiled. "Thank you, no. But perhaps you can help me. I am looking for a friend who may have frequented your café. He's approximately your age and goes by the name of Gabriel. I believe he would be a regular, someone you or one of your coworkers might recognize."

Coren looked at his suit and glossy dress shoes. She rolled her eyes, her smile fading into pursed lips. "Another detective?"

Septis nodded. "Detective Smith."

"I guessed. You know, a couple of you guys came by this morning when we were in our morning slam. The lunch rush isn't much of an improvement on your timing. I'll tell you the same thing I told them—I haven't seen Gabe since his seizure here several days ago." She stopped talking, as if recalling the memory. "It was horrible. If he's not at the hospital, he's with his father, I would think."

"We thought as much." Septis stood and moved to the

door. "I apologize for being redundant, but I have not yet spoken with the other detectives. Do you have a description of the boy's parent?"

"Well, Father Joseph Adam came in here only once. Thin guy, fifty-something. Black hair, British."

"British?" Septis asked.

"That's right. Oh, and he was trying to help Gabe get his application accepted at NYU, if that helps. Hey, shouldn't you be writing this down? You know, a little organization might help keep you guys from stumbling into each other's investigations." Coren looked at him, her gaze falling to the black jacket and overcoat closed around his chest. A hint of crimson trickled through the fabric of his white shirt. "Are you bleeding, Detective?"

Septis pulled his coat tight and stormed out of the café.

Joseph Adam, he thought, *where are you?*

CHAPTER TWENTY-TWO

Classes started seven days after Gabe learned of his secret, and for the most part, he had been separated from his father and Carlyle by a busy schedule. To his dismay, he had yet to cross paths with Micah. Her classes were more advanced, with the benefit of starting a semester early.

Gabe relished getting stuck into the college life, having done all the things necessary to accomplish that transition from a regular seventeen-year-old boy to an actual university student. Books and school supplies were bought. He even attended a special orientation for those entering the semester late where he was given a list of courses assigned for his curriculum.

Life felt normal.

Much of the undergraduate module for a theology major consisted of familiar subjects. Being force-fed Bible studies for so many years turned out to be useful after all, though he'd rather eat one of his textbooks than admit it to his father.

Even with that advantage, classes were still tough. He left his final course for the day and walked back to his dorm room, feeling the heft of his new backpack pull against his neck and shoulders. Homework was already piling up, and with his free time dwindling, Gabe wondered how any college student had time to waste in a student pub.

One paper was due within the week, and several teachers were using the Socratic Method, a particularly cruel teaching technique that, in an earlier class, had ended with some poor, unprepared girl standing in front of the class as their professor peppered her with questions for which she had no answers. Gabe could barely watch the ten-minute barrage as the professor's point was made—*miss an assignment and risk the same fate.*

Gabe decided the classes weren't necessarily harder than in high school, but the focus on the work was way more intense. Much, however, remained the same from New York. Each class still ended with a stampede toward the door.

Back at the dorm, Gabe discovered a note on his door. He pulled it off and opened the envelope. *Come to the Vault Room. 5 p.m. Don't be late. Dad.*

"So much for normal."

Outside the Norman Gallery, Micah paced in the snow, biting her nails. Her brow was scrunched together, fixed in a worrisome expression as if she'd just received bad marks on a test. Gabe approached and noticed a police constable in the doorway to the building, checking people's identification before they entered.

That's new, Gabe thought.

Micah's eyes went wide as they met his, and she rushed to meet him. "Bad things, Gabe. Bad things," she said and grabbed him by the arm, pulling him close.

"Misplace your halo?"

"Don't be an ass," she snipped. "Someone tried to break into the vault."

"What? Did they get in?"

"No, but that's not the problem." She motioned to the officer rifling through some indignant student's backpack. "There's an investigation. The curator is involved, and he and Carlyle don't exactly see eye to eye."

Gabe followed Micah through the gallery and down the stairs to the vault's office. Other than the unusual amount of strangers inside the small space, everything seemed in order.

"Figured it might look a little different," Gabe said. "Did they break in and clean the place?"

"Nobody physically tried to break in. It was a hacker trying to disable the security system," Micah said.

Gabe noticed a technician working on the LCD screen next to the vault door, explaining something to his father as he worked. The screen had been removed and dangled loose to the side, making way for wires connected to the technician's laptop.

"For the third time, you bloody Cyclops," Carlyle shouted, "what's inside the vault is none of your concern."

The recipient of Carlyle's verbal assault didn't flinch. Instead, he removed a pocket watch from his coat and placed it on top of the pocket-sized notebook he held. His glass eye remained fixed and as expressionless as his long face while regarding the time. The intended impression was clear—he was an important man, and this interaction was a needless bother.

"Curator?" Gabe whispered to Micah.

She nodded. "Mortan Balor is his name."

"Professor Carlyle, please," Balor began, his tone pompous in a way that suggested he was talking down to the Scotsman. "There's no need to be rude. The university values very much your contributions to the field of religious history, but we are concerned about the contents of your vault and what might prompt a—what is the term? Yes, a cyberattack. As the appointed liaison to the local authorities, I feel it is imperative that we fully cooperate with each other and that, of course, means full disclosure."

"Even if I wanted to show you what was inside, which by the way *I do not*, I lack the power. To do so would violate the conditions on which my benefactor grants this university its annual donation. I would hate to inform them that the board wishes to breach their agreement and seek donations elsewhere," Carlyle said.

Balor snarled, curling his lip into a forced grin, and then his singular gaze turned to Gabe and Micah. "And who are you? Students? Do they have information pertinent to this inquiry?"

Gabe felt uneasy as the curator evaluated him and Micah like they were something to detest.

"Pupils of mine," Carlyle said. "They were scheduled for tutoring this afternoon."

Balor flipped a page in his notebook and licked the tip of his pen. "Do they not have names?"

Gabe felt suddenly accused of something as the man studied him, the one good eye staring down his beak nose, waiting for an answer.

Carlyle nodded to Micah, and she said, "Micah Pari."

The pen went to work on the page. "And you?"

"My name is Gabriel Adam, sir."

"An American? Interesting. A coincidence, I'm sure, that their timing is so peculiar to this incident. Surely it will please the board to know that the Head of Divinity takes such a specific interest in attending to his students," Balor said to the professor. "Nonetheless, the university would simply like assurances that what is contained inside the vault is not a danger to the student body or the integrity of this institution."

"It isn't," Carlyle snapped. "There, now. You've been assured."

The curator seemed to stiffen. "Very well. I will submit a detailed report to the board and the president."

"Please do give them my best," Carlyle said with a patronizing smile.

Balor folded his notebook and placed it inside his coat pocket as he slinked out of the room and up the stairs.

At the vault door, the technician was stowing away his instruments. Gabe's dad then led him to the exit and thanked him for his work. As soon as the upstairs door shut, he turned to Carlyle. "He said the network's firewall held but could not say where the attack originated. But I think it's safe to say it was local. Why would they attempt to deactivate the security, if they couldn't physically enter the vault?"

"Indeed," Carlyle said. "Is it possible you were followed from New York?"

"Anything is possible at this point. Although as vulnerable as we were on that trip, it seems logical that the advantage would have been taken. I'm not certain there is a connection between the events at the cathedral and this."

Carlyle grumbled something that gave the impression he agreed but then said, "Unless the enemy believes there is something of greater value kept inside the vault. Something that might give the enemy absolute power over all."

His dad caught the professor's implication. "Certainly not. Kept here? That would suggest the enemy is as blind as we are in this ordeal."

"I concur," Carlyle said. "And perhaps they are."

Gabe looked at the vault and felt, he assumed, much like Balor did. "So what *is* in the vault? What's so important that you need"—he pointed to the huge metal door—"that?"

"The vault holds only one item that warrants such protection," Carlyle said. "But it is useless to the enemy. What the vault doesn't hold, and what the enemy might believe to be contained inside, is significantly more important."

"If they do believe it's here, they'll stop at nothing," his father said.

Carlyle nodded. "As they should. That book is the key to our victory."

"Are you going to tell us, or should we start guessing?" Gabe asked.

"Carlyle thinks the enemy believes the *Apocalypse of Solomon* is here," his dad said. "It is a book that dates back to the Old Testament and foretells the End of Days, the same one that also predicts the second dimensional war."

"A book? Have they never heard of a library? Or the Internet?" Gabe asked.

"You won't find this book in either place," Micah said. "The *Apocalypse of Solomon* suffered the same fate as the texts found in the Dead Sea Scrolls—destroyed in the fourth century because they weren't good enough for the Roman Empire's master plan for Christianity. A heresy, collected and burned, each and every copy."

"You've been paying attention in class," Carlyle said. "Please continue."

"The Romans were, if anything, quite efficient," Micah said. "Paper and the ability to write were sort of a luxury in that time, so finding and burning them all was hardly a bother. Some rebelled, though, hiding copies in clay jars in the desert or anyplace else that was outside Rome's watchful eye. Like the Nag Hammadi Library and the Dead Sea Scrolls, the *Apocalypse of Solomon* survived in a similar way, kept in the possession of Carlyle's people."

"Exactly," Carlyle said. "The Qumran Essenes and our ancestors before us were meticulous historians who recognized that the cryptic text told of the signs alluding to the End of Days and took extraordinary measures to protect that information."

"What signs?" Gabe asked.

"There are many. Get a mirror, and you'll find one on the back of your head," Micah said.

Gabe looked at the vault. "If the enemy is wrong to believe it's here, then where is it?"

"Only two exist," Carlyle said. "The only physical copy

is kept by the Vatican, and though I have not seen it, its age may render it unreadable. The other is standing right in front of you."

"In front of me?"

"I *am* the book," Carlyle said.

CHAPTER TWENTY-THREE

*J*ohn Carlyle is a rogue, Mortan Balor thought as he wrapped up his day in the office above the Norman Gallery. He packed his itinerary for tomorrow, already detailed down to the minute, along with several folders of inventory notes and scheduled events, all placed neatly into a leather satchel. Before he closed it, he grabbed the small framed picture of his deceased wife from the desk and secured it safely inside the bag.

Outside the window that overlooked the castle courtyard, lanterns began to burn to life in the fading light typical of northeast winters. Below, two figures exited the gallery, a male and a female. He recognized them as the American and the girl from Professor Carlyle's office.

That man has no business influencing the minds of students, he thought.

Frustration over the professor's complete lack of deference to order and rule sparked anew. Balor decided that the best course of action would be to make a formal complaint to the board and perhaps draw their attention to his negligence as a school head. If they determined his errant methods were more dangerous to the reputation of the university than losing the funding provided by Carlyle's mysterious benefactor, the professor could be removed, and along with him, the anarchy his presence caused at the college. The man kept irrational hours, coming and going from the new museum regardless of whether or not the building was open. And to deny all school officials access to lists of what was kept inside the vault? Enough to drive mad any curator who held the slightest pride in keeping an accurate inventory. Balor thought about how hard he had worked to make the Norman Gallery a respected addition to the university, and it deserved to be run with professional distinction. Professor Carlyle's departure would be good riddance indeed.

Balor smiled at the possibility as he watched the American and girl part ways to their respective dorms.

A jingle chimed and vibrated in his jacket pocket. He removed his mobile phone to see a message—*new text*.

Text? He'd never used this function of the device and didn't appreciate others sending them, thinking it rude not to take the effort to make a phone call like a civilized person. With the press of a button, the message appeared.

Mr. Balor, I have information that might be useful to police investigation. I know what is inside vault. It is dangerous. I wish to share with you my discovery but remain anonymous. Do not wish academic retaliation. Meet me in 15 minutes at the Ice House behind the Count's House under Prebends. Come alone. Onetime offer. Signed, Prophet.

Balor scanned the message again, focusing on the word *dangerous. I knew it.* Such a message was not a surprise. *Lunatics like Professor Carlyle are never tolerated long, even by the student body. In the end, order must be maintained*, he thought. An excitement flourished at the prospect of returning normalcy to the Norman Gallery. Carlyle's end might soon be in the palm of his hand.

He checked his watch. Not a minute to spare if he wanted to get to the riverside on time. Balor hoisted his satchel and fled his office.

In the cold of the night, he hurried across the cathedral grounds and then made his way down South Bailey Street until he came to Durham Gate. Passing its singular arch, he took one of the paths that led down to the trail found at the bottom of the deep gorge carved by the river. Balor knew that his anonymous source, this Prophet, had picked the perfect location to maintain anonymity. At this time of evening, it would be dark and isolated, and not another soul would be found in the area.

Near the Prebends Bridge, hidden along the path beneath a thick overhang of trees, a tetrastyle miniature Greek temple appeared, known as the Count's House. It was a heritage site dedicated to a Polish noble who had died centuries ago in the city. The building's A-line roof was supported by four pillars and had benefited from a recent renovation into a public garden. A black iron gate blocked the entrance into the building, and another to the side led to the rear.

It had been pushed open.

Balor stepped through the gate and walked around the small temple. In the near pitch-black, he regretted not bringing a flashlight. The steep incline of the hill formed a natural wall that enclosed the back of the building. Though he couldn't see, he knew the area well from summers spent walking the river. Balor hoped to find the Ice House, a cave-like open structure built into the hill that tunneled into the earth, guarded only by a rusty gate. As the name suggested, it had been used to store ice before the age of modern refrigeration, but if his memory served correctly, it more closely resembled a tomb rather than a house.

Using what little light the screen of his mobile phone projected, he found the tiny Ice House nearly buried in a pile of snow-covered fallen leaves. The rubble retaining wall supporting the waist-high rock structure looked in disrepair. Money from the city's renovation plan had apparently not reached this far off the main path.

Behind him, he heard the sound of crunching twigs and snow. There a dark figure stood, several yards away. Balor could see that the person was rather large for a student, and he could not make out any of his features because he was clothed in a dark outfit.

"Are you Prophet?" Balor asked.

"Mortan Balor?" Prophet asked in a low voice. He stepped forward and held out his hand as if to present something.

The evidence, Balor thought. "You do a great service to your university, sir. I am indebted to you and can assure you that your involvement will never be spoken of after tonight."

"I believe you."

The last thing Mortan Balor saw was a focused stream of blue light erupt from the Prophet's hand.

The curator crumpled to the ground, his chest smoking from the burning hole that passed through his heart. Part of the hill behind Balor caught fire for a moment and then fizzled out in the wet snow.

The Prophet knew the man's sacrifice was for a greater purpose, a greater good, though he was surprised by his lack of regret for having to kill him. He had accepted this as his fate. His duty. *There will unfortunately be others, too.* He approached the body and began searching, patting down the clothes. In the pocket of the dead man's trousers something jangled.

The master key to the Norman Gallery.

He pulled out the key chain and smiled, placing the prize in his coat. This gave him the access he had been denied in the attempt to hack the vault's system. He acknowledged the mistake. Now he understood more force would need to be applied if he were to get what he wanted. The change in strategy suited him, a direct course of action preferred to hiding in the shadows.

The Prophet dragged Balor's corpse to the small rusty gate and cleared away the debris in front of the Ice House to allow it to open. With some effort, he pushed the dead man deep into the tunnel and then buried him along with his satchel in fallen leaves.

His plan to secure the treasure inside the vault was now nearly complete. Only one step remained—create a distraction. The Prophet looked at his watch. *No time to waste.*

CHAPTER TWENTY-FOUR

An hour later, Gabe met Micah on the Palace Green having already returned to their dorm rooms to dispose of heavy schoolbags and catch up on the day's homework. She had taken the opportunity to change into an outfit that looked more suitable for an evening out. Her long hair and the high turtleneck of the fitted black sweater she wore put her freshly glossed lips and dark eyeliner on display like a piece of art in a gallery. Gabe felt underdressed in his usual blue jeans and brown jacket.

She didn't say much as he followed her down the hill into Durham's city center. His thoughts returned to the conversation at the vault and what Carlyle had said. Ancient texts, dimensional wars, the End of Days, and living books. His life had become fully cemented in the weird. Before these ideas led him into an endless loop of questions, he regarded the girl ahead. He couldn't help but notice the way she placed one foot in front of the other as if she were walking a line. Her legs were hypnotic. Like her cinched waist. And rolling hips. And . . .

She turned and her eyes met his. For a nanosecond, Gabe

felt a sting of embarrassment, like he'd been caught in a forbidden act, but she hadn't noticed his stare.

"God, I'm famished. Haven't eaten all day," Micah said as they crossed Elvet Bridge. "Fancy a bite at the New Inn? It's a decent hangout for students. Good music."

Gabe stopped, snapped from his trance, and the nagging questions returned. Micah had promised to discuss their situation at the vault over dinner and a drink, but he needed answers. Now. "How can you think about socializing? There's taking things in stride, but you're acting as though none of this is a big deal."

She rolled her eyes. "How would you like me to act? Shall I run through the streets, shouting at the top of my lungs about the end of the world?"

"No. But I would think you'd at least be a little concerned. This might be familiar to you, but I'm having some difficulty taking it all in." Gabe watched the boats pass under the bridge on the River Wear. "What did Carlyle mean, that stuff about being the book?"

"Once upon a time," Micah started, her tone childish and mocking, "the Essenes were, outside of the Vatican, the only custodians of the book. Like ancient librarians, know what I mean? So, when Rome cracked down on illegal texts, they secretly passed it within their society from generation to generation, like some kind of verbal rite or whatever. A ritual of a sort. They memorized the book, I think. In one of my theology classes we learned of a transcription practice used by Jewish scribes to copy the Torah bit by bit. Word for word. The Essenes probably used a similar method."

"So the Essenes are the only ones left who can understand the book?" Gabe asked.

"It's worse than that. Carlyle is the last of the Essenes."

"Seriously?" Gabe almost laughed. "What if he gets amnesia or something?"

"Indeed," Micah said. "A troublesome new development he discovered when the Vatican lost contact with the last Protector. That's why he's been instructing your father in the early fundamentals of the book and the Essene tradition. In the text's passages are some of the most important clues to our roles."

"Why aren't the others here, then?" Gabe said.

"We don't know the identity of the third archangel or his Protector. They kept that stuff from Carlyle and your dad in case you or I were compromised. Only the Vatican has that information. Apparently, they lost contact just before you arrived," Micah said. "And with the fourth, Phanuel, who knows? We have only rumors that he even exists. For some reason, he never got a Protector. Hopefully they're both in hiding."

"And what if they're dead?"

Micah furrowed her brow, finally showing some measure of concern. "That's why Carlyle and your father are so worried about what happened in New York and the security breach at the vault. They believe it's an organized effort against us. If you think about it, the strategy is sound—end the war before we even have an opportunity to wage it. I think it's safe to assume that one of Mastema's fallen was responsible for your friend's death and the destruction of your church."

Gabe wanted to laugh again at the fanciful suggestion of

evil angels but resisted the impulse.

Micah must have sensed his disbelief. "You'd better learn to accept this reality. This isn't some fantasy. One day soon, if what Carlyle and your father believe is happening comes true, we will be called upon to stop these forces. We each have a power within that should begin to manifest. Once it does, you'd better have control, which means the sooner you believe, the quicker you'll be prepared. By all rights, these manifestations shouldn't occur for another couple of years. That is why Carlyle is so insistent on intensifying our training. He hopes to bring them to the surface."

"What sort of power?" asked Gabe.

Micah joined him at the side of the bridge and gazed at the water. "I don't know. Only weird descriptions in agnostic texts give us clues as to the nature of our abilities. But there is more than just our power. Carlyle has mentioned that the *Apocalypse of Solomon* contains specific references to weapons of a more physical nature, which we are to acquire. Like the Ring of Solomon. You may have read about it in other texts as well—texts that were also omitted from the Old Testament and Torah."

Gabe laughed out loud this time. "I meant to check those out but never really got around to it."

Micah smiled with him. "Why am I not surprised?"

"So? What does this almighty ring do?" Gabe asked.

"Well, for those of us who are not so well-read, the ancient books describe it as so powerful an object, that legend says Solomon used it to wield control over demons. They became slaves to build the First Temple in Jerusalem. If there is any truth to that, the enemy will remember its power and be intent on preventing it from falling into our hands, though from what Carlyle has said, it's lost to time anyway."

"It is a fascinating story—I'll give you that."

"It's more than a story. Your nightmares have told you that much, just as mine have. It's out there somewhere and is powerful enough to conquer nations."

Gabe recalled his vision of Alexander the Great and the gift he received.

"Best learn to accept it," Micah said. "And until we discover more about our enemy, we need to be prepared for the worst. We don't even know what to look for in the enemy, or for that matter, who they are. If one were to walk down this very street, it's doubtful that either of us would know."

Now it was Gabe's turn to feel worried. Other images from his visions flashed in his mind, a blue-eyed man in a suit, his shirt covered in swirling patterns of blood. "I might," he said.

CHAPTER TWENTY-FIVE

The pieces began to connect in Gabe's mind.

"What do you mean?" Micah asked. Her voice dropped to a whisper. "You've actually seen the enemy?"

"My visions," he said, looking to Micah to see if she had a similar experience. She appeared surprised. This was new to her. "Apart from seeing the end of the world, I kept seeing this . . . man."

"What was he like?" Micah asked with a hint of nervousness.

"Very businesslike. Like an attorney, maybe. He was well dressed, wearing all black. Tidy shoes, expensive suit. There was something about him, though, something not quite real. It's as if he wore a disguise. Like his fancy looks and nice dress weren't really him. Also, it didn't match what was behind the eyes. They were so blue . . . so . . . cold.

"He spoke to me in what I think was Latin and then said, 'It shall all come to pass.'" Gabe paused, reliving the memory.

"Oh, my God," Micah said. "I've read that phrase before. Recently, in fact. It comes from Thecla's Apocrypha."

"Who's what, now?"

"I overheard Carlyle talking with your father about our

training—something about using a kind of acceleration technique. An anointing oil I'd never heard of, like a drug of some sort, but I didn't catch the name. Your father objected and warned Carlyle of Thecla's Apocrypha."

"I don't understand," Gabe said.

"I didn't, either, so I looked it up at the library. Thecla was a follower of Paul's apocalyptic ministry in the first century. Apparently, she somehow acquired something called the Entheos Genesthai and drank some. This is the accelerant that Carlyle was talking about." She seemed to tense. "Do you know what Entheos Genesthai is?"

"Are you serious? Under what circumstance would I ever need to know what . . . whatever it's called is? I don't know what the hell you're talking about most of the time anyway. It's all Greek to me."

"It's all Greek to *everyone*, idiot. It *is* Greek. Literally, it means 'becoming God within.' Look, I'll put it to you this way. If you've ever had any interest in substance experimentation while you're at university, you'll be able to get it all done in one go with that stuff. I don't want anything to do with it. Honestly!" Micah said as if referring to some recent scandal.

"But you're not supposed to drink it," she continued. "That's bad. It's too powerful. Like an overdose, you know? Only these witch doctor types were supposed to administer it and only in the tiniest amount exposed to the skin on the forehead. It sounded to me like an ancient version of peyote and the way the Native Americans used it to commune with nature. So, she drank it, a whole vial apparently, and fell into a trance. The story reads that she started describing visions she was having, given to her by God. Visions of the End of Days. According to what I read, she kept saying 'It shall all come to pass.'"

"I'd rather not hear the details. The less I actually know, the less stressful all of this actually is, and the happier I am. Blissful ignorance. Unenlightened. That's where I'm best. I'm sure it's just coincidence. How about that bite?" Gabe turned from the river to leave.

She frowned and shook her head, as if something had left a bad taste in her mouth. "We don't tell them about it."

"About what?"

"The man from your vision. Carlyle and your father don't need to hear it. If Carlyle said he could get the Entheos Genesthai, then that means it exists. It's not just a legend, and I'm not about to become a lunatic like that girl did in the story."

Gabe thought about it. She had a point. Besides, he couldn't see how knowing the man's face would help.

"Bollocks to food. I need a drink. And a bit of company." Micah grabbed his coat and spun him around, back toward the castle Undercroft.

CHAPTER TWENTY-SIX

The Undercroft Pub was, as Carlyle had first described, a dungeon of a place with stone arches that held up low ceilings. Gabe half expected to see chains hanging from the walls, but instead there were beer signs, beer mirrors, and posters of half-dressed women holding beer. A jukebox played the latest mix of British indie rock and American pop music.

Students gathered around the tables and bar, chatting and having drinks—beer, mixed spirits, ciders, and shots of all sorts. Gabe found it strange to see people his age carrying on in a pub.

Some of the guys at the bar were hitting on the barmaid who was, in Gabe's opinion, worthy of their attention. She brushed them away, as she did her peroxide-streaked auburn hair that cascaded to her face. She peered through the remaining strands and caught his glance. With a slight smirk, she made another drink.

Micah managed to find an empty table near one of the louder groups of students playing a card game that involved a bucket. She fell into a chair. "Mind getting the first round? I mean, if you're not too busy trying to pull the barmaid. A stout, please."

"I wasn't trying to . . . *She* smiled at *me*."

He walked to the bar and wedged between two groups of students. One hooligan tried to sneak a free pull off one of the kegs, which earned him a swat from the barmaid.

Once Gabe got her attention, she came right over, looking pleased to get away from her admirers. "Something to drink?" she said in an Irish accent.

"A stout and a, uh . . ." Gabe looked at the different beers on the wall and realized he had no idea what to order. He thought beer was just, well, beer. "Two stouts, please."

"Canadian?" she asked.

"American, actually."

"I haven't seen you round the pub. Are you a student from one of the other colleges?" She poured the stouts from the tap, filling each glass halfway up.

"No. I go to Castle. Just transferred in."

"Well, hope to see you round, then." The barmaid finished pouring each pint and knifed off the rim of the glasses, scraping away the extra head. "Cheers," she said with a wink and handed them over.

"Yeah, cheers," he said. Gabe paid for the pints with a few coin pounds and returned to his seat next to Micah.

"I thought she was going to bloody jump your bones, the tart. Could she have been more obvious?" Micah sneered toward the bar.

"What?" Gabe asked. "She was just getting the beer."

"Well, she fancies you. Played right, you might get more than a drink. A trip to the general practitioner, likely."

Gabe rolled his eyes and Micah laughed.

There was a short silence between them. "God, this day. Can you believe it?"

"I don't want to talk about it anymore," Gabe said. "Seriously. I'm having enough trouble trying to digest what I've already heard."

"You're starting to accept it, then?" Micah asked.

"I don't know. Maybe. Maybe I'm just going along because I'm sick of fighting with my own sanity. I mean, I'm in *England*. It's like I'm living someone else's life. Or dreaming. Like when I wake up, I'll be back in New York. It's all so weird." He drank his first sip of the dark stout and nearly choked. "Good Lord. You could chew this! *Disgusting*."

"You'll get used to it." She winked.

"I'd rather not," he said and pushed the glass away.

The table next to them broke out in a fit of laughter. One of the guys closest to Micah leaned over and asked, "You two fancy a game of kings?"

"I don't think—," she started.

"Sure," Gabe said, cutting her off. "Anything to get me out of this conversation. You'll have to catch us up on the rules."

He looked at Micah, who feigned a hurt expression. "You may need catching up, but I don't," she said. "I'll have you know I'm the queen of kings."

"She reckons she's a player, lads," the student said to the rest of the crowd. He motioned for them to join the group and said, "I'm Yuri, by the way. We're from Collingwood College."

"Gabe. Nice to meet you."

Yuri smiled at Micah, brushing some of his shaggy blond hair out of his face, and did a mock bow. "Highness, is it?"

"Micah will do. What are you lot doing at the Undercroft? Collingwood's pub not good enough?"

"Oh, don't be coy. We know all about you Castle girls. Very keen is what we've heard." Yuri laughed, elbowing the guy next to him.

"What a coincidence. Because that is exactly what we've heard about you Collingwood boys. *Very* keen," Micah said, letting her wrist go limp and mockingly elbowing Gabe.

Some of Yuri's friends caught her implication and broke into a fit of laughter.

CHAPTER TWENTY-SEVEN

The drinking games lasted several hours into the night with the group in a constant state of laughter nearly the whole time. It was nice to just be a normal student, even if for only one night, and Gabe guessed Micah felt the same way.

He received a lot of attention for being American, then more attention for being a likable American. Several of the girls who joined in showed some flirtatious interest, including one particularly forward girl from Glasgow, which he certainly didn't mind. He noted Micah receiving similar advances from Yuri and the other guys.

At some point, the barmaid announced that the Undercroft had to close. Like the other students, Gabe was not ready to turn in.

Yuri seemed to be in charge of the mob and jumped onto a chair in the middle of their group. "Down to the club or back to mine for the Wall of Death?"

An overwhelming shout for the Wall of Death erupted from several of the students.

"To Collingwood Palace, then!"

Having switched from beer to energy drinks early in

the night, Gabe had an ungodly amount of caffeine surging through his system. He felt up for anything.

Yuri jumped down and threw his arm around Micah, leading the crowd toward the exit. Gabe cursed himself for not having Yuri's confidence or his tall quarterback's build. Sure, several of the girls were pretty enough, but none of them held a candle to Micah. She was witty and likeable, with a wicked smile and a magnetic look. Had he not known her, she would have been the first person he noticed if he'd just walked into the room.

Rowdy and unfazed by the late hour, several of Yuri's friends sang a soccer fight song at the top of their lungs for the entire half-hour walk from Castle College. Micah followed, clapping and joining in the chant as they crossed Kingsgate Bridge and then climbed Church Street toward Collingwood College. Gabe wondered what the police presence was like in Durham and how many nuisance laws they were breaking with all the noise.

Near the New Inn, the mob turned a corner and converged near a row of townhomes. At the first house, Yuri pressed through the group to unlock the entrance. He opened his door wide and said, "Welcome to Collingwood Palace. Beer in the fridge, spirits in the cabinet. What's mine is yours."

It was difficult not to be instantly jealous of the entertainment system sporting a flat-screen television that Gabe suspected doubled for the local movie theater. Clearly, Yuri was the man to be affiliated with at the university.

Several guys cracked open beers, turned on the giant screen and satellite programming to the sports channel, and spread out on the couch as if they lived here.

A loud pop across the room startled Gabe. Yuri approached Micah with a freshly poured glass of champagne and a bottle of bubbly.

He then pointed to Gabe and said, "As an honored guest to our beloved United Kingdom, I think you should be the first to attempt the Wall of Death. Prove to us that you Americans know how to have as much fun as us Brits."

Gabe saw an opportunity to gain some favor with the other students and maybe even impress Micah. "Bring on the Wall of Death, then."

Yuri took Gabe, Micah, and the rest of the spectators into the kitchen where a series of five bottles waited, turned upside down and affixed to a dispensing mechanism on the wall that looked as if it had been stolen from a pub. Each bottle attached to a spout with a handle that released their contents.

"The rules of the Wall of Death are as follows: you'll need to assume the position, as it were, under each of the spouts and prepare yourself. I, as king of *this* castle"—the Collingwood students roared with applause at the jab at the other school— "will pour a fair but yet to be determined amount. You are to drink it, swallow, and then immediately move on to the next bottle until the circuit is completed. Spill very little, if you please. Now, just so you're aware, we have a whisky, a vodka, a cider, a peach schnapps, and a lager."

The description of the lineup made Gabe's stomach turn.

"Step up, sir," Yuri said as if taunting him. "And if I may make one suggestion . . . breathe through your nose."

Gabe maneuvered under the first spout and opened his

mouth. Before he was ready, the whisky flowed. He choked but managed to get it all in. Yuri was being liberal with the quantity. Gabe swallowed, and his throat felt like it was on fire. Then he was under the second spout. Vodka filled his mouth. For a split second he thought it might come up through his nose, but he persisted, his eyes watering, nearly blinding him. Then the cider, repulsive and sugary. The taste combined with the previous two and caused his stomach to lurch. Not wanting to think about it, he moved on.

"Come on, Gabriel," Micah shouted.

Fueled by her encouragement, Gabe opened his mouth for the peach schnapps. It was almost a relief in taste, but feeling it mix in his stomach with the others caused him to break out in a worrisome sweat. He was running out of breath as the lager hit his mouth.

This has got to end, he thought.

With his mouth filled, he was forced to swallow. Yuri continued to pour. A small amount splashed onto the floor. Before Gabe could quit, the game mercifully ended.

The carbonation of the lager seared his throat, and his eyes burned.

"We have a result, ladies and gentlemen!" Yuri shouted.

Gabe stumbled and choked as the students cheered. His stomach told him at any moment he could be sick, but he fought the urge in the presence of Micah. Somebody handed him a towel. The room spun.

Yuri smiled like a game show host as he slapped Gabe on the back, perhaps a little too hard. "Welcome to England, my son. Hell of a job for a Yank."

Micah laughed and applauded. "Well done, Gabe. Hell of a job for anybody."

"We'll see. You're next, Micah." Yuri grabbed her by the waist to position her in front of the Wall of Death.

"No, I've had too much already," she protested.

The crowd roused, insisting, even more excited for her attempt. If his head hadn't been spinning so hard, Gabe might have been able to help her. Instead, Yuri poured the whisky into her open mouth while holding her captive under the bottle.

A lot fell from the spout, and Gabe wondered if he had taken the same amount. She was already choking by the time she finished the whisky. Half the vodka portion fell to the floor when she stood up, choking and laughing along with the rest of the crowd. She playfully hit Yuri on the shoulder.

He, of course, had the crowd cheering her name.

When Micah finished straightening her clothes and wiping her chin, laughing the whole time, Yuri handed her the champagne flute she'd neglected. Gabe wondered how such a jerk move got such great results.

CHAPTER TWENTY-EIGHT

Gabe sat on the couch next to several students he didn't know and watched them play soccer on a video game console—the latest and most expensive one, naturally. Ever since the Wall of Death he'd been trying unsuccessfully to sober up, downing nothing but water. He couldn't stand the sight of hard alcohol, and the beer had lasted about five minutes, leaving only fruity liquor and some rancid cider drink that came in plastic two-liter soda bottles. It smelled like socks. *Old socks.*

Some time had passed since he'd seen Micah, and, thankfully, the girl from Glasgow who had pestered him all night for attention had stopped flirting, only to pass out on the couch in an unflattering position. Gabe wanted to go back to his dorm room and give up on the evening.

The clock on the wall caught his eye. He couldn't believe how late it was, or more accurately, how early. In the back of his mind lingered the notion that something wasn't right and that he should stay and make sure Micah was okay. *She can take care of herself,* he thought. *Anyway, who am I to act like someone's guardian angel?* He laughed at the unintended joke in his head.

The students playing the video game gave him an odd look.

"Inside joke," Gabe said to them and pulled himself away from the deep cushions of the couch, already thinking about his warm bed. The night was done. He took a moment to find his balance and then made his way toward the exit.

Upstairs, a door slammed, and Micah shouted something.

Everyone stopped what they were doing and looked toward the foyer, Gabe included.

Before he could even comprehend what was going on, Micah stormed down the staircase, practically bouncing off the walls. "Bastard!" she shouted to no one in particular. She reached the front door and pushed past Gabe.

"What's wrong?"

"That . . . perverted . . ." She turned and shouted up the stairs, "Bastard!"

He followed her out the door and tried to keep up.

Yuri stumbled down the stairs behind them. He was shirt-less and probably drunk, the cold having no effect. "Gabe, my son, why don't you go inside and fix yourself another? Me and the young miss have a bit to work out of her."

Gabe grabbed him by the arm and prevented him from pursuing her. "Why don't you go back to your palace and call it a night? She's obviously not interested."

"Get your hands off me," Yuri shouted and, in an explosion of anger, shoved Gabe to the ground. He hit hard, the wet snow soaking into his clothes.

Micah turned around to see Gabe on his back. "Just who do you think—?"

"Bloody tease! Get your ass back inside, you stupid bitch."

The degree to which Yuri's temper rose seemed to catch Micah by surprise. Gabe could see her recoil from the maddened look on the blond boy's face.

Then a searing pain in Gabe's hand traveled past his wrist and up through his forearm to his shoulder, like he had grabbed hold of a lightning bolt. He could no longer maintain his balled-up fist, and in that instant he realized he was up and had punched Yuri in the jaw.

He toppled to the ground like a falling tree and then started to get up but instead collapsed again in a heap. Several of his drunken friends came out to see the commotion. Because of their dulled wits, it seemed to take them a moment to work out what had just happened. Once they did, Micah and Gabe became the target of vicious verbal abuse and insults, though none of them thought to challenge the kid who had just felled their leader with one blow.

Gabe gave his hardest look to discourage any of them from getting physically involved. It was all for show—only a bluff. His hand had disappeared into the pain and left him unable to fight on, even if they were all drunk.

Micah pulled Gabe away. "Let's go. They're not worth it."

He turned to see Yuri being helped to his feet by several of his friends. He looked steady and, strangely, focused with a dagger stare, no longer the out-of-control drunk from the moment before. Gabe thought he saw a smile behind the blond locks that fell into his rival's face.

They hurried away, past the New Inn and toward Kingsgate Bridge. Once again, Micah practically dragged him by his coat.

Gabe cradled his hand under his arm. She finally noticed

and slowed down.

"Do you think they're following us?" Micah glanced behind them. "There's been enough drama for one night." She looked at his hand. "Is it broken?"

"Don't know. Hurts like hell, though."

"Let's have a look."

Gabe winced as he held his hand out for Micah. It was swollen. A bruise had formed just under the knuckle.

"Can you move your fingers?"

Reluctantly, he tried and they all moved. "Yeah, sort of."

"They're probably not broken, then." She bent down to scoop up some fresh snow off the sidewalk. "Come here. Give us your hand."

Gabe held out his hand again.

Micah piled the snow on his knuckles. "No one's ever defended my honor before." She laughed. "I thought people only did stupid things like that in those black-and-white movies Carlyle likes to watch."

"That's me. Old-fashioned, I guess."

"Well, anyway, for what it's worth, thanks."

"My pleasure," he said. The pain in his hand was replaced by the stinging cold, but soon it went numb.

Gabe and Micah stared at each other in silence.

Her gaze darted away, and she looked up the street toward Collingwood. "What a prat, they are. I swear the posh ones are the worst. With their Pimm's and pashmina. They buy you a drink and think they have a free pass into your knickers."

Gabe laughed a little through the discomfort. "I have no idea what you just said."

"But you know what I mean. He *was* an ass."

"I thought so, too. The snow is helping. Thanks."

They took their time as they strolled along the empty street, occasionally stealing glances at each other. Neither of them dared to speak, though Micah kept smiling and biting her lower lip, as if she wanted to. But Gabe didn't mind the silence. Just being in her company was enough.

Along the way, they stopped at a small church playground across the street from a cemetery. Gabe sensed a sadness or regret as she stared at the swing sets under the trees. She seemed to drift in her thoughts. Micah left his side and entered the playground through the open gate. She walked to a merry-go-round and brushed the snow off before sitting down. He followed her in, unsure of what to say or do. If only awkward was something he could shed, like his jacket.

"When I was a kid, Carlyle used to take me to parks like this. I think he wanted me to feel like I still had a childhood, even with everything that had happened." She patted the seat beside her, beckoning him to sit. "I know how you feel, Gabe. About everything. I miss the promise of those days, too. The hope of that future. We have more in common, I think, than I want to admit."

He joined her, and she kicked the ground. They spun slowly, picnic tables and seesaws passing by. He looked into Micah's eyes and saw an inner conflict waging.

Once again, she grabbed him by his jacket. This time, she pulled herself close and kissed him on the lips, holding herself to him for just a second.

Her breasts crushed against his chest. Gabe's cheeks

flushed, and his heartbeat doubled. He no longer thought about how cold it was or how much his hand hurt. In fact, he no longer thought of anything except the soft wetness of her full lips, the warmth of her body, and how amazing it felt to be kissing Micah.

She pulled away, and Gabe could see that all her confidence and light had returned.

"In case you're wondering, he never had a chance," she whispered with a smile. They held each other's gaze until her eyes narrowed, and then her smile faded. "Do you hear that?"

"Hear what?" Gabe listened to the night. Behind the hush of the wind and falling snow he heard a very distinct sound coming from the direction of the castle.

"It's the alarm."

CHAPTER TWENTY-NINE

The cold air burned in Gabe's lungs as he ran after Micah through the castle gatehouse, his hand throbbing again as blood flowed harder to the bruised hand. She was faster than him, and in the darkness, he had trouble keeping up.

She stopped in the courtyard, searching as the Norman Gallery's alarm blared into the night. "See anything?"

"No. It's too dark," Gabe said and followed her to the entrance. The door was slightly open.

"It's been picked, or someone has a key," Micah said under her breath.

"We should call the police. Or Carlyle."

Micah didn't respond but instead pushed the door open and walked inside.

"This is stupid," Gabe protested. "If we get caught, that curator will have us expelled. He'll think we did it. He suspects us already."

She turned and put her finger to her lips. "If we catch the intruder," she whispered, "we can find out what's going on before the authorities interfere."

Gabe knew he couldn't change her mind. They crept

down the hall, past the maze of new glass cases and model displays as quietly as possible, careful not to disturb the delicate exhibits.

"Look," she said.

The door to the stairway leading to the vault was unhinged and lay broken against the wall. Smoke drifted up from a scorch mark by the doorknob as if it had been electrocuted or blowtorched. Gabe could smell more fumes drifting up the staircase.

"Something's on fire," Micah said and rushed down into the dark.

Gabe followed her, his arm over his mouth to avoid inhaling smoke.

Inside, the lamp lay on the floor, its bulb sparking and flashing. Books and papers were strewn about the room, some of them smoldering. The gate had been destroyed and bent back at an awkward angle, but the vault remained sealed.

On the surface of the heavy door was a charred scar crumpling the metal in a way that looked like a bomb had been detonated there. The amount of force needed to cause steel to warp like that was unimaginable.

"It held," Micah said.

Above the basement came the sound of shattering glass.

Micah looked at Gabe. "The intruder."

She stormed past him and up the stairs.

"Micah, wait. It could be dangerous." He ran after her, thinking of Richard's horrible fate. Upstairs, he found her crouched down by an overturned exhibit in pieces on the floor. Something caught her attention outside—a shadow sprinting into the night.

She tore after the specter, through the entrance and into the freezing air with Gabe following close behind. The intruder ran down Owengate Street, past The Shakespeare Tavern, and toward the city center.

Micah stopped and pulled Gabe into the narrowest of crevices between the buildings. "This way is faster, down the castle wall stairs. It will cut off the intruder's escape."

Wide steps, narrowly spaced, made the steepness of the descent tricky to navigate. Gabe had trouble keeping his balance, and the darkness prevented him from seeing any-thing in front of him.

His eyes adjusted, and he found a medieval wall made of stone on his left following the path, which left no more than four feet of space from the back of the buildings of the market shops. Crates and cardboard boxes from store inventory obstructed the uneven ground.

"Quickly and mind your step!" Micah said.

The warning came too late. Gabe lost his footing and stumbled, falling onto the damp concrete. He used the castle wall to regain his composure and get back to his feet, but Micah had disappeared into the alley. Gabe hurried, wanting to catch her before she did anything that might get her in trouble.

As he neared the bend in the alley that led to the street, a blinding white light flashed, illuminating the path. It looked like lightning but not in the sky. Spots filled his vision, and his eyes burned.

"Micah?" Gabe shouted, feeling the way ahead along the

wall with his hands. Someone moaned nearby. He stumbled from the alley and into the open, still blind. His boot caught on something, and he fell to the ground, splashing into puddles of snow and ice.

CHAPTER THIRTY

abe's eyes began to readjust to the night enough to see his legs. Micah lay under them, whimpering and in obvious pain. He untangled his feet from her coat. "Are you okay? What happened? Can you move?"

She rolled over onto her back and rubbed her head, checking her hand for blood. "Too many questions . . . ears ringing."

"Too many? Are you serious? I thought you were dead."

She started to move, which let out the air that had been held in his lungs. "He got away," she said and sat up.

"I noticed. What the hell was that light?"

"You saw it, too? I thought they were stars from a punch." She rubbed her head again, obviously feeling the pain. "No knot but I still think he hit me. My whole brain feels like it's been microwaved. Help me up."

"Maybe you should lay there until I get some help."

She looked at him, eyebrows arched, indignant.

"Or I can help you up." Gabe stood, his knee aching as he did so, and grabbed her under the arm to lift.

Micah was able to stand, but it seemed to take all her effort. "I need to work on my sea legs. Did you see anything?"

"No. Just a flash of light."

She moaned. "That's unfortunate."

"Let's get you back to Carlyle's. He'll know what to do."

"No," Micah said. "He's not going to know, because we're not telling him."

Gabe's objection must have been plain on his face.

Micah dusted the snow off her clothes and stood taller, defiant. "If he finds out, we'll be locked up until the End of Days. I don't know about you, but I already feel like a prisoner in my life. Telling Carlyle won't make anything better for us, and it won't do anything to help them figure out what's going on. There was an intruder; he got away. Nothing changes that. That also means you're not telling your father, either. He and Carlyle are beginning to share a brain."

"That's ridiculous. You were just *attacked*."

"Not up for discussion."

Gabe could see in her eyes that she was serious and that unless he wanted to lose her trust, he would do as she said. "So what do we tell them? They'll know about the vault, if they don't already."

"We'll tell them we were out, and we heard the alarm. That's it."

"And the light? How do you explain that?"

"A stun gun or something. Maybe a Taser. I don't know."

Gabe wasn't sure, either. Two trails in the snow extended from her feet to where she had lain on the street, as if she'd been dragged, standing, several yards from a bald spot on the ground where the snow was melted away. Micah had not noticed it yet. Gabe thought about asking her, but she looked worried enough.

She tried to walk but wobbled, falling into Gabe's arms.

"Fine. We'll do it your way. But I'm taking you back to your room."

"I need to call Carlyle first. Let him know about the alarm." She pulled out her phone from her pocket and tried to turn it on, but nothing happened. "It's dead. I thought I charged it. Give me yours."

Gabe handed her his new phone. "My dad just gave me this, but I don't have anyone's numbers in it yet."

"That's okay." Micah dialed a number, and when Carlyle answered, she told him the news. As Micah had promised, she left out any account of the chase through the city center or her injury, then hung up. "He already knew. He wants us to stay away from the vault and suspects Balor will be on his way, along with the Durham police. Carlyle doesn't want to complicate the situation by us being there."

Gabe was thankful for that at least. Micah was in no condition to deal with adults. He wasn't, either, for that matter.

"Let's get you home, then." He put her arm over his shoulder and held her waist to steady her balance. As they walked up the hill to the university, he glanced back at the new flakes beginning to cover the exposed patch of concrete. The only explanation was that the snow had been instantly melted away, but that didn't make sense.

Nothing does anymore, he thought.

CHAPTER THIRTY-ONE

BC One blared from the clock radio accompanied by an electronic alarm that beeped like the warning signal of a reversing truck. Gabe woke and thought he was about to be run over. Correction—he felt like he *had* been run over. He squinted to a rush of daylight. It hurt, like a migraine twisting to life.

In the glare, he caught a glimpse of the red numbers on the clock's digital face. He was already late for Carlyle's study at the vault.

Noon, he thought. *So much for breakfast.*

With one slap, the alarm quieted.

Muscles ached from head to toe. A film that tasted like chalk covered his tongue. He wanted—no, he *needed*—water. By the gallon, if possible.

A stab of pain shot through his hand as he sat up in bed. There he discovered a mosaic of purples, greens, and reds surrounding two knuckles.

Memories from last night trickled through the alcohol-soaked synapses of his brain.

She kissed me, he recalled. The notion kept repeating itself as if it might become easier to believe, but it happened—he was there. For the most part at least.

He moved and felt another shock of pain. His knee throbbed when it bent, and then the rest of the night came back. *The intruder. Micah lying on the ground. The strange patch of missing snow.*

Carlyle and his father needed to know about the attack, but Micah would never forgive him if he went back on his word. Gabe decided to keep it to himself for now. He'd work on her later and hopefully change her mind about keeping it secret.

In the meantime, he needed to see about the break-in.

Gabe entered the vault, now cleaned and straightened from the intrusion with the exception of a dented lamp shade and the broken mirror. Even the blast mark had been scrubbed from the fresh dent in the vault's door. Micah sat at the desk, turned away from the entrance, with her nose in a book and her face hidden by a curtain of hair. She didn't look up when he walked in. Gabe tried coughing a little to get her attention, but she kept reading.

Trouble, he thought.

Carlyle and Gabe's father looked caught in one of their intellectual sparring matches, their discussion a series of animated whispers and hand gestures. Probably something to do with the security at the vault.

Gabe ignored them and sat down beside Micah. "What's going on?"

She didn't look up.

He let his book bag fall to the floor in a heap, hoping to get her attention.

"We'll be with you both in a moment," his dad said with a dismissive gesture.

"One second," Micah said rather loudly, without a glance.

Gabe's heart sank. He recalled the kiss at the playground. "Look, I know what you're thinking—last night was a mistake. We drank too much," he whispered.

She kept reading, lost in the book.

"It's fine. I won't let it get weird," he continued. "But what happened last night, the *other thing* . . . we need to tell them about the—"

"There," Micah yelled and closed the book. She pulled her hair away from her ear and removed two earbuds connected to a small music player hidden in her pocket. Its black cords were invisible in her hair. "Sorry. Was I shouting?" She leaned over and kissed Gabe. "How are you feeling? My head's killing me."

Gabe's mouth hung open, and he noticed a silence had filled the room. The hushed debate had stopped. He turned to Carlyle and his father. They looked frozen, eyes wide as if someone had punched them both in the gut.

"What was that?" his dad asked. "Did I just see you two kiss?"

"Did you kiss him, Micah?" Carlyle asked.

"Yeah. So, what's on the agenda for today?" she asked.

"What's on the . . . ?" Carlyle fumbled through his documents and books, none of which, Gabe suspected, were written on the complexities of raising a teenage daughter.

"You two can't bloody kiss. You're Watchers!"

"I don't care if I'm the Pope. I can kiss whomever I please. Including Gabe, unless he should prefer I didn't."

"I'm just here to learn," Gabe said.

Micah cleared her throat and cocked an eyebrow.

"But the kiss is good, too."

She winked and nodded, as if to say, *Damn right it is*.

"You weren't meant to *be* together," his father said. "I mean, you're meant to be together, of course. But not *together*." He made a horrible colliding motion with his hands that nearly caused Gabe to dissolve from embarrassment.

Micah rolled her eyes and began fixing a nail. "Calm down. It's just a kiss. It's not like we've had sex."

"Oh, my God." Gabe put his face in his hands.

Carlyle and his dad nearly choked on their tongues as a frenzy of arguments spun around the small room. Gabe couldn't understand a word from any of them as the bickering rambled on.

"Right, then!" Carlyle slammed his hand on a book like a gavel, bringing the room to order. "For the meantime, you two are not to see each other outside the context of what we're doing and learning here. Is that clear? There is too much at stake for the both of you to be anything less than totally focused on our cause."

"Whatever." Micah's tone said something else entirely.

"Yes, sir," Gabe responded.

For an awkward moment nobody looked at each other.

"As you both know, there was another attempted breach last night on the vault," Carlyle began. "All the security cameras had been disabled, and the police have discovered that whoever entered the gallery had access. A key, it seems."

Gabe remained quiet, staring at his feet.

Micah put on a show of feigned ignorance. "Is the curator going to shut us down?"

"No," his father said. "There will be no internal investigation by the board or the gallery. Mortan Balor has gone missing."

"That man had access to the Norman Gallery," Carlyle said. "I've spoken with the Vatican. They're investigating his background. It's possible he may have been compromised."

His dad sighed. "We've also come to the conclusion that your need for acceleration is justified."

Gabe remembered Micah's warning about Thecla.

His father continued, "Whoever is conspiring against us clearly has the upper hand. We can no longer afford to treat time as a luxury."

"The accelerant," Carlyle said, "is a ritual device used in ancient ceremonies where the devout would attempt to commune with God."

"Entheos Genesthai," Micah said. "We know all about it. And what it can do."

If Carlyle was surprised, he didn't show it. "Good. Then you must now understand how dire our circumstance is to resort to such extreme measures. I've made the request to the Vatican, and we should have possession of the substance shortly. Since we are now pressed, I believe it is time to share all I know about what secrets the vault holds."

"Before you begin," his dad said, "I'd like a word with Gabe in private."

"Agreed. Perhaps Micah and I have some things to discuss as well."

Upstairs, Gabe followed his father through the glass exhibits of the gallery to the entrance to the Norman Chapel at the end of the hall.

The small ancient room was the pride of the castle's exhibits, and inside, they would have privacy from the foot traffic of the hall. Soft candlelight bathed the vaulting pillars and low-hanging stonework ceiling of the eleventh-century Saxon architecture, giving the prayer room a solemn atmosphere appropriate for what Gabe knew was coming.

His dad walked across the herringbone floors to the altar table at the end of the room, his footsteps echoing around the tightly enclosed space. He looked conflicted and unsure of what he wanted to say. He hesitated as if choosing his words carefully, his hands folded in front of him.

"Nothing makes me happier than to see you happy, Gabriel. Especially in light of what you've been through. I'm glad you and Micah are getting along so well. Truly, I am. You both have a common empathy that draws you together. I understand that, but you must know that whatever your feelings are right now, you were not meant to be with Micah."

"First of all, I don't know if we are *together*," Gabe said. "We're just getting to know each other, so you and Carlyle can stop acting like I've put a ring on her finger."

"She kissed you. That's hardly nothing."

"It was only a kiss, okay?"

"Regardless of your casual feelings toward this behavior, it is the beginning of what will certainly become complicated in the future. There is something you need to know about Micah."

"What, that she's the archangel Michael?"

"Obviously, but she is also the *Michaelion* to whom Constantine attributed his victory over Licinius—*the* turning point of the Roman civil war that established Christianity," his dad said. "Micah is believed to possess powers great enough to favor an army. Obtaining control of the Michaelion will be central to our enemy's plan. She may be one of the greatest weapons in this war."

"A weapon?"

"Yes. You all are. This war won't be fought on a super-natural plane. Unless we stop the End of Days, there will be nations and armies involved. Guns and soldiers. Different factions playing against each other. And now, because the archangels are human, and humans are corruptible, you've each become the greatest advantage to achieving victory."

"And this has what to do with a kiss?"

"Everything and nothing. It is a distraction. You both need to focus on the reality of who you are. More importantly, you don't need to get attached to her. Her path will likely be different than yours. Should we be unable to keep the spark of Armageddon from lighting and this war from spilling over into the nations, she will be called to lead the armies."

Gabe laughed. "Micah leading an army? An army of what? Fashion designers?"

"This is serious. The archangel Michael presided over the nations of man. Also, as a practical matter, she is the archangel *Michael*. Once you partake in the ritual of the Entheos Genesthai, we expect you both to begin to recall who you were as archangels. You can see where there might be some . . . complications there."

"That's a bit narrow-minded, Dad."

"That's not what I mean."

"Then what do you mean? Like we'll recall our former selves?"

"We believe so, yes."

"So we'll become somebody else?"

"In a sense. But no more than we all grow and become more than who we were. You will always be Gabriel Adam. You are who you are. What you'll recall won't affect your personality to any great extent but rather your knowledge on how to fulfill your roles. At least that is what we think." His father failed to hide the uncertainty in his voice, and he looked at the altar.

"But you don't know, do you?"

"You are a smart, strong young man. And Micah is a smart, strong young woman. I have no doubt that when this is over, you'll both continue to be yourselves and hopefully free to pursue whatever you wish in life. For now, you and Micah need to concentrate on the tasks at hand and not each other."

He took a step toward his son, his demeanor even more severe. He leaned in and whispered, "Archangels are not immune to the lure of the enemy. They have fallen before. The darkness is listening for you. It can hear your presence in this world. And though it cannot see you, its focus is certain. Its plan in motion. Make no mistake—any departure from your path will invite temptation. Any opportunity you give, it will seize. Take care of who you are and who you are to become, because that, ultimately, is the prize for which our war is fought."

CHAPTER THIRTY-TWO

Gabe entered the vault room with his father to catch Carlyle and Micah in mid-embrace. They parted, and the Scotsman wiped a tear from her cheek before returning to his desk. He seemed softer somehow.

Makeup ran on Micah's face, and she tossed her hair as if it might help her gain some composure.

Carlyle pointed to the chair next to her. "Please have a seat, Gabe." The large man seemed to have trouble finding his thoughts. "The enemy, as you know, has moved faster than we anticipated. How they've managed to enter our world without our knowledge remains a mystery. Whatever they've done to breach the seal, if indeed it has been breached, is beyond our knowledge. It's possible that the supernatural connection that remained allowed for a doorway to open under extreme circumstances, but what's done is done. Our last order of business before you undertake the Entheos Genesthai ritual is to introduce you to our only weapon—the Gethsemane Sword." Carlyle excused himself to the vault.

Micah sat in silence. Gabe wanted to reach out to her and comfort her, but she stayed hidden behind the curtain of black hair hiding her face.

When Carlyle returned, he carried a long rectangular case wrapped in what looked like a burial shroud. The ornate material, with embroidered roses and crowns, draped over the case like a tablecloth. It was paper-thin and fluttered in the air as he walked.

He put the case on the desk and removed the cloth, then folded it and set it gently to the side. The wood lid had but one latch, which he unhinged and opened.

Micah and Gabe looked inside to see a flash of metal and a red handle wrapped in gold embroidery.

"This is the Gethsemane Sword, a Roman short sword that cut Jesus during his capture at the Gethsemane Garden. It is said that to the shock of the soldier that wounded him, Jesus then blessed the sword and tended to the wounds of the Romans wounded by his disciples." Carlyle removed the sword from the box and held it out for closer inspection.

The weapon captivated Gabe. Its blade forked at the end like the tongue of a snake, forming a double-tipped point in the steel. Grooved slots lined the inside of the V shape, allowing for something to slide into place. Symbols had been etched up the metal in a vertical line, one after the other, from tip to hilt. They looked like hieroglyphs he'd seen in documentaries about the pyramids in Egypt, only cruder.

"Is it broken?" Micah asked.

"No. Incomplete. When Rome crucified Jesus, they speared him to hasten death. That spear tip makes up the other half of the weapon. Eventually, the sword was given to the governor of Judea, the Roman Prefect Pontius Pilate, who took the two pieces and fashioned a trophy sword as a gift for Emperor Tiberius Caesar Augustus and as a boast of Pilate's success in quashing the discontent of Judea."

"So then, why do you have it here?" Gabe asked.

"Because as the sword tumbled through the ages, from frontier to frontier and from general to general, it was used as a symbol of Rome's might to be held by its army's most successful leaders until it landed here in northern Britain, the last battleground of the empire's expansion. It is a relic of Rome's unfinished business, much like Hadrian's Wall." Carlyle paused and presented the blade. "Incidentally, the spear tip was made of iron stone. Thus became the *stone in the sword*. Later translations would inverse the words, giving us the sword in the stone, from which an entirely separate legend grew. What I have in my hands is the true sword Excalibur, the legendary weapon used in the defense of the invading tribal hordes of what is today Scotland. The sword has remained here ever since."

"This is King Arthur's sword?" Micah asked.

Gabe stared, slack jawed, and then caught Micah's glance. She lingered for just an instant and then looked away.

"Yes," Carlyle said. "Though the legend is only inspired by fact. The Roman Army knew him as Lucius Artorius Castus, the last general to earn the trophy. This sword was actually of far greater value than the Romans ever could have guessed. According to the *Apocalypse of Solomon*, an object that has been blessed by an anointed being can be used to evoke the power of God if done by one who is ordained to wield that power. Ordained in such a manner as say, an archangel."

"So where is the stone?" Gabe asked.

"Safe and secreted from the blade until needed," Carlyle said. "They are kept separate should one fall into the wrong hands. It is only by the grace of God that we possess these pieces now or that they weren't lost to history. There will be a time when you awaken the sword to the power you possess and harness its use for our cause. Which one of you will do it, and when that is, remains to be seen."

CHAPTER THIRTY-THREE

Nearly a week had passed since Gabe last saw Micah at the vault. With Carlyle giving up his daily lectures in favor of study and preparation for the Entheos Genesthai, Gabe found himself more alone than usual, especially for a Friday. Mostly, he'd used the extra free time to catch up on his suffering schoolwork, though the distraction of mind-altering drugs and the feeling of abandonment from Micah left him less than inspired.

When his last class of the afternoon ended, the professor pulled him aside before he could escape. She was kindhearted but demanding and easily his hardest teacher. Luckily, the class, Christianity in Context, was one of his best. Still, he knew what was coming from the look of disappointment on her face. After his last paper, a pathetic analysis of the effect of the Jewish Temple's destruction on the writing of the New Testament Gospels, it was only a matter of time before she said something about his steadily slipping grades.

"Big plans this weekend?" Ms. Bernstein asked.

"No, ma'am. Not any more than usual at least. Catching up on my work more or less," Gabe said.

"That's why I stopped you." She produced his paper, the

first page riddled with red marks. "I have to say, there has been a distinct shift in the quality of your work. Factually, it is accurate. Probably more accurate than the rest of the class. Your grasp of the subject matter is not in doubt. But your writing—it's rushed. As if you don't care."

"I do care, Professor."

"Which is why I'm offering you an extension on this paper, an opportunity to put your best foot forward. You have wonderful potential, dear boy, which not so long ago you wielded almost effortlessly. I'd like to see more."

Gabe hung his head, not used to the sinking feeling of a bad grade.

Ms. Bernstein handed him the paper. "Is there something outside of class interfering with your work that we can remedy? Are you having difficulty acclimating here?"

Interfering? Gabe repeated the notion in his mind. Her question made him want to laugh out loud. *Where do I begin?* "No, ma'am. I've been temporarily distracted. It won't happen again."

"Fine. Have the revised paper back to me by Wednesday of next week. Do try and enjoy the weekend, Mr. Adam."

Gabe exited the building near the courtyard of Castle College. Gone were the usual gray skies, replaced now by cloudless afternoon. Sunshine reflected off the snowy ground and the white branches of the trees, as if Durham had been covered in a blanket of glitter. But instead of giving him the happy, fuzzy feelings everyone else seemed to have plastered across their faces, it merely aggravated his bad mood. Worsening the stress over his poor academics, the shock of brightness ignited that tiny, familiar pain in the back of his head.

He walked down the hill into the city center, across the bridge, and past The Swan & Three Cygnets, hands cupped over his face like horse blinders to shield out the glare. As Gabe attempted to cross the intersection of New Elvet Street, the sound of a cab's horn caused him to jump back to the curb. It missed him by inches and sped away up the hill toward the New Inn.

The fright turned the dull ache in the back of his head into the full-on beginnings of a migraine. As if to get in on the action of what was quickly becoming the Worst Day Ever, his stomach growled as hollow as an empty keg.

At Yuri's party, someone had mentioned how a morning fry-up would be needed for the next morning's hangover— something to do with greasy food did the trick. Gabe recalled his first day with Carlyle and how he'd cooked everything for breakfast in one skillet.

Comfort food. Exactly what he needed for this depression that was beginning to consume his day.

One thing he learned about the traditional pubs was that they served food at all hours. Even breakfast. The pub seemed like the best place to undo his funk.

Gabe found The Court Inn across Elvet Bridge on Court Lane. Inside, ceilings hung low with dimmed light. Without

The Revelation of Gabriel Adam

any patrons, the inn maintained a steady quiet, which his headache appreciated. He snagged a menu and a table off in the corner and made his order with the barkeep.

A short while later, the generous helpings of beer-battered fish and French fries more than met the medicinal grease requirements to cure his mope. He felt better with every vinegary, greasy bite. Enough to even try the green peas.

Above the bar, a television was tuned into an international cable news channel, with the volume on low. The barman seemed hypnotized by it. On the broadcast, the world stood on the brink of war over the Western Alliance's interest in oil fields and the promotion of democracy in a cultural region that didn't seem to appreciate either. The breaking news banner trickling across the screen reported that in a sudden change of policy, Turkey, the region's staunchest supporter of the Western Alliance, now protested any aggression toward their neighbor to the east and threatened to cause unrest in the region by mobilizing its military to the border.

The Turkish president had begun to adopt an extremist view of his country's first religion, despite the very outspoken dissention by his own people and of one of his top military commanders, General Simon Magus. The experts sitting behind the desk salivated to suggest the possibility of a coup d'état. On the screen, they christened the news as the Genesis of World War III.

In light of his circumstances, Gabe wondered if there was any validity to the claim. He recalled his father's description of how the nations would be pulled into their conflict. *Is it beginning already?*

As he finished his lunch, the door chimed and a man entered. He took a seat facing Gabe at a booth across the pub. The barman went to ask if he needed anything, but the man said nothing and waved him off.

Gabe scooped up the last of the tiny green peas and shoveled them into his mouth on the edge of his knife. He noticed the man staring and shrunk in embarrassment. His caveman manners were probably a bit offensive in the land of teatime.

"Sorry," Gabe said and held his hand up apologetically to the gentleman, but he remained still. If not for the thousand-mile stare, the man would be unassuming. His short stature and bald head framed in thick round spectacles were nothing noteworthy.

But his eyes. They seemed unfocused and vacant, but they did not wander.

The man's constant gaze left Gabe feeling uneasy. He pushed away his plate and grabbed his backpack.

Before he could get out of the booth, a power surge caused the television and the lights to dim. The air felt charged with electricity. Hair stood up on Gabe's arm. Then the screen flashed static, and the plastic-looking anchorman froze in midsentence.

The barman didn't move, either. He looked like a statue reaching up to adjust the television.

"Your fears of the world are not unfounded," said a nearby voice.

The man now stood at Gabe's shoulder. "The signs foretell a war amongst men that shall ignite the War of Wars. It is the beginning of what is to come." He held a wooden box about the size of a cigar humidor. "I am Enoch," he said. "Greetings, Fortitudo Dei."

Gabe felt the blood rush from his face. Memories from his visions flooded into his mind. *The bleeding man.* Yet Enoch looked different, shorter and bald as opposed to the commanding presence of the black-haired man. "What happened to the bartender? What did you do?"

"Only what I must."

Gabe flinched and pushed himself farther into the booth. He felt trapped. The air warmed where Enoch stood. "Are you an archangel?"

Enoch cocked his head, but his expression did not change. "No. I am an ally to this realm. I am of the Earth. I have seen the deepest rivers and the stream of life. The birth of mountains and the fires of creation itself. I am an arbiter of war and lay the paths of angels. My rule is over the tribes of man. I am Gnostic and eternal. It is my charge to ensure that mankind remains subject to the balance maintained by this world."

The lights flickered again, and Gabe felt his body involuntarily tense. The man's use of language gave the impression that he was from another time, yet his dress and appearance looked modern. Gabe tried to maintain his calm while struggling to understand the man's contradicting presence.

"Do not be afraid," Enoch said. "I am not to be feared."

There was little comfort in his words. "Why are you here?"

"I am here because there is a need for me to be. The Vatican has many friends. Precautions have been taken for me to come here in secret."

Gabe looked at the man's key chain clipped to wool pants that matched a plaid button-down shirt. *Not the outfit of a supreme being*, he thought.

"This is not my true form," Enoch said, as if reading Gabe's mind. "I have claimed this vessel through the art of possession."

The expressionless face. A voice with no emotion. No light in the eyes. Gabe couldn't believe that the flesh and blood before him was a stolen shell. "That's impossible."

"Your reluctance to believe is troubling. Possession was necessary," Enoch said. "Though I am not tracked through any physical means, I do require physical form in order to commune with humankind. This man will be discharged back to London unharmed with no memories of his missing time."

"If you are able to possess humans, then why possess one in London, only to travel here?" He motioned to the frozen barkeep. "There are plenty of people in Durham."

"In doing so, I must exert a significant amount of my power, leaving a tear in the fabric of this world. The one who hunts you, the one who seeks your end, would feel such a ripple in the stream of life running throughout this realm. Through me, your enemy will seek to find you."

"What about Micah? Why is the enemy after me and not her?"

"The enemy cannot feel the girl yet and will be unable to until she discovers her full power, which is the same with the others. But you, Gabriel, are his opposite in every way. You each possess converse abilities of one another—each a different side to the same coin. The enemy can feel your presence like a scent on the wind. If the enemy were to succeed and deprive the others of your strength, his abilities would consume them in despair, and this realm would surely fall."

Enoch held out the small box and opened it, revealing several vials of liquid ingredients. "I have brought you all that is needed to create the Entheos Genesthai. Use it sparingly. Once mixed, the potion is very powerful and will open up time and the realm of creation to those who choose to be enlightened. Use the greatest of caution, for only the Watchers may consume it and the procedure is delicate."

The word *delicate* sounded like code for *dangerous*. Gabe looked at the vials as Enoch handed him the box and turned to leave. So many questions begged to be answered. "Wait," he said, moving to the edge of the booth's seat. "Why is this happening? We were told there is a seal or something that prevented the realms from interfering with each other. And the others? There are supposed to be four archangels."

"The enemy has advanced faster than you are aware. They have breached the law against immortality by exploiting the nature of the vilest men and women. The dimensional seal holds, but while a pathway to Earth has been opened, it is only limited. Only one demon is through, but a trickle may soon become a flood. Phanuel is lost. As to his safety, I cannot speak. It is possible that he is fallen or that his essence has changed and blinded me to his existence. Raphael's fate is also unknown. I can feel his presence lingering upon the Earth, but his location is hidden even from me. Only a great source of energy could hold power over my own."

Gabe felt as if he'd been kicked in the stomach. "There are only two of us," he said under his breath.

"You must take Entheos Genesthai to the Essene immediately. Following the ritual, you must then go to retrieve the

Ring of Solomon. Make haste, for the enemy will be seeking it as well. Without the ability to unite the four archangels, it remains the only hope for ensuring the integrity of the seal and stopping the Apocalypse."

"The ring?"

"It is kept in the Ark of the Covenant, safe in Zion." Enoch took a step forward and put his hand to Gabe's forehead. "You still have much to learn about faith. Zion's secret should not be spoken out loud for fear of those who may be listening from the shadows."

He seemed to concentrate, mouthing unspoken words. Gabe shut his eyes, and he could hear Enoch's voice in his mind. *"Go to Axum in the land of Ethiopia. There lies Zion. There lies the Ark of the Covenant, guarded by its master."* His last sentiment came as a warning. *"Time is of the essence. You should leave immediately. It is no longer safe in England."*

The television returned to life. Gabe opened his eyes to see the barman's hand finally hit the screen. The anchors continued their reports as if they'd simply paused for a moment. When Gabe turned back to Enoch, he was gone.

CHAPTER THIRTY-FOUR

abe sat alone at the Undercroft and dialed Micah's number on his cell phone. She didn't answer. He waited several minutes and then tried her again, but the line went to voice mail on the second ring. *Screened.* Gabe pressed the end button and crammed the phone into his pocket.

He knew a migraine would eventually strike. It was inevitable. As inevitable as the hell he'd pay for not going straight to Carlyle with the box of vials. But he couldn't. He thought of Micah's story about Thecla. If the legend was true, what was inside his backpack sitting in the corner of his dorm room scared him to death. He wasn't ready to become someone else or risk turning into an insane freak. Despite Enoch's warning, he couldn't face his fears. *I am a coward*, he thought.

With his head swimming, he went to the bar and ordered pint number three from the cute Irish girl.

The more he drank, the more she reminded him of a red-headed Coren from back at The Study Habit in New York. If he squinted, he could almost see her. Some of her sarcastic humor would be much appreciated right about now.

He missed his life. His *real* life.

All he really wanted to do was have one more normal night, one where he could be a teenager like the rest of his peers—just one more night where he was himself and not some Being from Another Dimension.

Through his deepening beer-induced haze, he thought of the vials. They weren't going anywhere. Neither was his father or Carlyle. *What's the hurry? What's a few more hours?* He began to negotiate with the more responsible side of his mind, making compromises, promising to take the Entheos Genesthai directly to his father after he built up some courage. And one measly night was all he needed.

Just a little time to get used to the idea that I'm going to become a nut job.

Across the bar, Yuri walked in alone. Gabe made eye contact with him but quickly picked up his glass to shield his face, pouring the entire stout down his throat.

Too late. A minute later, two pint glasses were placed on his table. "My favorite American," Yuri said.

Gabe kicked his chair back and stood up. "Piss off. I'm not in the mood."

Yuri lifted his hands and held them wide open. "No, mate. There's no trouble. I just wanted to apologize. Totally my fault. I deserved the kicking I got. Seriously, I earned it."

The nearly faded bruise on the side of Yuri's face matched the one on Gabe's hand.

"Look," Yuri continued, "I was a right ass. Tend to get that way on the hard stuff, which is why I don't take to it that often. Lost the plot, I suppose."

You'll get no argument from me, Gabe thought, but he took his seat.

"Tell Micah that I'm truly sorry and I want to make it up to her. To both of you." He put his hand out to shake Gabe's and then noticed the brown and yellow bruise. "Bloody hell. It's not broken, is it? You got me good; I'll give you that." He rubbed his face. "I just transferred in from another university. I don't need any enemies. Had plenty of them at my old school. Friends?"

Friends was a stretch, but Yuri seemed sincere. Besides, Gabe didn't have the energy to debate the offer. "Sure. Whatever."

"Great. Then you don't mind if I join you."

"You know, I was actually trying to—"

Yuri plopped down at the table and made himself comfortable before Gabe could finish objecting.

"You look bent out of shape if you don't mind me saying."

Gabe gave in and picked up the new beer. "Been a tough day. I can't even begin to explain it to you."

"I can relate. Where's Micah?" Yuri asked and looked around the bar.

"Good question."

Yuri smiled. "So, girl troubles then, is it? I didn't know you two were an item. That explains a lot. Sorry about that."

"No big deal. It's just, well . . . I've got this"—Gabe thought a moment—"this *class*. And it's asking too much of me right now. *Way* too much."

"Micah's a classmate, I presume?"

"Yeah. And it's an intimate class, you know—very small."

"So it's hard to avoid her."

"Exactly. And the subject matter . . ." Gabe rolled his eyes and waved his arms around. Beer sloshed onto the floor. "It's just weird. We're studying stuff you wouldn't even believe. Stuff I'm not even sure I believe."

"What subject?"

Gabe thought for a second about all the secrecy, but he was too mad to care. "Religious studies."

"You're in the Theology module? That explains the jihad you pulled on my face." Yuri laughed. "Interesting subject at least."

"Yeah, not really. It's crazy. But boring. I'm not much of a religious guy, I guess."

"It's a load of bollocks, I think. Religion is just another way for people to suppress each other. It's politics, you know? Assuming there is an omnipotent creator out there, be it God, creativity, or Elvis Presley—whatever your preference—do you think mankind is smart enough to understand it? Doubtful. Just look around. We're plagued by imbeciles and the dim-witted. Anyway, you might consider being a bit more careful about selecting your courses."

"Well, this particular one was required. Special studies under Professor Carlyle."

"John Carlyle? He's a legend. Or at least his temper is. There's a rumor that he ripped a Glasgow phone book in two with his bare hands. Can you imagine that? What's he like?"

"Eccentric," Gabe slurred, taking another sip. "He's serious and demanding. And gets involved with his students' private lives. Said I couldn't see Micah." Gabe caught himself, realizing he'd said too much. "I mean, he didn't say I couldn't, exactly, just that student relationships might interfere with the classroom dynamic."

"Ah, well. Plenty birds at Castle. With that accent and American bravado, you should be fine. I've been meaning to ask you about that tattoo on the back of your head. You had your toboggan off for a moment the other night. Have to say, I was surprised. Didn't figure you for the counterculture type."

"My birthmark?" Gabe said and then silently cursed his own dimmed wits.

"It's a . . . birthmark?"

"No. I mean, I've had it since birth, so you know, I think of it as a birthmark. It's a tattoo."

"Your parents got you a tattoo when you were born? What the hell is that all about?"

"Hippie parents. Something to do with a family lineage, I guess you could say," Gabe responded. "Truthfully, I still don't understand it." *Close one*, he thought, satisfied by his quick recovery.

"That's . . . odd."

"Tell me about it. It's kind of a sore subject."

"No bother. I understand. My family life is a bit odd, if I must say. Though not so much these days, being on my own and all."

"Really, they grew out of it? Mine are entrenched."

"No, actually. My parents died when I was younger. I've been in foster care ever since. But they did manage to leave a bit of a trust fund for me when I turned sixteen. So, sans proper parental guidance, there's always the lovely substitute of money."

"Sorry about that. I didn't mean—"

Yuri waved his hand. "No. Seriously, I was quite young. I don't honestly remember either of them. Just vague memories. Sunday school. Holiday. That sort. And it's not like I've been left wanting."

"Wow. Why don't we talk about something more serious?" Gabe laughed. "Any horrible tragedy you know of that we've missed?"

"We're a tragic lot, you and I, eh?" Yuri laughed, too.

"Oh, I got one: my home in New York, which was a church by the way, burned down, and somebody was murdered in the process. How's that?"

"Jesus. You're having a laugh, right?"

Gabe looked deadly serious at Yuri and then smiled. "Yeah, I'm only joking."

"You're a bit off, aren't you? You need a sense of humor transplant or whatever." Yuri laughed again. "I'll tell you what, though. I can understand your frustration with Professor Carlyle. I've got several grievances with the authorities at Collingwood."

"No offense but you seem the type that has a grievance with any authority."

"Maybe I do. I'm the only authority I need in my life. There's too much structure in this world. Take the university, for instance. What business is it of theirs what you do in your private life? They expect us to act like adults and then treat us like we're to be coddled. That's ludicrous, and that's not how the real world works. You should tell that Carlyle to get bent. Properly."

"I'd love to."

"Seriously, I would. Let him know you're no pawn in

his game. No prat to be pushed around. Nothing like a little affirmative rebellion to get some respect, I say."

"You think?"

"Damn right I do. If you don't respect yourself around him, he'll never respect you. You can see whomever you damn well please, and he can't do anything for it."

The words sank to the very core of Gabe. His own freedoms *were* being taken away from him. And now they were asking him to take the Entheos Genesthai and give up everything that he was. How did he not see this before? *Yuri's right*, he thought as he finished his beer.

"Another round? I'll buy," Gabe said.

CHAPTER THIRTY-FIVE

Inside Rixy's Nightspot, music synchronized with a ballet of colored lights showering the dance floor while lasers ricocheted around the club. Gabe couldn't help but feel too young for the crowd, a fake waiting to be discovered by the adults. Still, he nodded to the DJ's beat, trying to stay lost in the new experience, the responsibilities of tomorrow forgotten.

The air inside the discothèque felt warm and thick with humidity from body heat and smelled of sweat. From his perch at the bar, he could see an undulating sea of people moving hypnotically to the music.

Yuri was amongst them on the prowl. Watching him work the crowd was like watching a con artist work a hustle. And it was a sort of art, too. He was a confident, decent-looking guy. Blond hair, athletic build. By most standards, Gabe expected him to see some success with the women. But not *every* woman in the club. No matter whom Yuri approached or what she was doing, each girl seemed captivated by his presence. They smiled, blushed, and swooned—all eager to dance or chat with him. The only time they looked bothered was when he moved on to the next girl.

Yuri stumbled back to the bar and threw his arm around Gabe. "C'mon, mate. Time to get off the reserves and into the game. Get in there, son. These birds are effing gagging for it." He snorted and took a long pull of his beer. "I swear to God, I'm through half of them already. Bloody townies. Easier pickings than at the student pub. But there'll be none left, if you don't quit this wallflower business."

"I'm the shy type, I guess," Gabe said, not wanting to leave the comfort of the bar.

"Nah, you're just being lazy is all." Yuri dragged him off the stool and toward the dance floor.

They stood at the edge and surveyed the scene. For a moment, Gabe thought the floor was moving, his head floating in the last beer. He tried to count how many he'd drank during the evening, but he couldn't put the numbers together.

"Look—that one. She's the one for you." Yuri pointed to the middle of the floor.

A tall and statuesque girl danced alone. She had her blonde hair pulled up and knotted in the back with a long ponytail. Strands of silky hair cascaded down her face. Blue eyes were half open as she swayed to the music. Her black-and-white minidress clung tightly to her athletic body and hugged every curve as she danced.

"She's out of my league. *Way* out of my league."

"Don't give me that shite. That's the old Gabe talking. There are no leagues. Don't you see? It's our world. Everything is for the taking." Yuri pulled him closer and whispered into his ear, "I guarantee you can get her. You only have to *want* her. Project your desire, and she'll be helpless. I promise."

His insistence put Gabe off. "I don't know."

"You need proof? A demonstration? Watch this. I'll show you how it's done. See that girl over there?"

Another girl, flanked by her three friends, was shooing away some poor guy trying to talk to her. She laughed with her girlfriends as the guy slinked off.

"She doesn't look interested in being hit on."

"It doesn't matter what she thinks. Just watch."

With that, Yuri walked over to her. She turned and faced him with a wicked look in her eyes, obviously not happy with being interrupted again. But Yuri persisted, and in a matter of seconds, the girl's expression softened as if she'd succumbed to some drug meant to numb the senses. Even in the dark of the club, Gabe could see her cheeks flush.

Yuri bent down and kissed the girl deeply right in front of everyone. Gabe expected the girlfriends to protest or at the very least look disgusted with their friend's behavior, but they wore an altogether different look on their faces—common desire.

Yuri broke off the kiss and wiped his face as he walked back to Gabe, leaving her standing in a daze. "See. It doesn't take anything. You just have to want it and let them know you want it. It's in you. Reach inside and project your desire." He locked eyes with Gabe. "If I can do it, then you can do it. We're different, you and I, from this rabble. That, I promise. These townie girls won't know what hit them. Now, no more talk." Yuri shoved him toward the blonde girl in the black-and-white dress. "Go get her."

Gabe tripped slightly on the step up to the dance floor. The DJ spun another beat, this one faster, heavier. Its bass pounded against Gabe's chest, and it felt good. The gyrating crowd made reaching the girl difficult. Heat emanated from their bodies, the warm air void of oxygen, yet blood surged through his veins, powerful and determined.

Something drew Gabe toward her, whispering in his ear: *Why not?*

She was older, sexy beyond measure, more so the closer he got, her hands running through her hair as she danced alone. Her piercing blue eyes locked with his and beckoned him to come. Her lips parted, glistening wet in the moving lights.

Gabe did want this girl. The closer he got, the more she seemed to want him as well. He stopped trying to understand why and just accepted that she did. Her dance moves became provocative, hands up and down her body and over her dress, her curves, begging him forward.

Just then, a large bald man walked up behind her with two drinks. His tattoos fit the rest of his look with pierced ears and a shirt that was several sizes too small. Gabe hesitated, but the girl kept dancing, her eyes still calling out.

The man shook the girl's shoulder, but she didn't acknowledge him. She *was* in some sort of trance. He shook her harder this time, and she blinked. It seemed to wake her up but not before the man followed her line of sight to Gabe.

The man's muscles stretched, the spandex shirt nearly ripping as he flexed in anger. He clenched his square jaw and balled up his fists. Watching him react, Gabe almost expected fire to shoot out his nostrils. It would have been laughable had this guy not charged like a bull, throwing people out of his path to get to Gabe.

A sound whooshed by his ear, and a bottle sailed past and struck the bald man in the face. It shattered in a frothy splash of beer and glass. Blood spewed from his brow as he fell to his knees and cursed loudly.

Yuri leapt past Gabe and kicked the man in his bloodied face. The blow sent him crashing onto his back. The girl screamed, and then the club became a frenzy of excitement as security fought through the crowd to get to the commotion.

"Come on! Let's get out of here," Yuri said.

CHAPTER THIRTY-SIX

Yuri pulled Gabe along as they ducked through the crowd condensing around the screaming girl and slipped down the stairs of the club to the street, stumbling out into the frigid night.

"I thought that guy was going to kill me," Gabe said, feeling alive with nervous energy. He followed Yuri as he casually walked toward the order window of a street-side kabob shop.

"And he would have if not for me. Don't you forget it." Yuri placed his money down and got a kabob, which he shoved into his mouth, spilling lettuce onto the road. "Hungry?" He chewed the bite and held up the sandwich, offering some to Gabe.

"No. I'm too wired to eat. God, that was awesome."

"Just another day in the life, mate. Shame, the club. You looked to have that blonde right where you wanted her." Yuri continued to stuff his face as they neared the Framwellgate Bridge.

"Something was weird about her. Did you see? It was like . . . I don't know." Gabe tried to make sense of it, but in his excited state thoughts tripped over each other. "What happened?"

Yuri stopped walking and threw his kabob into the

street. He wiped his hands on his shirt. "What do *you* think happened?"

Gabe shrugged and started laughing. "I have no idea. Beginner's luck?"

"Something more than that, I think. I wasn't sure you had it in you. But you definitely exceeded my expectations." Yuri stared at him. The hint of a smile formed at the corners of his mouth.

"What?" Gabe asked.

"We're a formidable team." He looked up at the Castle Keep, visible atop the hill. "Ever feel like you're being held back? Like you're stuck in a situation with no way out?"

Gabe thought of what he had to do in the morning, and his anxiety returned. "All the time. What are you getting at?"

"The future. Do you think you're going to find it here at a university? Under the oppression of their rules and silly superstitions?" He had a fire in his eyes, a severity that made Gabe uncomfortable.

"I'm suddenly feeling a little tired. Maybe it's time we called it a night."

Yuri stepped forward, pressing harder. "You're bigger than this; you just don't know it yet. They're holding you back—can't you see? And they have no idea. *No idea, Gabe.* That makes them dangerous. To us all." He was in Gabe's face now. "I know people. Powerful people. And they know things, can teach us things. Things that we'll need for the future. Stuff you would have to see to believe. What do you say? We could even trash Carlyle's office as a parting shot."

Gabe took a step away from Yuri. Even through his

muddled senses, he knew this wasn't right. "What are you talking about? I'm not leaving Durham. I can't. I won't. I have responsibilities here."

"You don't know what you're turning down. I won't be able to ask you again. Time is of the essence."

Yuri's words sounded like a threat. The crowd from Rixy's Nightspot caught up to them, and the street swarmed with clubbers. Surrounded by people, the two students stared at each other, not saying a word. Gabe felt like he was seeing Yuri for the first time, and the calm intensity in the boy scared him.

"I have to go," Gabe said.

"Last chance, Gabriel."

Gabe didn't look back. He ran, stumbling toward the castle with one question repeating in his mind: *Who is Yuri?*

CHAPTER THIRTY-SEVEN

abe lay in bed, the club music still hammering inside his head. His heart fluttered in a spastic, weird way—a residual effect, he figured, from the mixture of energy drinks and beer that coursed through his system. He needed something to drink, water to quench his thirst and flush the horrible taste out of his mouth. The comfort of the bed, however, refused to let him go. Buried underneath the covers and piled upon a healthy dose of regret, he felt a migraine building in the back of his head.

He remembered leaving Yuri by the bridge and his offer to meet his friends, though the way he'd described them, they sounded more like business partners. Gabe wondered if Yuri was involved in some sort of illegal enterprise. Maybe selling drugs or gambling. With the way he threw money around, it didn't seem that far-fetched. But there was something dark about him, something more menacing than the average jerk that Gabe couldn't quite figure out. Regardless, he wanted nothing more to do with him.

The club's bass continued to pound in Gabe's head until he realized it wasn't a memory from last night. Somebody was at the door and banging hard.

In an instant, he was wide-awake. *The vials*, he remembered.

He threw back the covers, forced himself out of bed, then grabbed a pair of shorts from a pile of dirty clothes in the corner and tried to put them on. Seeing his reflection in the mirror on the wall, he realized that he was fully dressed in yesterday's outfit.

That's convenient, he thought and threw the shorts back onto the pile.

He barely had the door unlocked when his father barged through. "Where the hell have you been? The Vatican informed Carlyle that the vials were delivered to you by the messenger. Is that true? We've been calling your mobile since last night, for God's sake!"

"Sorry. I didn't know." Gabe looked at his phone. "It was on vibrate; I didn't feel it go off."

"No excuses." He took a step back. "You stink like a pub."

"Dad, keep your voice down. The other students—"

"I don't give a damn what the other students think. You are not *other students*! Do you even realize that we thought something had happened to you when you couldn't be found? There are things out there that want you dead. *Dead*, Gabriel. Where are they? Where are the vials?"

Gabe slumped back onto his disheveled bed. "In my backpack."

His father opened the zipper and removed the small box. He opened it and sighed, his posture decompressing and the red fading from his cheeks when he saw that the vials were safe. "If something had happened to you, to the vials, we would be lost. There is so much riding on you and Micah. Why can't you see that?"

"I'm sorry. It's just . . . Micah told me what those vials can do. I needed time—"

"We're out of time. This is *your* life, whether you want it or not. You have got to take responsibility and realize that you have a higher purpose than"—his dad looked him over—"drinking yourself like some fool into a stupor like *other students* do. You have a greater purpose. Do you not yet understand that? Even after all you've seen?"

His father stood, gently closing the lid on the small box. "You need to persevere. There is still much to prepare for and even more that will be asked of you. Did the messenger tell you anything?"

"His name was Enoch. He looked normal enough but he didn't seem . . ." Gabe couldn't say the word *human* to complete the thought. It would only sound like fantasy. "He said we are to perform the ritual and then seek Solomon's Ring inside the Ark of the Covenant."

His father's legs seemed to give out. He fell into the chair by the desk. "Solomon's Ring is in the ark? But it has been lost to time."

"They are both in Zion. In Axum, Ethiopia." Gabe felt awkward saying Enoch's thoughts out loud.

"My God. You are certain? That is what he said?" He drifted, lost in thought. "Discovered at last. We will need to make travel arrangements immediately. I'll contact Carlyle and let him know, so he can prepare Micah."

"There was more. Enoch said Micah and I are the last

archangels. The others are lost or turned. He didn't know."

His dad looked as though the wind had been knocked from him. "Then the hour is later than we thought. I'll take the vials to the vault. Be there in thirty minutes. You'll need to pack. We're leaving Durham."

CHAPTER THIRTY-EIGHT

Inside the vault, Carlyle and Micah waited, looking frustrated. Gabe walked in with his father, who had been waiting for him upstairs in the gallery. Several candles flickered in the blackened room, casting shadows on the walls and looking more like a dungeon than ever. Micah didn't make eye contact with him as he sat in the chair in front of the desk.

But Carlyle stared daggers. "Enjoy your break, boy?"

"I'm sorry. I wasn't in the right frame of mind yesterday," Gabe said.

"Hopefully you won't be in the same frame of mind when the enemy makes an attempt on your life," Carlyle said and stood from his desk where the box and vials were laid out. "I want to hear it from you. Where exactly did Enoch say we would find Solomon's Ring?"

"Ethiopia. A city called Axum, though he also called it Zion. He said we would find the Ark of the Covenant there and the ring."

"Idiot," Carlyle snapped. "Do you know how valuable that information is? How many would kill you just to hear it whispered? If there is an argument against the existence of

God, you are it. Because what god would entrust a damned fool like you with anything greater than tying your shoes?"

Gabe kicked his feet under his chair, just in case.

His father held up his hand in an effort to hold back the Scotsman. "There's no point in berating him now. Gabriel is well aware of his mistake. The question is, why Ethiopia? It was my understanding that the ark was in Jerusalem near the piece of land that once held Solomon's temple."

Carlyle leaned against a wall and rubbed his forehead. He deflated, the rigid posture of anger from a moment ago giving way to a more academic slouch. He nodded and tapped the frame of his glasses. "Beneath the Dome of the Rock or somewhere in that vicinity was always the strongest possibility. Though Axum has a history connected to Solomon as well. Ethiopic Christianity tradition suggests that the ark was stolen by an illegitimate son born to King Solomon and an Ethiopian queen known as Makeda of Sheba and secreted away to her kingdom. When Christianity made its way down the Nile far enough from the influential reach of Rome, a denomination of the religion grew around this legend. Unlike Rome's version, this sect was rooted in the Old Testament, much like Judaism. There has always been a claim by their followers that the ark was hidden from Solomon in Ethiopia, though archeologists and religious scholars never found credence in such boasts as its religious leaders refuse to allow a formal study or, for that matter, access at all. They deemed it merely a tourist gimmick."

"And now Enoch reveals the truth," his dad said.

"It seems he has. We should make arrangements to travel

there as soon as possible." Carlyle turned to Gabe and Micah. "But for now, we have more pressing matters to attend. I have prepared the ingredients of the vials for you both."

Gabe saw two small pewter cups filled with an unassuming clear liquid on the table.

"You are about to take the Entheos Genesthai, the Oil of the Anointed King. It will awaken an inner pathway to the energies of creation, and many great secrets will be revealed."

Gabe looked to his father for reassurance, but he only stared blank-faced at the vials.

Micah bounced her leg nervously, as if she were about to undergo major surgery.

"Much will be revealed to you. You may experience things that are not from this generation but of a generation from a long ago distant time. You may see events from a future, which have not yet come to pass. Your innermost self will come alive inside you."

"Okay. Let's have it, then," Micah finally said. "If I'm being honest, I don't know if I want to know anything more about it. Just give me the bloody stuff."

"Right. No point in postponing the inevitable," Gabe said and at last looked to Micah. Their eyes met, and they understood one another.

She took his hand and squeezed it before letting go.

Carlyle blessed the liquid with a silent prayer. When he finished he handed Gabe and Micah each a cup.

"A toast?" Gabe offered in an attempt at levity.

"To the future," Micah said.

"And the past." Gabe touched his cup to Micah's, careful

not to spill any of its precious contents, and drank the small portion.

The syrup went down without much fuss, like a berry-flavored cough medicine. In a matter of seconds, heat began to emanate from the pit of his stomach. An uncomfortable fever quickly spread to his extremities, causing a prickling sensation in his hands.

He heard Micah gasp. She started to hyperventilate. She screamed and fell out of her chair. Gabe watched as Carlyle caught her. Gently, he laid her convulsing body onto the floor and put a folded cloth behind her head.

Gabe was just aware enough to know that the same was happening to him and barely understood that he was now in his father's arms, being laid on the floor as well. Candles were placed around their heads. His breath seemed to catch in his lungs. He tried to focus on the interior of the vault, but the candlelight grew at the corners of his eyes.

As his perception of the room drifted away, the straight lines of the ceiling and walls bending and curving, he saw the ghostly liquid image of his father kneel down. Gabe heard the echo of his dad's breath, and then the candles were extinguished by a darkness that washed away the world.

CHAPTER THIRTY-NINE

omething crunched under Gabe as he lay on the hard, warm surface. He opened his eyes to see the familiar onyx floor now covered in shards of mirrored glass. As expected, the harsh light from the fixture beat down against his shoulders and back. He looked above him, wondering how much time the light had. But instead of the fixture, he saw a sky of endless blue. Its sun shined brilliant, bathing him in its rays.

Carefully, he brushed aside some of the glass and made room to push up from the floor. Bits of mirror stuck to his chest and face. He pulled at his shirt, and the glass fell back to the floor, jingling as the pieces hit. The rest he picked from his skin as he surveyed this world.

The black floor, covered by a sea of endless broken mirrors, met the horizon in every direction. Gabe knew he had just taken the Entheos Genesthai. All his memories and thoughts were clear in his mind. Gone was the confusion and fear of his visions, replaced by a feeling of peace.

"Do you wish to understand Solomon's power?" asked the familiar voice of a woman. "How he attempted to use it to rid your realm of the demons left behind after the banishment of

Mastema's kingdom?" Her words seemed to play in the air, coming and going as she spoke. "Do you, Gabriel?"

The voice came from behind. Gabe turned to see a singular mirror standing in a small space that had been cleared of the broken shards. He approached his fading reflection to see a scene appear in the glass.

A bearded man wore a ring of gold, its jewel engraved with a pentalpha. He sat on a balcony that overlooked a building site in an ancient city.

"Solomon and his Jerusalem," whispered the disembodied voice.

The king observed a nearly completed temple, rendered in marble and stone, at the top of a hill. Gold-encrusted pillars stood side by side, guarding the entrance. Solomon wielded the ring in masterful strokes, like a painter using his brush. Distant forms labored over its completion, but they were not men. Their demonic forms resisted against the ring's power that bound them to its authority, compelling them to work.

Shrieks of protest carried on the wind.

Gabe's reflection returned to the mirror as the image faded. "Is this what I am to do? Build the Temple?"

"The task was Solomon's and his alone. Your path is laid before you in many directions. Do you not see?" asked the voice. "To ensure that you walk the right one, you must know your true self."

True self? Gabe gazed upon his face, noting that he looked normal enough for a seventeen-year-old. He then turned from his reflection. Other mirrors appeared, assembling from the pieces of glass on the floor. They surrounded him, and he counted seven in all. In some, his reflection. In others he saw the burning light of fire shine from within the glass. Again, ancient scenes reflected in a few, but one held his attention.

He approached, and in the glass he could see the front of the cathedral in New York, its wreckage smoldering in ruin. Richard's mutilated body hung upside down on a cross stuck from the ground.

His father appeared nearby, bound and curled in the grass. Beside him a smokelike specter shimmered against the flames of the church. Gabe felt a surge of panic as his father struggled. He reached out to the glass, knowing what would happen, but something had to be done.

In a flash of blinding white light, Gabe was there in the streets of New York. Clouds of fire loomed over the city's skyline. Central Park burned in a towering fire. He'd seen it before, but this time something was different.

"Fortitudo Dei," hissed a voice in the air. Shadows and smoke of the specter swirled together into something physical, and in its shape formed the bleeding man, standing over his father.

Gabe felt something in his hand. He looked down and saw the Gethsemane Sword, complete with the stone of the spear affixed to the end. The blade burned hot, the air around it shimmering like a mirage. Subtle vibrations of power radiated from the hilt.

The man reached out, and a smokelike shadow leapt from his fingertips and wrapped around his bound prisoner, constricting like a serpent's vise. He laughed and said, "Your weakness betrays you, boy."

His dad writhed in agony, dying on the ground.

Gabe stood, unable to move, frightened by the display of dark power. *What can I do against such a thing?*

Before he could act, the woman's voice, sad and filled with regret, echoed in his thoughts. *"Why do you doubt yourself, dearest Gabriel? Perhaps you were not meant for this after all."*

He hoisted the sword for a strike and leapt at the man. The feathered weight of the weapon allowed the blade to fall through the air like a guillotine and cut through the man's black suit with a calculated blow.

The bleeding man merely smiled as blood spilled from his chest. He reached back and swung his arm like a club. Gabe was struck on his face so hard, the impact lifted him from the ground, and the sword flew from his hands.

He rolled on the street and tasted blood in his mouth.

The man squeezed his hand into a fist, and the shadows surrounding his father balled into a furious, swarming blanket, like ants on a carcass. After a moment they stopped their attack and pulled away, withdrawing into the man's outstretched arm. Laughing, his form splintered. As he had in Gabe's vision before, the man then broke apart into fragments of smoke and disintegrated like ash into the winds.

His dad's body looked contorted, broken, and bleeding. Gabe knelt down beside him, but it was too late. His father was dead. He felt cheated, having done what he knew was right, and yet he failed. The storm of the coming Apocalypse rolled over the city, a consuming wall of fire that Gabe welcomed in defeat.

CHAPTER FORTY

We can't win, Gabe realized.

He opened his eyes to the darkness of the dorm room. The alarm clock read 10:30 p.m. In the chair beside his desk, his father slept, wrapped in a towel for warmth.

The vision. The memory caused his stomach to clench violently, the pain sudden and unbearable. He rolled to the side of the bed, and the remnants of the Entheos Genesthai lurched from his stomach and onto the carpet. He spit into a shirt from the floor, careful not to make much noise. His dad adjusted in his seat, but his eyes did not open.

Gabe took stock of himself in the bed. He didn't feel any different. Unless feeling worse counted. Carlyle had said they would inherit powers and stop the Apocalypse, yet the vision told Gabe that he wasn't even capable of saving his own father. He had seen the truth: *The enemy will be victorious. The End of Days can't be stopped.*

Images of his father lying dead in the street, his body ravaged from the bleeding man's shadows, filled Gabe's mind, and then he thought of Enoch. At the Court Inn, he had said something about the enemy's power. Gabe thought hard, trying to remember it exactly. Something about the enemy being able to feel him within this realm's stream of life.

He is my reflection, Gabe thought, and the full realization of what that meant thundered down upon him. *He can find me. I am leading the enemy here.* He glanced at his dad sleeping in the chair. *To my father.*

Gabe now understood what a danger he was to those around him. The visions had been clear on the enemy's capabilities, and he was not willing to see such promises fulfilled.

The decision came quickly.

It was rash, he knew, but his mind was made up. The enemy would have no need to focus on his father if Gabe separated himself. He saw no other choice. Running away seemed the best hope for those he loved.

He pushed back the sweat-soaked covers and got out of bed, silent as a thief. A backpack lay in the corner, ready for Ethiopia. In its front pocket, a stack of money and a credit card given by his father in case of an emergency. Gabe only hoped there was enough for travel and food.

His father would never understand. How could he without having witnessed the vision?

With the exception of what he wore, most of his warmer clothes hung in the closet, but the door usually squeaked. If he risked opening it, his dad might wake. *I'll have to make do with what I have*, he thought.

A twinge of guilt caused him to hesitate. *At least he deserves an explanation.* On his desk, he found a scratch sheet of paper. As quietly as possible, he scribbled a note and placed it on his pillow.

Gabe grabbed his bag and opened the door. He looked back at his father and wondered if he would ever see him again.

"Good-bye," he whispered.

Committed, Gabe stepped through the door without a sound.

CHAPTER FORTY-ONE

abriel Adam walked out of Castle College into the night, unaware that he was being watched. Prophet had made certain of that. Ever since the boy had arrived in Durham, his every move had been scrutinized, his routine learned, and his schedule memorized.

This evening, however, had proven to be quite peculiar. Gabriel and his father had joined Micah and Carlyle for an unscheduled meeting in the vault room. Sometime later, Prophet watched as the boy and girl were moved from the building by wheelchair.

They seemed unconscious. Hours had passed without a sign.

And now, the American emerged, alive and well and alone. Something felt different about this particular night. Gabriel seemed different, his aura changed. New power yet to be harnessed grew inside him.

He must have it. He has to have it, Prophet thought.

The moment proved too tempting to let slip away. An opportunity had presented itself. *Now is the time—before Gabriel learns of his potential.*

If he moved fast enough, Gabe thought he could still catch the last train at the station with a few minutes to spare. Unless they somehow found a car, his father and Carlyle would have to wait until the morning to catch up. But it could be even longer, considering how much time it might take before they even realized he had left the city. He adjusted the strap on his shoulder. The missing backpack would eventually give his intentions away.

Gabe cursed himself for not having a better plan. Its entirety amounted to getting to Ethiopia first. The most obvious place to begin the journey was London, which meant he'd be on the train for a while, so it was crucial to catch that last train. If discovered by his father or a more sinister element, he could disappear into the city.

He wanted to continue the fight. But how? Who would know about this war and not disclose his whereabouts to his father?

In the bitter cold, Durham was a ghost town. Even so, he didn't want to risk being spotted. It would not be long before his father found the note and went searching through town.

Gabe thought it best to take the trail by the Wear and follow the river around the bend, all the way to Framwellgate Bridge. Crossing the river there, it would only be a sprint to the station. The route would take much longer, but he had time if he hurried, and there was little chance of being seen on the path tonight.

An old staircase near the outside of the cathedral grounds

led to Kingsgate Bridge. Beside the bridge, another staircase took him to the trail below. He could barely see in the dark, though the path was well worn by joggers, students, and tourists. He followed along, using the river to guide him.

Moving quickly, he closed in on Prebends Bridge, in the gorge just below South Bailey Street. His lungs ached with each cold breath, but the pace had managed to warm his muscles.

As Prebends came into view under the moonlight, he made out a figure standing on the path.

Gabe slowed to a walk. He felt something, as if all his senses were opened to the surroundings. His vision sharpened, his hearing acute. He could smell the river, trees, and mud mix with the scent of a figure standing on the path ahead.

Gabe approached, and the person's features became clear.

"Odd time of night to be jogging by the river, isn't it, mate?" Yuri asked.

CHAPTER FORTY-TWO

"What are you doing down here?" Gabe asked.

"Looking for you, obviously."

Yuri stepped into the moonlight. He looked calm, somehow pleased with himself.

"Well, you've found me," Gabe said. "I'm in a bit of a rush. Mind letting me through?"

"Can't do that, my friend. Got a bit of business with you. You have something I need. Something you took from that bloody vault. By the way, what do you prefer I call you? Gabe? Gabriel, perhaps? Or would you rather Fortitudo Dei?"

As soon as he saw Yuri under the bridge, Gabe knew their last encounter had been something more than a casual coincidence. "It was *you* all along. *You* were the one trying to get into the vault."

"A task that proved to be more difficult than expected. Even after I killed Balor and stole his keys." Yuri wavered, as if ashamed of what he'd done.

"And burning cathedrals in New York? I suppose arson is another hobby besides murder?"

"Never been, actually. I hear it's lovely."

"There are things bigger than you and me. Bigger than

murder. Whatever you know or think you know about the vault is wrong."

"You mean things like saving the Earth from a war between the dimensions?" Yuri laughed. "Can't be done. Not by Carlyle's lot at least. You should know that by now. Has the good professor not done a proper job training you in the Essene way? Those ancient traditions are laughable. Their superstitions will be the end of us all. But then, I suppose you're Constantine's man through and through."

Gabe didn't answer.

Yuri must have sensed his inner conflict. "Oh, still not a believer, are we? Won't the Vatican be ever so disappointed. Perhaps I've misjudged you. Those religions are as outdated as they are obsolete. The path to the light must be forged anew."

"So, you're with the enemy?"

"That vile rabble? Don't be daft. We have our own agenda. Earth is the reward." Yuri paused. "Man's stewardship has become a burden to this world. An infection of festering hate and intolerance built upon religious beliefs perverted by generation after generation."

"What the hell are you talking about? You sound insane."

"Call it clarity of mind. This realm needs a new authority. A new governance. Join us, and we could rule the world ourselves and set things right again. Bring peace and stability. *We* could be gods again!" He had the same feral look in his eyes, dangerous and unhinged, that Gabe noticed last night.

"Out of my way."

"Not going to happen."

Gabe knew he wouldn't stand aside. *I've beat him before.*

He dropped his bag and charged Yuri. As the distance closed between them, a splinter of doubt entered his mind. Yuri simply smiled and stood his ground.

In the instant Gabe reached him, with his fist clenched and swinging, Yuri bowed his head, narrowed his eyes, and held out his hand, as if gesturing to halt.

A bluish-white light illuminated from Yuri's hand. The image of Micah lying in the snow flashed in Gabe's mind. He realized his mistake and hesitated, tripping forward, unable to stop his momentum.

Yuri opened his eyes wide.

His outstretched hand caught Gabe in the chest, and then something else happened that took him by surprise: a muffled blast of heated, glowing energy expanded outward, lighting the river and forest around the bridge like a fireworks display. Both boys flew apart like two supercharged magnets of opposite polarity.

CHAPTER FORTY-THREE

abe tried to focus, disoriented by the spots in his eyes. He couldn't hear a thing through the ringing in his ears. Debris from the explosion—branches, leaves, and dirt, some of it smoldering in the air—fell from the sky like rain.

The ringing faded into the noises of the forest. A tree nearby cracked and toppled over. He rolled out of the way just in time as it crashed down. Gabe's arm wrenched with pain shooting through his forearm and shoulder.

Some thirty yards away, Yuri looked to be in a similar condition. He staggered to his feet and braced himself against a tree by the river's edge, laughing hysterically as he pulled leaves out of his long blond hair. "Well, I suspected that might happen. Worth a try, I suppose. Spectacular that was, don't you reckon? Your girlfriend was lucky I missed. Though I suppose it wouldn't have mattered, since it seems archangels really can't harm each other with their power."

Archangels? Gabe thought. "Who are you?"

"Phanuel to some. Uriel to others. But most everybody else calls me Yuri."

"Everybody believes you're dead," Gabe said.

"Not dead. Just lying low. I don't play well with Carlyle's type, so I figured I'd go a different route, know what I mean?"

"Carlyle can help you. He can teach you—"

"Teach me what?" Yuri asked, cutting him off. "How to harness my power? News flash, in case you're too stupid to see—it's harnessed. For once, open your eyes and use your head. Quit being his manipulated pawn."

"And yet here I am by myself."

"Yes." Yuri paused. "Quite the enigma you are."

"So, if we can't hurt each other, let me pass," Gabe reasoned.

"I'll let you pass on one condition: give me the ring."

How does he know about the ring? "What ring?"

"Save that bollocks for someone else. You wouldn't have left without it. Give it to me! We cannot allow her to use it."

Her? "You're wrong. I don't have it."

"It's too dangerous. You'll lose it to the enemy. Give me the ring, or I'll kill you where you stand and take it from your corpse, I swear."

"You can't. In case *you're* too stupid to figure it out—you can't use your power to harm me."

Yuri reached into his jacket. "There are other more conventional ways to harm you, my friend." He brandished a formidable-looking knife.

Gabe broke off a thick branch from the fallen tree to defend himself. "I don't have it," he repeated and dug a heel into the dirt, ready. "I don't even know where it is."

Gabe could see that the lie about the ring's whereabouts had given him away as concealing something. His face must have twitched. Or his eyes revealed his intent to deceive. Whatever his tell, Yuri had called it. He smiled and raised his arm, the sharp point of the knife aimed accusingly at Gabe.

"Liar, liar," Yuri hissed. The blade glistened in the moonlight.

CHAPTER FORTY-FOUR

From atop Prebends Bridge, a voice echoed down to the river. "Gabriel!"

Gabe looked up to where his father stood. Two silhouettes moved over the river.

"Who's that with you?" Carlyle shouted.

"It's Uriel," Gabe said.

Yuri stopped his advance and turned to the two men on the bridge above. He raised his hand, and a volley of light crashed against the bridge wall with all the destructive power of dynamite. Thrown rock and debris shattered and fell to the river.

A cloud of dust plumed into the air, swirling vaporised stone about, concealing everything in a fog. Gabe choked on the fumes and watched part of the bridge disintegrate. His heart stopped in his chest as rubble from the wall splashed nearby in the river.

Yuri screamed, "You're forcing my hand, Gabe. I don't enjoy this. But I'll find Micah, and I give you my word, she will see the same fate. All you need to do is give me the damned ring!"

Tears filled Gabe's eyes. He felt the burn of anger, the overwhelming fear of what this betrayal cost. "No, you will not." Gabe held up the branch and wielded it in front of him like a sword.

"Think you can take me again, do you? Let's see about that." Yuri lowered his hand and started toward Gabe, knife at the ready. He closed the gap between them with astonishing speed, nearly disappearing into a blur.

The knife stabbed through the air, but Gabe moved at the last moment and managed to parry the blow with the branch. Another slash caught his jacket, and the blade nearly drew blood, but a second block with the branch spared injury.

The defensive flailing worked but also threw him off balance. Stumbling backwards, he swung hard at Yuri's mid-section. The branch smashed against ribs with a crack.

Yuri howled and reeled from the blow. Still falling, Gabe tried another swing but couldn't generate enough momentum. Yuri caught the branch, ripped it out of Gabe's hands, and kicked him hard with a boot to the chest.

Gabe slammed against the fallen tree, his back bent over its trunk. He rolled off and slumped to the ground, unable to move or breathe, lungs starved for air. There was little doubt in his mind that ribs had been broken.

As he waited for the cutting blow, Micah suddenly appeared behind Yuri on the path and hoisted the incomplete Gethsemane Sword above her head.

She screamed as she rushed toward Yuri. A mistake.

Yuri spun at the sound and splintered the branch against the side of her face. She crumpled to the ground with the sword and curled in the mud, her body still. Quiet.

Gabe watched helplessly, trying to find his breath as Yuri

turned toward Micah. He held the knife back for a kill. In the instant before the blade fell upon her came a brutish roar from the path. Carlyle charged at Yuri, his large, muscular hands nearly on the boy's throat.

For a fraction of a moment, Yuri seemed genuinely surprised by the man's rage. He let go of the branch and turned his back to Micah, squaring his shoulders to aim at Carlyle.

Gabe tried to move on the ground, but the searing pain in his side stopped him cold. He tried to shout—anything—but there was no breath to give voice.

Once again, rivers of light escaped from Yuri's hand. Time stood still as the beam traveled over the path, a wide and constant flow barreling toward its intended target.

For the first time since childhood, Gabe prayed. *Please, God. No!*

Carlyle seemed to lean into the oncoming attack. Before the energy struck him, Gabe saw the large man's face, sad and knowing. His eyes glistening with sorrow. The light swallowed him and continued into the side of the hill, slamming into earth and throwing debris into the air. For a moment, Yuri seemed to have lost control of his abilities.

Then a sound. A cry—as if a soul were tearing in two.

The beam stuttered and then ended in silence. Carlyle had simply disappeared. *Gone.*

Yuri looked at his hands, like he was trying to understand why his power had failed. He moved his fingers back and forth, as if studying their malfunction.

A cough escaped his throat, followed by a gurgling noise.

Blood drooled from his mouth. As his body swayed, Yuri looked down to see the forked tip of the sword protruding from his split sternum.

"Huh," he managed and collapsed next to the riverbank, dead.

CHAPTER FORTY-FIVE

Next to Yuri, Micah sat on the ground, her mouth stained red with her own blood. She breathed in short gasps. Letting go of the sword, she rose and walked like a ghost to where Carlyle last stood.

There was nothing there but burning dirt and leaves. She looked back to the student she'd just killed and dropped to the ground in a fit of sobs.

By now, his father had made his way from the bridge, his forehead bleeding and caked with the dust of pulverized stone. He rushed to Micah's side and shielded her from Yuri's corpse with his jacket. He then took her back to the bridge staircase and sat her down.

Gabe felt his own eyes tear up.

His father returned and grabbed him by the arm, hauling him to his feet. But Gabe's legs wouldn't respond. He simply couldn't move and slumped back down to the mud.

"Get up, Gabriel," he said in a quiet, academic voice. "Help me with the body."

His father picked up the hilt of the sword and removed it from Yuri's still form. The blade dripped blood, which splattered onto the ground. He proceeded to wipe it off on

Yuri's clothing, then bent down to brush the blond hair away from the back of the neck. A small circular birthmark was clearly visible. "Damn it. This *is* Uriel."

Gabe looked at the mark.

He betrayed us.

His father rolled the dead boy onto his back. Yuri's head turned to face them, eyes fixed in their sockets. His father picked up Yuri's body and dragged it toward the river. "Gabriel Adam! Quickly! We haven't time. Authorities will be here any minute now."

Gabe snapped back to the moment and took in his surroundings. His father was right. The area looked like a war zone. People would be coming to investigate. Gabe got to his feet and seized Yuri's limp legs.

"Help me roll him into the water," his dad said.

They placed the body on the bank, and his father shoved it in with his foot. It rolled in with a sickening splash and disappeared under the water, carried away by the River Wear.

Gabe lost control of his nerves and vomited onto the mud.

"Are you hurt? Are you okay?"

"No," he said, answering both questions.

"We have to get Micah out of here. She looks traumatized. Probably in shock."

At the top of the hill, a police siren could be heard by the cathedral.

"The dormitory, it seems, is no longer an option." His father grabbed the sword from the mud. "Get your bag and let's go."

He started toward Micah with Gabe following closely behind.

They made their way through the city to Carlyle's house, managing to arrive unnoticed by the curious townies stumbling out of their homes throughout Durham's city center to investigate the commotion. It seemed a cruel place to hide out, Gabe thought, but there was nowhere else to go.

His father fumbled with the door lock, trying to work it open. With the deft use of a credit card and a barge of the shoulder, the door gave way. He ushered Gabe through, half carrying Micah as she leaned against him.

Gabe listened to the distant sirens gathering on the hill by Castle College until the door slammed shut.

Inside the dark room, the smell of tobacco pipe lingered. Dying embers smoldered in the fireplace and reminded him of the life that once lived in the house.

Micah slumped onto the couch and stared off into space. Gabe wanted to console her, to help her, but the guilt he felt stole his courage. He knew that if he hadn't run, Carlyle would still be alive.

More than even the plotting minds of the Vatican, Carlyle had known the protocols for stopping the End of Days. The ultimate authority. Even if the Vatican had a copy of the *Apocalypse of Solomon*, no one would be able to interpret its meaning.

Now they were lost.

After a while of sitting in silence, each of them trying to come to terms with what had just happened by the river, his father walked upstairs with the Gethsemane Sword.

Gabe waited in the dark for a minute, and when being in Micah's company became unbearable, he followed him to the second floor. At the top of the stairs he stood in the doorway to Carlyle's office unseen like he had by the entrance to his father's office so many years ago when he listened to his father's conversation with Aseneth.

Now his dad was rifling through Carlyle's belongings, apparently convinced something might help point him in the right direction. For all of Carlyle's militant insistence to be ready to confront the enemy, he was quite a disorganized man. Stacked books and papers were piled high, wall-to-wall, with little thought of order. There was so much to sift through that Gabe thought it fruitless to even try. None of the materials looked useful.

In the corner his father found several long, rolled documents leaning against a bookcase. They looked like maps or building plans. Near the group was a reinforced travel tube used to hold them. Gabe could see an attached carrying strap, and the case looked to be made of nylon or a similar material. His dad unscrewed the top and slipped the sword inside. It fit perfectly.

After a moment his father set the container aside and began yanking pictures off the walls. Behind one, Gabe noticed a safe. His dad seemed driven, as if finding the small metal box had been thought out before. He spun the dial in several directions until its door opened. From it, he took out a piece of paper. His shoulders slumped, as if he'd expected to find something else. "Where were you planning on going tonight, Son?" His back remained turned toward the door.

Gabe didn't realize he'd been noticed. "London."

His father held up the paper over his shoulder, his head hanging. "Looks like you'll get your wish. Right now, I think we could all use some rest. Go to bed. We're leaving first thing in the morning."

Without another word or so much as a glance to his son, he fell into Carlyle's desk chair and put his hand to his face to rub his temples. Gabe thought of the hours following the incident in New York when his father refused to look at him.

"I'm sorry," Gabe managed.

"We'll talk about it tomorrow. Just try and sleep if you can. We have a long journey ahead."

CHAPTER FORTY-SIX

I n the early morning light, the doors to the Great North Eastern Railway shut and left Gabe with a sense of finality to his time in Durham. The little town and its university life had just begun to feel as much like a home as anyplace he'd lived, but now those days, like the ones in New York, would find their place in his memory.

The train was sparse with passengers, allowing room to comfortably spread out. His father sat across the aisle from Micah, who had curled up against the window, her eyelashes still wet from crying.

Gabe felt like being alone. He found a spot in the middle of the compartment and put his backpack on the booth table, then sat across from a pair of empty seats. Outside, England passed by, covered in snow. The magazine he'd read on the plane from New York came to mind. Rolling hills and patchwork fields, barely distinguishable in the blanketed white of the country.

After an hour of traveling, the train slowed and eventually stopped. One of the conductors entered their compartment. "Tickets," she said.

Gabe produced his from a pocket, and the woman promptly checked it and scanned the card with her device.

"Slight delay," she said. Her tone trailed in exasperation, without a hint of apology. "Mechanical difficulties. Not more than thirty minutes, and we'll be under way." She moved down the aisle calling out for tickets.

Gabe watched the flurries dance in and out of the windowpane until his father rounded the table and sat down in the seat facing him.

"How are you doing, Son?" he asked.

"I don't know."

"Micah's been asleep the whole time," his father said. "I think she's still drowsy from the sedative she found last night in Carlyle's medicine cabinet."

Gabe rested his head against the window. "What have I done?"

"What do you mean?"

"Carlyle is dead. It's my fault," he said, unable to hold back tears.

"Gabriel Adam, listen to me. His death is *nobody's* fault but the enemy's."

"If I hadn't run, he would still be alive."

"This is not your doing. I'm sorry I wasn't awake to counsel you on your experience with the Entheos Genesthai. I can't imagine what it was like."

Gabe allowed his mind to drift. "I saw the future. I know it was real. And the enemy, he can feel my presence. That's how he found me back home in America. You're all in danger if I stay. You'll be killed. It's already started."

"We've suspected that about the enemy. It was the only conclusion that explained why they have not come for Micah. But that is our risk to take. Carlyle understood that. And nothing is ever certain. Especially the future."

"I knew him," Gabe said. "Uriel. Or Yuri. Whatever. Micah and I thought he was just a student from another college. Collingwood. That's what he told us, anyway. We went to his house for a party earlier in the semester. He always hung around the Undercroft. Or showed up wherever I was. I should have known, but I didn't really believe all of this. I mean really, truly believe. And even when I could no longer deny what was happening, I wanted to push it away and pretend it wasn't real."

"Did you ever speak about what we were doing here?"

"No. But I think he always knew."

"That would make his constant presence something more sinister than coincidence, don't you think?"

"I know it now. He was the one trying to get inside the vault. He killed the curator. That's how he got in."

His dad didn't seem surprised by the news. "Then we were undone from the beginning. You can't blame yourself. No more than you could blame Micah. The enemy uses deception to its advantage. It can play to your emotions or exploit weaknesses that you don't even know you have. You didn't believe. That's understandable. What reasonable person could instantly accept such a belief on faith?"

"I believe. In Micah. In me. In what we are. I just wish it was happening to someone else."

"It's happening to all of us. If you believe, then faith

will come. We have been blessed with a small victory in that regard." His dad reached into his pocket and pulled out the note from the safe. "In the meantime, I need your help."

"What is it?" Gabe asked.

"Final instructions from Carlyle. Though in his typical fashion, like he did with installing the vault, he's taken an unfortunate precaution. It's a riddle addressed to me. That old fatalistic bastard," he said with a sad grin.

His dad placed the note on the table and turned it so Gabe could read it.

There was an address to a bank in London and an account number for a safety-deposit box. At the bottom of the note it simply read:

Joseph, to seek what is inside, you must go back to the day when the genesis of a love lost was a love gained.

"Since there was no key, I'm assuming that the safety-deposit box is accessed by a combination code. Obviously, Carlyle believed it could be derived by me through this riddle."

Gabe read the note again. "It's a date."

"I guessed that, too. But what date could be so important that I should instantly know it?" If he was truly lost by its meaning, he didn't show it. He seemed to be baiting Gabe for the answer.

"You know the answer, don't you?" Gabe asked.

His father smiled, caught in his ruse. "I do. But I wanted you to see for yourself. Can you deduce the riddle's meaning? We've spoken about it before, years back."

A love lost . . . , Gabe read again, and then the memory came back as it had last night. He was hiding outside his father's office years ago while he spoke on the phone. "Aseneth. She's the love lost."

"That's correct. Carlyle and I knew her well from the Nicene Project in Turkey that involved the Vatican and the Essenes."

"But what does *a love gained* mean?"

"Think. When did I leave Aseneth?" his dad said, his smile growing.

"After I was born."

"My son, the detective. To be specific, I left her the day you were born to be by your side, the very day I received the call."

Gabe never realized it all had happened so quickly. "So that makes the combination . . ."

"Your birthday. The most important day in my life. A date Carlyle was certain I'd never forget." He put the note back into his jacket pocket.

Gabe felt his heart swell as his father beamed at him.

The train lurched forward beneath them. Soon they were back up to speed.

CHAPTER FORTY-SEVEN

In a cab taken from King's Cross Station, they arrived at a bank in the West End of London. Micah had not said a word the entire trip, but occasionally, Gabe stole a glance from her before she would again get lost in the passing scenery of the busy city.

As they came to a stop, Gabe felt as though he'd been dropped into every car fantasy he'd had since becoming old enough to drive. Cars worth more than he'd ever make in a lifetime lined the curbs of the street. A gleaming red one rumbled by and parked in a space by a marble-sided building, which had a white sign that read in black lettering, City of Westminster.

They exited the black cab, his father helping Micah with the nylon bag that contained the sword. "Neighborhood of the Royals," he remarked, nodding to the sign as he led them to the entrance.

Inside, the foyer's carved stone and tall ceiling lit by natural light gave the impression that the space might make a fine museum. His dad spoke to a woman at a concierge desk, and they waited until a young man arrived to greet them. He looked every part the banker, from his tortoiseshell glasses to his custom-fitting suit. "My name is George. You are one of the holders of the account?" He checked his papers and turned to Gabe's father. "I'll be assisting you with your business with us, Mr. Adam." He turned, stiff, and said, "This way, please."

His dad walked with George, and Gabe and Micah fell behind. As George led them through the winding corridors, he bragged about how the bank was used by many of the nearby museums to house various treasures in their high-security safety-deposit boxes. He stopped outside a large vault door. "I'm afraid only those named on the account may enter," the banker said.

"Wait here. I'll only be a moment," his father said and followed George through the vault and into a long hallway of safety-deposit boxes that reached all the way up to the ten-foot ceiling.

The vault closed behind them, leaving Gabe alone with Micah.

"Let's get this out of the way," she said, her tone hard-edged. "In no way was Carlyle's death your fault." She seemed to struggle to find words. "Yuri fooled me as well."

Gabe stared at the marble floor. "He played me. But had I not run—"

"If you had not run, the inevitable would have happened anyway. Only perhaps Yuri might have been more successful. When you left, you forced his hand. Think if he had taken us all by surprise. It could have been worse." Micah leaned against the wall, unable to totally keep her emotion in check. She frowned and wiped away a tear as it slid over her cheek.

"You okay?" Gabe asked.

"No. I keep thinking that if I had let you tell your father about the attack in Durham, none of this would have happened. That is a mistake I'll have to live with forever. I think, deep down, I was more like you than I wanted to admit. I never wanted this responsibility. More than anything I just wanted to be normal."

"I still struggle with it. But we couldn't have known. Telling them about the attack wouldn't have revealed Yuri, either. So none of it matters, really. Carlyle and my father would have only insisted on us being more careful, but that wouldn't have stopped what happened."

"I want those bastards dead—whoever is with Yuri. Carlyle wasn't my father, and to be honest, never wanted me to treat him like one, but he's the only family I've ever really had. And now he's gone."

"I'm so sorry, Micah." Gabe fought back tears of his own.

"You know, I also had a vision about the future," she said and reached over to hold his hand. She squeezed gently, the surprise of the gesture nearly stopping his heart. "It was about you, Gabe. A demon killed you. And then it killed Carlyle and your father. I managed to get away, but the world still ended in ruin." She drifted off again, anger flaring in her eyes, her hand slipping from his. "It was so real."

Gabe wanted to comfort her, to hold her and tell her that she was beautiful and everything was going to be okay, but in truth, he wasn't sure everything would be okay.

Before he could say anything more, the vault opened and his father exited with George, who held a black box with a number pad on top, much like a telephone.

"I'll take you to a private viewing area," he said and led them again through the bank. In an adjacent hall, he opened a door to a small room filled with a wooden table and leather chairs. George stood in the entrance and allowed them by. He then put the box on the table and turned to leave. "If you need assistance, please use the intercom on the wall."

They walked in, leaving George in the hall to close the door behind them.

With quick precision, his dad entered the numbers into the keypad and opened the box. Inside was an elongated object wrapped in a cloth adorned with embroidered crosses and symbols matching the marks of the archangels.

He removed the item from the box and unraveled the treasure. Their eyes grew wide, and Micah gasped, putting her hand to her mouth. He held a spear tip, its slotted end notched with grooves that would slide perfectly into the forked blade of the Gethsemane Sword.

"My God," his father said. He quickly rewrapped the spear in the cloth and placed it inside the sword's container. "It's time to go. Ethiopia is waiting."

CHAPTER FORTY-EIGHT

The longer he watched from across the London street, the more Septis realized this short, bald man—this pathetic waste—concealed no threat. Nor was it Enoch, and yet some of Enoch's aura had been imprinted on the human, like a fingerprint left at the scene of a crime. Of its origin, Septis felt certain. Never would he forget that scent.

But the power had faded and abandoned this shell. He could smell Enoch in everything surrounding the human, covering it like musk, yet his true essence was elsewhere. Hidden, perhaps, by the fools of the creator's legion. The conundrum left Septis confused. Confusion made him angry.

The man walked through the neighborhood and entered a building off the sidewalk.

Had this been a trick? Was he being mocked? Had he been baited to England, lured away from his search for Joseph Adam and his son by the showing of Enoch's power in order to distract from the boy's movements?

The mistake in New York continued to haunt him. Mastema's patience would not last much longer. Yet Septis could feel it all over the human—the remnant of power. He decided to proceed with caution and caught his reflection in a passing window.

Appearances, after all, can be deceiving.

Septis flicked his cigarette to the ground and moved toward the flat. He placed his hand on the door, shadows slipping from his fingers to unlock it. He entered, silent, undetected. Shadows reached from darkened corners and found their master, concealing him from sight.

Inside, the human put on a kettle while some mindless daytime game show played in the background on the television set. Leaving the kettle to boil, the insect returned to the couch and watched the program, hypnotized by the sounds and images.

Sickened, Septis could hardly stand to be in its presence. *How could such a meek and worthless species inherit the Earth? Blind is the ignorance of God. His likeness indeed.*

The human started to laugh at something, but suddenly couldn't find the ability to continue. It gasped and choked, struggling for breath.

Septis had grabbed the throat. Lifting the human from the couch, he held it off the floor. Eyes bulged in shock, yet to register the attack. Septis pulled it closer and inhaled.

Fear.

The human flailed about, dangling from the arm, attempting to scream. The gravity of the situation set in, and the thing calmed to a terrified stillness, awaiting its doom. Septis positioned thumb over the jugular vein to feel the pulse. Blood pumped through its veins.

He wondered if the human might die from shock before ever providing any entertainment or information. The pulse settled to a steady, measurable rhythm. "I will ask you questions," he said. "If you lie, I will know, and you will be dead. I swear it. Where is Gabriel Adam?" Septis loosened his hold to allow it to speak.

"Who? I don't know him! You've got the wrong house," the man struggled to say.

Septis felt no change in the heartbeat. *Truth*, he thought. "Where is Enoch?"

"Please, I don't know what you're talking about. You've got the wrong . . . *gah*!"

Septis squeezed, ending its protest. *This maggot tells the truth again, yet Enoch's stench covers the thing like a perfume.*

The man tried to say something else, but it only frustrated Septis, so he crushed the neck, snapping the spine. Eyes went vacant as the body fell limp. A last breath hissed out of the gaping mouth.

Septis let go, and the body dropped to the floor in a heap.

He thought for a second, trying to restrain his rage. *The trail is cold again.* As the berserker inside begged for release, his concentration wavered. *I am undone by my own failure.*

The kettle whistled loudly.

The flame. An idea occurred to him. *Answers can be had by means other than asking.* He looked down at the lifeless form and took off his overcoat, laying it on the back of a chair.

He found a soup cauldron and lit the stove. Then he poured in some of the boiling water from the kettle.

Like a dog gnawing at an infected paw, Septis bit his finger and held it over the boiling water, allowing several drops of blood to fall into it. He then rolled up his sleeves, revealing ceremonial scars cut into his skin.

He dragged the body near the stove. As he kneeled over the head, a grotesque, crunching noise followed the sound of blood spilling onto the linoleum floor.

With red-soaked hands, Septis placed two eyeballs into the cauldron. He bent down again and went back to work on the corpse. Sounds of ripping, popping. In his hand, a tongue, dripping and mangled.

He placed it into the boiling cauldron and stirred the liquid with his bare fingers.

The broth bubbled into a thick crimson froth. He placed his palms over the substance and began to chant.

Shadows grew from every corner of the wall—from every crack in its surface. They flowed like oil into the cauldron as he spoke, enslaved by his will. The liquid sloshed and boiled over, sizzling in the flame of the stove. He finished the incantation and opened his eyes.

It was done.

He drank the potion right out of the cauldron.

Vertigo struck him instantly. He stumbled on the body and fell into the corner, spitting and writhing in pain. The kitchen hutch toppled, sending plates and cups shattering onto the floor.

Septis put his hands in front of his face as if something

had appeared there. His eyes turned to deep, black pools.

Muscle memory from the tongue moved his mouth. Visions seen by another's eyes appeared in his mind. Words stammered back through time, as if rewinding the human's life, until Septis felt a moment different from the rest, draped in a familiar energy. He drew toward the memory, focusing his mind to slow, and relived the man's experience.

Mumbling at first, he spoke, the voice alien to his own. "*. . . Entheos Genesthai. Use it sparingly . . . The potion is very powerful and will open up time and the realm of creation . . . Only the Watchers may consume it . . . Solomon . . . the ark . . . the ring . . . Zion . . . Axum . . .*" The vision climaxed and Septis roared, the sound shuddering through the house like an earthquake.

Windows inside the house burst, sending broken glass onto the street.

Septis felt consumed by the excitement of the revelations. *Enoch possessed the human in order to counsel Fortitudo Dei.* His eyes opened wide as new life and resolve invigorated his scarred form. In his mind, the remnant of what was the bald human dwindled into oblivion. Once more, his thoughts were his own.

"Ethiopia," he whispered in his own voice. A smile crept across his face. "Axum," he said louder. "The ark is in Ethiopia."

Septis stood and walked with a renewed purpose toward the front door. He lit a cigarette as he left. Flames the color of its ember ignited inside the building.

The trail is fresh again.

CHAPTER FORTY-NINE

The window to the hotel room looked east into the desert sky and allowed the Egyptian sunrise to spill its rays through the lace curtains, turning Gabe's makeshift bed on the floor into an oven. Combined with the incessant car horns that beeped through the night and the thin rug, which offered little comfort on the hardwood floor, Gabe had accumulated a grand total of no sleep whatsoever.

Under the covers, sweat trickled down his back. He wished he'd joined Micah last night on the king-sized bed. The thought had crossed his mind. Several times.

He kicked off the damp comforter and sat up.

She slept, benefiting from another sedative. His father snored on the couch. Gabe regretted not taking one of the sleeping pills his dad offered before the last flight.

He felt worse than tired. It was a bone-deep kind of exhaustion that had drilled into his waking thoughts. His chest and side still ached from Yuri's kick, which last night had made it impossible to find a comfortable position on the plane.

He stood and stretched the soreness out of his back and

The Revelation of Gabriel Adam

then pushed aside the lace curtains and sliding door. On his way to the balcony, he grabbed the sword case propped up against the wall near Micah's bed.

The sky was awash in light. At first glance, Cairo was a sprawling orange mess, like a giant puzzle waiting to be solved around the Nile River. After a moment, the beauty of the city began to unfold, and he recalled the first time he visited New York's Metropolitan Museum of Art. Monet's dots of paint, much like the clutter, buildings, and streets of Cairo, somehow came together to become more brilliant than their individual parts.

Across the river, tall buildings lined up against the bank. Their piers were filled with boats of all kinds and extended into the blue waters. Trees lined a riverside walk below. Various ferries docked against its landing, ready for tourists and sightseers who walked by.

Beyond the busy district, lush grass and foliage extended from the riverbanks, the Nile a stripe of green that faded along with the rest of the city into distant orange sands of the desert rising on a hill in the horizon.

Gabe couldn't help but smile.

The hotel faced upstream on the point of an island situated in the middle of the river, with its waters flowing north to the Mediterranean Sea. Gabe leaned against the railing and watched the nautical traffic. Industrial ocean liners, haulers, ferries, small cruise ships, and boats with hoisted sails went about their daily routines, oblivious to this changing world that now felt bigger than it ever had before.

And at the same time the world felt smaller, closing in,

with fewer and fewer places to call sanctuary. *Fewer places to call home.* He couldn't remember what it was like to not endure a sense of urgency.

Above a building to the northeast, the Union Jack flapped in the wind. The British Embassy sat next to the bank of the Nile. He wanted to run to them and beg for some sort of military or government assistance. *A gun, maybe. Though perhaps their army would be better.*

It seemed unlikely that the embassy would believe a story from three strangers about a coming apocalypse, but what was there to lose? Unless, of course, they had been breached or infiltrated by the enemy. The sting of Yuri's betrayal still weighed heavy on Gabe's mind. Suspecting everyone around him was a terrible feeling, but trust had become a liability. He trusted his father. Micah, too. Outside his two travel companions, anyone could be an enemy.

He pulled over a chair and sat down next to the railing. Thoughts drifted back to Carlyle—the look on his face when Yuri murdered him.

Carlyle knew. He knew that was his final moment.

Gabe unsheathed the sword. It had been cleaned—all the blood wiped from the blade by his father at Carlyle's place. Gone was any evidence of Yuri's death. Any hope of uncovering what he knew, lost.

And what about Raphael? Was he dead? Or turned like Yuri? The possibilities made Gabe's neck muscles tighten into a dull ache. As his anxiety returned he realized that his head didn't hurt. Even with all that had happened, he had not experienced a migraine since he'd taken the Entheos Genesthai.

"Africa . . . can you believe it?" Micah asked from the doorway.

Her voice saved him from his wandering mind. She stepped into the arid breeze and sunshine, looking deflated. Worn. Sad. Loose strands of hair danced around her face. They defied the light, the black somehow darker, more radiant. She brushed them behind her ear and held them against her neck.

"I was just thinking the same thing. How are you feeling?"

"It's like I can't sleep enough. Like I don't want to do anything but sleep." She paused, her words hanging in the air. "That pill leaves a bit of a hangover. Your father's still knocked out. And snoring. Loudly, in fact," she said, looking out over Cairo. "It's quite beautiful, isn't it? The Nile?"

Micah stepped onto the balcony. A flash caught her face. She turned to see the sword twirling in Gabe's hand, light reflecting off its blade like a mirror. "Could you give me that, please?" she asked.

"Yeah, sure. Sorry."

"It's just . . ."

"No explanation needed." He handed it over.

"Thanks." She put the forked end on the floor and let the blade reflect the sun into her eyes. For a moment, she was lost in its brilliance. "Do you think we have a chance, Gabe? You saw what Yuri was capable of. He's been coached. Trained. What if the same thing has happened to Raphael? There's something we're not seeing. Some clue we're missing."

Gabe thought of his father's warning about the power of the Michaelion. He wondered if Micah knew how powerful she might be. "My dad thought there might be a third party to this war. One that wants an outcome different than the enemy. Or us. Someone who might profit from a war. Yuri, I think, proved that my dad was right. If the battle is over authority in this realm, we have to ask, who or what could possibly benefit?"

Micah didn't have an immediate answer. She gazed out over the water to the buildings. The British Embassy looked busy. Gabe noticed it, too.

"Maybe man. Maybe government," she said, looking at the flag. "If this war is for power and control, then why not? Mankind is hungry for it. Always has been."

CHAPTER FIFTY

The riverside by the hotel bustled with activity. Groups of tourists moved like cattle through the crowds of locals, herded by water taxi drivers toward small boats tied to docks on the Nile. Merchant vendors in small kiosks were strategically set up to take advantage of the indecisive. They pestered the groups, shouting encouragements to buy their goods, each a one-man infomercial.

Micah and Gabe stood alone by the docks, waiting for Gabe's father to find transportation up the river. Gabe caught looks from passersby. He thought some were staring. *There are too many people here.*

"Quit it." She looked at him and adjusted the sword case on her back.

"Quit what?" Gabe asked.

"People are enjoying themselves, and you're standing there with that I'm-freaking-out look on your face. Like you're expecting a bomb to go off."

"Well, I am . . . sort of. People are checking us out."

"No, they aren't. If they are, it's only because you're drawing attention to yourself. You look as though *you're* about to set off a bomb. Relax."

"Whatever," Gabe said. "Crowds make me nervous right now."

"Not me," Micah said. Since Carlyle died, she seemed to be hardening. The bounce and wit had faded from her personality, leaving an angry edge to everything she did. Gabe wondered if the girl he had come to know and like was now gone forever.

"I don't see why we don't just fly directly there."

"Because, like your father said, traveling by plane leaves too easy a paper trail. If whoever Yuri was with is tracking us, it will seem to them that we are still in Cairo."

"And if the other enemy is onto us, the one Enoch said can find me?"

"We keep moving," she said, her tone cold and matter of fact.

His dad walked up behind them and slapped their backpacks. "Okay, we're sorted for the cruise."

Micah shook her head and rolled her eyes as Gabe jumped out of his skin.

His dad continued, "I've hired a boat to take us upriver. I found a captain who knows a pilot that can get us out of the country without hassle from immigration. Apparently, he runs reporters in and out of Khartoum from Egypt, so he knows how to keep a low profile. It will be expensive but necessary, I think."

"How long will the cruise take?" Micah asked.

"Could be a long journey, a full day at least, depending on how strong the current is flowing against us. But being on the river will effectively take us off the grid. Once we get to Luxor, we'll find that pilot and charter a flight to Axum. They're ready to board, so grab your things."

"Have you thought about what we're supposed to do when we get there?"

"I don't know, Gabe. Find the nearest priest and say, 'Hello, I seem to have come across a couple of archangels sent to lead man against forces of evil. Any suggestions as to what to do with them? Terribly sorry to bother.' One hurdle at a time."

"And if, you know, *it* isn't there?"

"This is where Enoch said we should go. If he is wrong, then God help us."

CHAPTER FIFTY-ONE

espite Gabe's efforts to sleep in the small cabin of the riverboat, his senses worked overtime. The air tasted stale, and the day's sweat coated his skin like a film of salt. Scents of gasoline and oil drifted in the air.

In the bowels of the boat, the engines idled their steady, soft rhythm, suggesting they were anchored for the night. Beside him, his father slept in the bed, snoring once again. Somehow he knew Micah was in her room next door, sleeping as well.

He could almost feel her there.

Snuggling with her new best friend, the Gethsemane Sword, he guessed.

A gray light trickled through the condensation on the window port, bathing the room in pale tones of blue. The hollow sounds of waves lapping against the hull echoed through the ship.

He felt so alert, so alive. So awake. Like during one of his super tall caramel macchiato binges at The Study Habit. *But more.* He decided to try for sleep later after some fresh air.

The calm water of the Nile shimmered in the moonlight

that was now yielding to the blue horizon of the breaking dawn. On the far banks, water was nearly inseparable from land. Gabe leaned against the rail, his legs worn from travel. A chill in the air caused him to suddenly shiver, his breath catching—an odd reaction, he thought, to have in a desert. Earlier in the day, the air had been dry and hot. Putting on anything more substantial than a T-shirt seemed stupid, which was exactly how he felt now, rubbing his arms for warmth. He faced the breeze blowing in from the land. It was steady, full of unfamiliar fragrances.

The night obscured the shoreline, but when he concentrated, his vision focused. It found the details of the bank in the distance, and the harder he looked, the more of it he saw.

Curious, Gabe thought. He tried to recall a time when his eyes had done this before. Then again, he realized it had been quite some time since he'd been this far away from city lights and under a full moon. He remembered discovering Yuri by the bridge in Durham and the weird clarity of the night.

Coincidence, he hoped and pushed the thought aside. He was aware of odd little changes in his senses that began after he consumed the Entheos Genesthai—heightened smell, sight, and hearing. Sure, they were insignificant compared to what he had expected out of the experience, but together they amounted to something more. He wasn't yet comfortable acknowledging the new abilities, however. Underneath all his insecurities, he knew: *I'm changing*.

The boat's deck was empty of passengers and crew, except for one young couple, lovers obviously, who were drinking a bottle of wine on a blanket laid out under a string of white lights near the bow. Gabe stayed far enough away from them so as to not impose on their privacy, though her constant giggling was starting to annoy.

Their flirtations weren't enough to distract from his senses. Suddenly, he caught a dank scent on the wind coming from downstream, from the direction of Cairo.

Brimstone. He tasted sulfur in the air and wondered why it should seem familiar. He had never actually smelled brimstone. Nor did he even know what exactly brimstone was, and yet there was the answer shouting in his head. Looking downriver he felt an odd feeling, a coldness growing beyond what his sharpened vision could see. The slightest of discomforts wormed into his thoughts like a warning. Something was coming, and he knew it like he would know an approaching storm by his aching joints.

After a moment, the feeling passed, along with the scent in the air. He turned to look upstream, wondering if the couple on the bow had noticed the smell.

The man caught him staring and looked irritated at the invasion of privacy, then cursed in another language. Gabe thought about trying to apologize but guessed it would be pointless given the communication barrier. They grabbed their bottle of wine and disappeared to the other side of the boat.

Above, the stars began to lose their fight with the lightening African sky. Gabe marveled at how his life had brought him here. He felt like a theater actor who didn't know the role, waiting for the director to show him how to play the part.

A yawn. The need for sleep was returning. His body relaxed,

his nervous energy somehow stolen by the cool air, and the cramped cabin seemed a little more appealing. Perhaps there was some more shut-eye to be had before breakfast.

"You're becoming quite the introspective boy, Gabe," a melancholy voice said. "I seem to keep finding you staring out into the world, lost in your thoughts. Not that I blame you."

Gabe turned to see Micah joining him by the railing. "What are you doing up?"

"Same as you, I suspect. Couldn't sleep. It's like my brain won't shut off." She followed his stare toward the horizon. "I heard you get up and thought I might join you."

They stood for a moment, silent, each looking out over the river into Egypt.

"I never thought I'd see the Nile," Gabe said.

"I know. I feel like since we've come all this way, we should jump in or something, just to say we've swam in it."

"It's freezing out here."

She folded her arms against her sweater like she agreed. "Have you at least felt the water?"

Gabe shook his head.

Micah bent over the railing and stretched her arm to the water.

Gabe moved closer, convinced she was going over. "Damn it, Micah. Aren't there crocodiles in that thing?"

"It's warm. Much warmer than the air. Feels good," she said. She stopped splashing in the river. "Pull me up," she said, her voice now filled with terror. "Pull me up now, Gabe!"

He yanked her back, grabbing her sweater. It felt hot to the touch, warmed by her skin as if she had been stricken with fever. Her face was white from shock, and her hand dripped with water. As he watched, the droplets of water turned crimson and fell into the river. "Oh, my God," he said. "Micah, you're bleeding."

She looked at her hand. Where there had been only water, blood now covered her fingers. "It's not mine. It's not my blood," she said, but she sounded detached, almost vacant in thought.

He reached to grab her hand but then heard glass shattering on the deck followed by a shrill scream from the woman on the bow.

Gabe's heart jumped into his throat, and he turned from Micah.

The man on the bow was bent over the railing, staring into the water as if something had been dropped in. The woman had fallen to the deck. Her hand was held to her mouth, and she dry heaved, unable to look at the river.

Spotlights on the boat sprung to life, illuminating the bow. A spattering of blood covered the woman's face and dress. The sight of it on her sent her further into hysterics. More glistened on the deck and on the railing. Gabe looked her over for any sign of an injury, but like Micah, nothing stood out.

A horn sounded. The man pulled back from the rail and ranted in his language. Words came fast and without much thought. He looked terrified, pointing into the river and emphasizing certain words. Even without understanding the language, Gabe could tell the man wasn't making sense.

Frustrated, he continued to stab at the river with his finger, then stopped his tirade and fell to his knees repeating only one word over and over. He stepped back and tended to his woman on the deck. She was in shock, sobbing uncontrollably.

Micah clutched Gabe's shirt. "I want to go. Please, Gabriel, take me inside," she said, her voice monotone and without emotion.

It was not immediately apparent what had caused the couple to react in such a way. *Perhaps a piece of jewelry fell in.* But the blood on her dress, the blood on Micah's hand—it didn't add up. As the boat's spotlights swept back and forth across the bow and over the dark water, Gabe focused on where the man had pointed.

Then he understood.

The water carried a distinct tint. Where the boat's white hull met the river water revealed the answer. No other substance on Earth had the same look or viscosity. Gabe turned to Micah and said, "The river. It's turned to blood."

CHAPTER FIFTY-TWO

Deckhands and passengers arrived to comfort the woman and investigate the disturbance. Her reaction spread like a virus as they, too, discovered the river of blood. Men shouted in foreign languages and dropped to their knees to pray. Others were more reserved and practical in their fear, seeking refuge on the higher decks.

Micah stood in a state, frozen.

Gabe put his arm around her shoulder and led her through the crowd to get back to his cabin.

Inside, his father lay half-awake under the sheets. "What's all that racket, then? Did we hit something?" he asked.

"The water . . . it's blood," Gabe whispered, out of breath. He grabbed a towel off the floor and began to wipe Micah's hand.

She stared at her open palm. "I did it—"

"What's going on?" his father asked again, interrupting her.

"The water—the whole river—it turned to blood!" Gabe said.

His dad sat upright and turned on the small lamp over his bunk. "What do you mean, blood?"

"What else could I mean? We're floating on freaking blood!"

"My God," muttered his father.

"Are we safe?" Micah whispered.

His silence was answer enough.

"Dad, what do we do?" Gabe asked, but before anyone could make a suggestion, the boat's engines throttled to life with a violent shudder. He steadied himself against the wall. His balance wavered as the boat altered its position in the river. The sound of the anchor chains coiling onto the deck vibrated through the walls.

He jumped onto the bed, nearly on top of his father, and put his face against the porthole. Adrenaline surged through his veins. With his hands cupped around his eyes to block out the room's light, Gabe peered through it, scanning the darkness.

The searchlight crossed the window.

"I think we're turning around. Going back downstream. There's a light in the distance on the horizon. Might be a city . . . I can't see." He swiveled back and forth in the window trying to get a look. "What if the blood is a sign of the enemy's presence?"

Micah's breathing slowed. She seemed to be calming and held out her hand, squeezing it into a fist as if to steady it.

"It's possible, but I don't think so," his dad said. "In the Old Testament, God used Moses to turn the Nile to blood. Perhaps this is no different. Perhaps it is a sign or a warning. That the End of Days is upon them."

"But Enoch said we were alone in this fight," Gabe said.

"No. It was me," Micah said. "I felt something inside me when I touched the river. I don't know what it was, but I felt it spill from my body, from my hand, and flow into the Nile. What's happening to me?"

Gabe turned from the window and fell against the wall, wondering what her admission meant for her. Another thought slipped into his mind. *Will it happen to me?*

His father stood and looked at the girl. "It is a warning after all. Though not from God. A warning from the Michaelion, the leader of men." He reached out to Micah and held her hand in his. "My dear, your power is growing."

CHAPTER FIFTY-THREE

The boat docked off a pier outside the riverside town of Qinā just as the morning sun broke the horizon. As they debarked from the cruiser, Gabe noted that the water had returned to its normal blue color. But whatever Micah had done had left its mark. Hundreds of single sail fishing vessels were landed on the riverbank, and several cruise ships docked along the boardwalk carried a crimson stain on their hulls.

It had not gone unnoticed, either. Thousands of locals and tourists gathered by the Nile to observe the strange occurrence, discussing what it meant while snapping their cameras. The growing crowd seemed calm, though in the distance Gabe could hear occasional screams from women or the berating shouts of frightened men who must have believed the stains on the boats to be something more.

"They seem only mildly curious now," his father said, walking up the boarding plank to the pier. "But wait. Soon the fear of the most terrified will spread from person to person. These people live among the Valley of the Kings, a land haunted by ancient tombs and temples built to powerful Egyptian gods. Their superstitions run deep. We have little time before chaos seizes the city." He handed Gabe his bag. "Wait here."

Gabe stood with Micah while his dad moved ahead to speak with the ship's captain. After a moment he returned with a name and an address written on an Egyptian five-pound note. "I got the pilot's contact information. The captain said he set up a meeting before we left Cairo."

"But he's in Luxor, right?"

"Correct. And we're in Qinā, an hour or so north by rail. I don't know if that means we're going to be late or early, but we should get moving. The station is within walking distance. Generally, we're safe in the city, and English, I am told, is common with the area being so prone to tourists. Just be aware and keep your eyes open." His father glanced at a group of Egyptian women walking by, draped head to toe in black burqas. "Micah, you should probably cover your head and face. It isn't that conservative here, but we'd do well to blend in."

Micah removed a garment from her backpack and fashioned a makeshift hijab headscarf from it, tucking one of the sides across her face. "The smell of fish is getting to me anyway," she said.

They walked farther into the interior of the city toward the train station. The streets of Qinā moved with the energy expected in a tourist destination. Palms and other trees lined the streets where visitors and locals shopped under the covered markets. The men dressed equally in Western styles and the long, robe-like jellabiya of the local culture. The colorful awnings fluttered in the morning breeze coming off the Nile.

Three-story buildings framed the roads, with laundry hanging outside windows and drying on telephone lines. Satellite dishes looked to be very popular, decorating every roof. Above it all, minarets reached into the cloudless blue sky.

At the Qinā Station, his dad purchased their tickets, and they boarded a train packed with passengers. With only standing room available, Gabe held the bar overhead and watched Egypt pass by in the window, the train hugging the Nile as it rolled south. Flattened land streaked by in flashes of green palms and fields of tall grain growing by the river.

Occasionally, he would glance at Micah to see how she was faring in the sweaty, hot compartment, but she didn't seem to notice. Instead, she once again focused on her hands, studying them as if they were now something foreign to her.

Luxor Station was a tourist's Mecca. The whole place looked like one giant theme park. Posters of ancient ruins and statues lined every wall, along with advertisements for sightseeing tours for the nearby Valley of the Kings. Last-minute souvenir stands crowded the area with maps for those arriving and trinkets for tourists who wanted to remember their experience with a plastic sphinx.

They took a taxi to the address written on the Egyptian pound, a hole-in-the-wall café off the beaten path in a neighborhood near the airport. Its interior was open like a garage to the patio area outside. Sticky strands of fly tape hung from the ceiling, each full of tiny victims, though it seemed to help little.

Inside the building, away from the unbearable heat of the midday sun, local men sat around circular tables, smoking and talking. A single television above the bar broadcast an Arabic news station, though nobody seemed particularly interested. In the middle of the room a solitary fan limped from its missing blade, clicking as it slowly turned.

Gabe and Micah followed his dad to the bar, but the patrons, all of them men, seemed to stop what they were doing and stare at the girl.

She stopped. "I don't think I'm welcome in here. How anyone ever meets a woman in this country is beyond me."

"Right. Perhaps you should wait outside," his father said.

"I'll go with her. Try and hurry. It's sweltering out there," Gabe said.

He followed Micah through the exit and stood close enough to keep an eye on his father, who tried to engage the man behind the bar. He didn't seem to speak English, so his father showed him the note. He pointed to a man sitting in a corner by himself, reading a paper.

The pilot, Gabe thought. He watched his father order two teas and then take them to the pilot's table, offering him one of the cups.

The pilot appeared agitated and folded his paper in a manner to make the point. He then held up his watch and threw his hands in the air.

"I think we're late," Gabe said, watching. "Or early, maybe. Either way, the pilot isn't happy."

His dad tried to appeal to him calmly. Then he bent closer, and Gabe watched his father hold out his closed hand and rub his thumb over his index finger—the international sign for money.

"What's going on?" Micah asked.

"I think my dad is trying to . . . bribe him."

"Is it working?"

"Looks like it."

"Good. I don't like being here," she said, swatting a fly from her face. "This heat is absurd, and it smells like rubbish."

Gabe turned to her, and behind her hijab he could see her angry eyes. "You okay?"

"We're in bloody Egypt trying to find a criminal to take us illegally into Ethiopia. And if you haven't noticed, I turned a freaking river to blood this morning. No, Gabe, I am not okay."

Gabe regretted asking, but he was encouraged that Micah seemed to be opening up. Opening to anger but opening nonetheless.

His father shook the pilot's hand before walking out of the café. "He's not a pleasant man," he said. "Like I suspected, we were late. Among his many subtle qualities is a militant stance on punctuality. Apparently, he had chartered a group of tourists to do a flyover around the Valley of the Kings."

"So we're screwed," Micah said.

"No. Luckily, greed is another one of his qualities, and money talks. And he's not asking questions. I think he's about to make his year's salary on us." He looked inside his wallet, and his nose scrunched up. "He'll meet us at the airport in an hour. But if this doesn't work, you may be right, Micah."

CHAPTER FIFTY-FOUR

At Luxor International Airport they arrived to a
churning sea of people. Angry mobs had formed
around various ATM machines, which had shut
down, overwhelmed by use. More than a few times
someone grabbed Gabe to plead something in Arabic.
When he couldn't respond, almost every one of them, whether
indigent or affluent, repeated what they said in English. They
all wanted one thing—cash to buy a plane ticket.

Micah and Gabe took advantage of a few spare seats
and rested while his father searched for their pilot. Gabe
had visions of a seatless, twin-prop plane stuffed nose to tail
with smelly passengers and tagalong farm animals. He could
almost see the chicken feathers floating through the cabin
on takeoff.

"This place has gone crazy. People seem to be out of their
bloody minds," Micah said as she brushed a long strand of
hair out of her eyes and placed the sword in its case in the
seat next to her. Even without a proper shower for a day, she
maintained a certain poise in her look and manner. The lack
of makeup had only brought out her natural beauty.

"I think this morning has caught up to us," Gabe said,

trying not to stare at her. He motioned down the corridor.

Television sets hung from the ceiling and broadcast several different news stations. People congregated under them, waiting for information and occasionally pointing at the screen. Images occasionally elicited unified gasps from the viewers.

On one channel, the camera panned to a woman drenched in blood from the river, passing a reporter. She looked stunned. On a different television, journalists reported near the riverbanks, giving on-the-scene commentary or talking to scientists and religious experts. One blurb below a scientist claimed in English *Red Algae Bloom Responsible for Religious Panic—Deemed Hazardous to Humans*. On yet another channel, an Islamic cleric was being interviewed. He looked unconvinced by the official explanation and seemed to be trying to explain or persuade the correspondent that there was more to the story.

The channel then changed to an international feed. A Vatican spokesperson stood at a podium outside St. Peter's Square nearly hidden behind a tangle of microphones.

"Micah, look," he said and gestured to the screen. "The Vatican knows. Maybe they know about us. Maybe they can help us."

"I don't think that would be a good idea. If an archangel can be compromised like Yuri, then I don't see why we shouldn't also be concerned with the Vatican. I think it's better we're on our own," she said.

Gabe sank into his seat, knowing she was right. The incessant roar of the airport crowd and the occasional hysterical scream played against his already frayed nerves. He felt jumpy, and the heat inside the airport choked the oxygen from the air.

"What's wrong with you?" Micah snapped and leaned away from him in her seat. "You're on my last nerve. Like a puppy in a thunderstorm."

"I think I'm freaking out. Things are changing so fast, I can't keep up."

"Deal with it," she said. "We no longer have the luxury to be scared."

"Really? What about you? Bulletproof all of a sudden? An emotionless robot?" Gabe asked, surprised by his quickness to anger. "Don't act so tough around me. You're human, too, and just as scared as I am."

"This is our task," Micah said. "And I mean to finish it, whatever it takes. Carlyle would want nothing more from us than that. We do what we can and, if possible, what we were meant to do. Whatever else is left of all this"—she motioned to the crowd and airport—"whatever is left of us, if anything, will be decided soon enough."

Gabe looked deep into her eyes. They exuded a strength and confidence in knowing who and what she was becoming. She'd accepted this new reality. He could only hope he would soon find the same inside himself.

His father pushed through the crowd and sat down beside them. He looked tired. "We're leaving. Now. The pilot's ready on the tarmac. He said the whole damned region is falling apart around us."

"What do you mean?" asked Gabe.

"News of the river has gone international. Videos of the

blood in the river taken by mobile phones have reached the Internet. Riots are breaking out along the Nile, all the way to Cairo. Some of the most powerful religious leaders are trying to take control of the government, convinced that what happened is a sign from God that gives them authority. There's talk of military action, which would close the borders and all airports. People are desperate to get out of Egypt but not just tourists and foreigners. It seems a large population of locals is fleeing, too, and for some reason, Ethiopia has suddenly become a popular travel destination. If we don't go now, we could be stuck."

They got on the plane, and Gabe sat in the cramped space of his seat. At last, he was overcome by the lack of sleep, and before drifting off, one final question slipped through his mind. *What exactly is waiting for us in Axum?*

CHAPTER FIFTY-FIVE

"Gabe, wake up. You need to see this." Micah shook his leg and brought him out of his slumber. He'd drifted off for a brief nap since renting the old Land Rover at the airport outside Axum.

The discomfort of the day's travel in the rickety plane ached in his lower back and legs. He tried to sit up in the seat but felt a sharp pain in his side. Something stuck into his abdominal muscle. He checked his ribs with his hand. None of them seemed to be out of place, but he still wondered if one had been cracked by Yuri's kick.

"What's going on?" Gabe struggled through a yawn.

The vehicle had slowed to a crawl, its engine drowned out by the sound of panicked voices. Not yet accustomed to the bright setting, he strained to see outside the Land Rover.

"We're in Axum city center," Micah said from the front seat. "Look."

An Ethiopian face bashed against Gabe's window, leaving a splash of sweat on the glass. All the weariness in his body jolted out of his system. The man pounded his fists against the door. Tears rolled down his face.

Gabe recoiled. "What's happening?"

"A good question," his father said from the driver's seat.

Hundreds, maybe thousands, of refugees lined the main road of Axum, standing next to shelters and tents in a mixed street of residential houses and roadside markets. Women, children, and men waved their hands and white cloths at the passing SUV. One small group knelt around a man who held a cross and his open palm to the sky.

The Land Rover passed a crying woman. She held her baby to the window.

"Something is going on here. I doubt Axum has a population that amounts to a tenth of this crowd."

"Looks like there's been some sort of . . . migration here," Gabe said.

"Like in the book of Exodus, you know? When Moses escaped to Mount Sinai," Micah added. "To the promised land."

"You may be right," his dad said. "My indications are that this road leads straight to the Church of Our Lady Mary of Zion. If the Ark of the Covenant and the Tabernacle of God are both found here in these hills like the Ethiopic Christians believe, the church seems like our best chance for getting answers." He peered through the refugees. "We're nearing a gate. The road is ending. This must be the place."

Gabe followed his father's gaze. Ahead, above the crowd, an oasis of tall, thick trees could be seen behind a large fence that reached nearly as high as the trees. He found the leafy foliage odd amongst the dry dirt- and boulder-populated orange landscape surrounding the rest of the area.

Spotlighted towers separated sections of the chain-link barricade that reached around the compound and appeared new from the freshly turned soil at the base of the metal posts supporting the structure. It looked more like a prison than a church. Gabe noticed buildings partly obstructed by the foliage, including a small square structure to his left, its gated garden bordering the larger fence surrounding the compound. Farther into the compound, the white dome of its largest building, resembling a mosque without a minaret, peeked through the greenery.

The crowd prevented the SUV from advancing. Another frantic man threw himself on the hood of the Land Rover. He pounded on the windshield and motioned to his mouth.

"We have no food or water. We cannot help. I'm sorry. Please let us through!" His dad honked the horn.

More and more people surrounded the vehicle, and the crowd swelled the closer they got to the gate. They shoved each other, trying to get to the SUV. It rocked back and forth from the bodies that stacked against the sides. Some were getting hurt, crushed. They cried out in pain.

Ahead of the vehicle, automatic gunfire crackled over the SUV.

The crowd cowered from the sound as they scattered and fled, leaving the vehicle exposed and alone on the street.

Men dressed in military fatigues stood atop a set of concrete steps that led to a fortified compound behind a gate covered in barbed wire. They shot their Kalashnikov machine guns randomly into the air. Warnings spat from the guards toward the refugees, scaring them farther away from the vehicle, emphasized by more shots over their heads.

One soldier pointed his gun at the Land Rover.

Micah cursed and tried to get the sword out of sight.

His dad threw the gear into park and took his hands off the wheel, holding them up. "Nobody make any sudden moves. I'll get us out of this."

Inspired by hours of action movies, Gabe's imagination let loose on what the weapons were capable of doing to a person. In his mind, bodies lay in pools of blood, torn to shreds by bullets.

The gunfire ceased, and then the soldiers leveled their sights on the Land Rover as its engine idled.

Gabe held his breath and waited for the worst.

CHAPTER FIFTY-SIX

In the steps behind the line of soldiers, a monk in a white robe appeared, his head wrapped with a ceremonial prayer shawl, which covered his ears and draped to his shoulders. He motioned to one of his men who wore a blue beret, different from the seemingly standard issue of desert yellow that adorned the others. The officer approached the monk and bowed his head.

"Look," Gabe whispered.

The monk pointed at them, and the officer shouldered his weapon. Then, with a snap and rhythm similar to that of the Kalashnikov's gunfire, he barked a string of orders to his platoon.

"Just cooperate, you two. This is all merely a misunderstanding," his dad said in an attempt to steady their fears.

Gabe watched three soldiers surround the vehicle, one for each occupant. Micah's door opened first, then his father's and finally his own. The soldiers yanked them from the SUV, wrenching them out by their clothes.

Micah tried to protect the sword but was thrown to the ground before she could get the case. She jumped up, defiant, but another soldier seized her and held her back.

The old monk saw this and shouted to the soldiers. His

father's hands were put on his head as another soldier searched his pockets.

On the officer's command, the other soldiers followed suit, searching Micah, then Gabe. Their hands were uncaring—squeezing their arms and legs, yanking at pockets. One of the soldiers pressed against Gabe's side, and he gasped in pain from the pressure on his bruised ribs. Soon the soldiers had their passports and wallets. With the Land Rover emptied of its occupants, the soldiers herded their prisoners toward the steps of the gate.

"We're seeking the Church of Our Lady Mary of Zion—," his dad said but was silenced with a slap to the back of his head.

The officer shouted again, this time enraged. Gabe couldn't tell whether he was yelling at his father or the soldier who'd slapped him.

The remaining men picked apart the Land Rover like vultures on a kill. They cut open seats, ripped panels from the doors. What little baggage was in the trunk was thrown into the street. One of the men picked up the sword's case and unscrewed the top. The blade spilled onto the ground along with the cloth-wrapped spear tip. Micah attempted to pull free from her soldier's grip but could do nothing with her arms held behind her back. The soldier tossed the material aside and held his findings up before presenting them to the monk.

The old man received them and shook his head. He then turned toward the interior of the complex and motioned for his officer to follow.

The soldiers responded to the gesture by shoving their

captives toward the steps.

Without any explanation, the Land Rover was driven away.

Gabe, Micah, and his dad walked at gunpoint through the gate. Once inside the compound, one of the soldiers shouted and pointed to the ground with the muzzle of his gun.

Gabe understood first and dropped to his knees with his hands still interlocked behind his head. He figured it was the best strategy to avoid getting a bullet. Prisoner executions looked as though they might be one of this army's specialties.

Micah glared at them, her jaw and fists clenched. Her gaze dropped to one of the guns. She wanted it. Wanted to use it, Gabe suspected.

"Please—," his dad started before having the barrel of the gun placed on his folded hands behind his head.

The message was clear: *No more talking.*

The more Micah simmered on the ground, the more Gabe realized she was about to make a move. *She'll be shot dead*, he thought.

Something had to be done to prevent her from getting herself killed, but the opportunity was slipping away.

Yuri had power. So does Micah. That means I have power somewhere inside me, he thought. *If I could only get to it . . .*

As if responding to his desperation, his skin began to crawl. Neck hairs stood on end. A feeling—alien and new— welled up inside. He felt like he might explode. His shirt became statically charged, tingling against his skin. Gabe felt a shock against his shoulder as a flash of electrical current arced from his shirt to the barrel of the gun.

The soldier behind him lifted his gun away and yelled to his comrades. He sounded terrified, his voice rising in octaves as he took a step back, shaking his weapon at Gabe.

His father and Micah watched, the look in their eyes a mix of fear and confusion as the energy spread from soldier to soldier. Gabe could feel it growing inside, and he knew he was losing control. Dog tags and buttons on the soldiers moved of their own accord, reaching out from their bodies, sticking to weapons and medals on their jackets.

The sensation was just like the one Gabe remembered from the vision. He'd felt it just before going supernova.

The officer gave an order to the soldier behind Gabe, his voice calm and deliberate, careful, motioning with his hand. Hesitant feet moved closer, and Gabe felt the cold steel of a gun barrel settle on his birthmark.

He looked to the ground. Grains of sand and tiny pebbles rolled away as if pushed by some unfelt wind.

Micah shook her head, pleading for him to stop, but he didn't know how. She mouthed, *What are you doing?*

Gabe shrugged. He had no idea, but he knew the soldiers would kill them unless he acted. The power inside him had built to a crescendo, and heat radiated from his palms. Gabe decided it was now or never. He seized the moment, fists clenched, and spun on his captor, only to see the butt of the machine gun thrusting toward his head.

Then there was a burst of pain followed by darkness.

CHAPTER FIFTY-SEVEN

Gabe opened his eyes, unable to focus on the ground moving beneath him. His legs dragged behind him through the dirt. Two men held him, each by an arm. A throbbing pain pulsed over his right eye. Something warm trickled into his eye and down his nose. He felt dizzy and nauseous, then, without warning, he vomited. The men who carried him stopped and let him finish. Once his stomach emptied, they adjusted their path to avoid the mess.

He gathered the strength to lift his head and fight the vertigo. Ahead was a small domed and primitive-looking square temple behind a protective gate. The structure looked not much bigger than some of the mausoleums in the old graveyards scattered around Durham.

They're going to bury me, Gabe thought as they unlocked the fence.

Around the entrance was a façade of handcrafted brick rising in the pattern of two columns next to the entrance, giving the surface a rough, textured look. Large windows flanked the brickwork. Their panes were shaped like Christian crosses and painted a bright yellow that contrasted the mosaic of green tiles bordering the glass. Above the entrance he could see a purple cross in a window peering out into the front garden within the fence.

Gabe's eyes fluttered. He fought to stay conscious. Images of Micah's face flashed before him, and he wondered if he'd ever see her again. A terrible feeling of regret filled him when he realized he'd never be able to redeem himself in her eyes. That she'd always only think of him as the reason she lost Carlyle.

The monk from the street walked by them, still holding the sword and spear tip, and moved ahead through the building's entrance, which was nothing more than a simple red curtain that discouraged passage to the interior.

Gabe glanced at the sky one last time before the soldiers took him inside. Atop the dome, a spire reached into the sunlight. *A wind compass.* At the north, south, east, and west points, four arms stretched out, each affixed with a unique design. Each looked very familiar, despite the jumbled thoughts in his head. He focused on the symbol pointing south. It was circular, with elliptical objects arranged to form a symbol.

Before he succumbed to the concussion, he remembered that first day in Durham, the day his father and Carlyle showed him the document from the Vatican, and in his mind he could see the symbol as clearly as he had when he looked upon it reflecting in the handheld mirror—*the mark of the archangel Gabriel.*

abe choked and spit water onto his shirt as he was roused awake in a fit of coughing. He opened his eyes in time to see the monk leave with two soldiers through the red curtain. One of them held a bucket.

Empty, obviously. He found he was once again able to think clearly. The vertigo had left his mind, taking with it his nausea from the moment before.

His hand went to his head, the soldier's cracking blow still fresh in his mind, and he expected to find a gash and some major swelling but felt nothing. On his fingers and palm he saw no signs of blood—only the wetness from the bucket's water.

He propped himself up with his hand, somewhat surprised at the ease with which he was able to do so, and discovered that the pain in his ribs had also gone, though the discomfort of being soaked still remained. Warm water dripped from his clothes. A quick sniff of his shirt made certain that it was only water that had doused him. On the floor, a gritty mix of mud had formed from the dust and liquid.

Gabe looked around the room and saw paintings on the domed ceiling—demons and angels locked in battle. These were the depictions so common in murals and paintings he'd seen in famous works by famous artists—red gargoyle-like devils and white-winged angels. The warriors were separated by the two halves of the arched support beam that ran through the center of the ceiling. On one half were the angels, glowing in white tunics, their halos suspended above their heads. Men and women fled on the green field that curved down into the walls, away from the battle at the center.

The opposing half looked like a land tortured and rotting. Dark skies had been drawn across the ceiling, with clouds lit by a hellish orange. Demons surrounded a larger being, a humanoid form made of fire. There was a face where the head should have been. Its black mouth hung open, and inside the eye sockets, deep blue flames burned. The beast was lashing out in anger. This was something different from any artwork Gabe had seen before. Something he wished he'd not seen at all.

It was like a nightmare pulled from Dante's *Inferno*.

The rest of the room was a little less frightening. Only a curtain blocked the entrance, so Gabe figured he was probably not in a prison. And it didn't look like a mausoleum with such a decorative interior. The building was more like a temple, though a very small one, similar to the Norman Chapel. A single marble structure, a sort of altar, had been erected in the middle of the square, stone room. It stood chest-high with a cloth draped across its surface. Gabe used the centerpiece to pull himself to his feet, surprised again by his sudden wealth of strength.

On the other side of the room sat a throne occupied by the elderly Ethiopian monk. He peered at Gabe from beneath the wrinkles of a furrowed brow half covered by the shawl wrapped around his head.

After a moment of silence, he held up the sword and stone with his bony, skeletal fingers. "I am wary of visitors who burden me with intrusion on our sanctuary of peace, especially those who bring such devices of ill intent," the old man said in perfect English through a heavy Ethiopian accent. "Who comes to this holy land bearing the mark and claiming himself to be the Strength of God?"

"Where are my companions? What have you done with them?"

The Ethiopian eyed Gabe, scrutinizing everything about his presence. "Arrested and imprisoned for trespassing on sacred grounds and for the illegal possession of weapons. Both punishable by death," he said with a smile. "As you may also be."

"Are they okay? Have they been harmed?" Gabe asked.

"For the moment they are detained and awaiting execution."

"Please, we were sent here to find assistance with very important things."

"And what sort of assistance can be found in the city of Axum?"

"My name is Gabe . . . Gabriel Adam. We've come seeking information."

"Information?" The man challenged. He placed the stone in a wood box next to the throne and put aside the sword. "These days, many come to Axum seeking information. The devout and the fanatic alike. The wealth of knowledge can be invaluable in such tumultuous times. Careful, we must be, to whom it is disseminated. What knowledge do you seek to find? You do not look like a follower of our traditions."

Gabe hesitated and wondered, *Can this monk be trusted? Has he been corrupted like Yuri?*

"Speak!" The Ethiopian stood and took a step toward Gabe. Only the large stone centerpiece separated them. "I do not have all day to entertain criminals."

Flustered by the man's aggression, Gabe couldn't think of a way to get information about the ark without revealing their purpose. Besides, lying had never been a gifted skill. Finally, he gave up. "Knowledge contained inside the Ark of the Covenant."

The Ethiopian laughed, waving his hand to dismiss the answer. "You are a fool to seek such treasures here. You, like many who have come before, journeyed a long way for nothing, I'm afraid."

"No. It is here. I've seen the mark of the Watchers on the dome. We were told by Enoch—"

"Silence," the man said, but Gabe's words seemed to make him reconsider. Leaning against the stone tomb, the man's demeanor changed. The lines of his face softened. "You claim to be Fortitudo Dei? The Strength of God?"

"I can prove it. I have the mark," Gabe responded.

"Which can be easily fabricated. I will, however, allow you to prove that you are indeed telling the truth. A test, perhaps. One that only the true Gabriel could pass," the man said, and another smile crept across his face. The Ethiopian took a step toward the boy and then raised his hand.

Unfamiliar with the man's customs, Gabe simply looked at his outstretched palm until there was a crackle of energy and a consuming white light that blinded him to the world around him.

CHAPTER FIFTY-NINE

Gabe landed hard on the dusty stone path in the garden outside, rolled, and skidded to a stop. The red curtain had wrapped around his head and shoulders, binding his movements. The blast had singed the material, and it smoked, threatening to set fire. Quickly, he disentangled himself, patted out the embers, and pushed the curtain away, careful to avoid getting burned. A quick examination of his body confirmed everything was still intact. His rear end hurt where he landed, but that was the extent of his injuries, apart from a few scrapes on his arm.

He knew exactly what had just happened. It had been the same by the River Wear when Yuri had unleashed his power against him, catapulting them both into the air. The effect was identical—a momentary loss of motor skills and fleeting dizziness—and Gabe imagined the sensation was similar to being shot by a stun gun. He shook his head, trying to rid himself of the ringing in his ears, and sat on the ground while the disorientation quickly faded.

Somewhere in the near distance he thought he could hear Micah yelling profanities, but it was difficult to tell with traumatized eardrums, but they, too, were recovering. Joining her voice, someone was definitely laughing.

The Ethiopian entered his field of view. With the sunlight behind him, he appeared as a silhouette. A broad, toothy grin accompanied a hearty chuckle. "You passed the test, my friend," he managed to say through a fit of laughter. "I believe that you are indeed the Strength of God."

"What the hell, old man?" Gabe started.

"Please," the Ethiopian said, holding out a hand, "let me introduce myself. I am Afarôt, the Healer of God and Sentinel of the Ark. We are brothers!"

He helped Gabe to his unsteady feet. Micah and his father, accompanied by their armed escort near the curtainless building, looked concerned. In a foreign language, Afarôt said something to the soldiers. They acknowledged the order, released their captives, and marched away, disappearing into the compound.

Afarôt turned back and asked, "I take it you are not harmed?"

"I'm fine," Gabe snapped.

"I do apologize for the rude welcome you've received to the Temple of the Ark," Afarôt said, still smiling as he held out his arm to formally present the ornate building behind them. "You must understand that many are seeking treasures in Axum. Especially now that the signs have begun. My men are committed to the security of these premises. And they are dedicated to my safety. Only I am to be the keeper of its secrets." He frowned, as if noticing Gabe's discomfort for the first time. "I am sorry for the test. As archangels cannot truly harm each other by means of our gifts, this was the fastest way to see if you really are who you claimed to be."

"You could have just looked more closely at the mark. Or asked for a freaking passport," Gabe said.

Micah and his dad moved closer so they could hear the man talk. His father took a step toward him, his brow furrowed in concern for his son, but Gabe waved him off.

"Yes, but this is the only *true* way."

"And if I hadn't been?"

"Quite messy, I'm afraid." Afarôt winked. "But worry not. I suspected you were Gabriel the moment I was informed by my men that you had entered Axum, but you can never be too certain until you are *too certain*. However, I did not expect you to fly through the door such as you have done. Your defensive technique is lacking, my friend. That is something we shall want to remedy. It has been quite some time since another Watcher has been here. Allow me to assume my true form."

The old man took a step back, and like sweat on his skin, a sheen of luminance formed that radiated from his body. Years faded away from his face. Lines softened, wrinkles vanishing as skin pulled tight against his face. His hair thickened from gray to black as youth flowed into his body.

Gabe could only stare.

Afarôt's posture grew sturdy and less feeble, standing taller and broader, his body no longer just a collection of bones in a bag of skin. The light then softened and dissipated. Where an old man had stood, there was now a teenager.

Gabe was amazed, like a child who had just seen a magician's greatest trick. It forced a smile to his lips. "How did you do that?"

Afarôt's age looked close to Gabe's and Micah's. "I am capable of many things, Gabriel. As are you. You see, in these parts of the world, authority is often exclusive to those of a certain age. Which of course helps when unwanted visitors who come seeking the ark knock at our door."

"You're another Watcher, aren't you?" Micah finally said. "I thought there were only four."

"You are not incorrect. There are indeed only four. I am the first and the last and have many names." He unwrapped the covering from his head and turned to reveal the mark above his neck.

"Raphael," his father said, recognizing the symbol.

"That is my familiar name amongst some cultures. Though I do prefer Afarôt."

"I'm Micah Pari." She offered her hand.

Afarôt shook it. While doing so, his expression broadened, eyes alight, and then he let out a hearty laugh. "No, certainly not the archangel Michael? The Creator's ways are mysterious, are they not? And you, sir? An Essene, perhaps?"

"No." His father hesitated. "I'm Joseph Adam, Gabe's father and Protector."

"Uriel is dead. He betrayed us," Micah said.

"Dead? That is interesting," Afarôt said, almost dismissing the news. "Are you quite certain?"

"Yeah. He's definitely dead," she said with a hint of pride. "I killed him myself after he murdered my . . . our Essene."

"Uriel murdered the Essene?"

"The enemy is on the move. Is the ark here?" his father asked.

Afarôt looked around the perimeter fence and made a move toward the interior of the compound. "Perhaps this is a subject matter best discussed indoors. Come; let us return to the main church. I have much to show you."

CHAPTER SIXTY

G abe sat alone in the crumbling first pew of the old church at the front of the compound just near the Temple of the Ark and waited for the conference between Afarôt and his father to conclude. The Ethiopian had asked to be briefed on the days leading to Axum, but Gabe neither had the energy nor the desire to relive those events. Micah must have felt the same and had wandered off, presumably to find some corner for her own bout of brooding.

The dilapidated interior of the neglected building remained quiet except for the muffled sounds of the street permeating through the walls. The anxious murmur of voices didn't mesh with the church's calming interior. Inside the sanctuary, the craftsmanship of the wood and stone carvings mirrored the swirling designs of the local culture, all rendered in a spectrum of colors dulled by time. The faded paint, splintered wood, and crumbling stonework suggested the Old Church was not long for this world. Its Ethiopian style contrasted the gothic styles of the European churches familiar to Gabe. Instead, the preference was to the bright and warm, much like the surrounding landscape. Much of the art reminded him of what he saw in Cairo. "The assimilation of Coptic tradition and culture from the distribution of goods and services provided by a stream of commerce," he could hear Professor Bernstein say.

Engravings of Scriptures and stained glass windows were held in the large blocks of the stone walls. One of the scenes in the windows caught his attention. The setting sun cast its panels in the softest of light. A haloed figure dressed in a pearl robe stood over a manger. Behind the sparkling figure, huge outstretched wings shielded a couple as they knelt beside their newborn baby.

Gabe wondered which one of the archangels the scene depicted. *Could be me*, he thought, yet the idea rang hollow. He had no memories other than his own, and even while he had accepted that he was something else, something different, he still only felt like Gabriel Adam.

But here he was in Ethiopia of all places seeking the Ark of the Covenant and the treasures found within, all while being pursued by an enemy that haunted his darkest nightmares.

He opened his hands and looked at his palms. *So ordinary*. Three times now, he'd witnessed his kind do incredible things with their hands. To envision using such abilities felt like make-believe. Fantasy. And yet he'd experienced something while Afarôt's men held them at gunpoint.

Closing his eyes, he raised his hand like the others, palm out, fingers together. He concentrated, trying to will forth some hidden energy.

Nothing happened.

There was no sensation or even the slightest suggestion

that power existed within. In front of the soldiers, it had nearly surfaced, but whatever it was, it seemed reactive, uncontrollable.

Not much use in that, he thought and looked at the decaying interior of the abandoned church. He couldn't help but draw comparisons to his world.

His old life had been reduced to only memories. He could now accept that. Things would forever be different. Though in the back of his mind, he wanted to believe that he would one day wake up from this dream. That somewhere another reality waited.

"Catching up on some alone time, are we?" Micah's voice startled him as she walked down the aisle. Something about her made her seem more at ease, returning a sliver of the brightness she'd once had.

"Just thinking about everything, I guess," he said.

"I try not to. Nothing makes sense anymore." She took a seat next to him and looked up at the angel in the window but didn't comment.

"I know." A moment passed. "Have you seen where we're staying?" Gabe asked.

"The rooms are a little wanting, but I suppose it beats being stuck traveling in a boat or a train again. To be honest, anyplace I could get some rest and a shower would feel like a five-star hotel."

"Trouble sleeping?"

"Not a wink since Cairo. There's this burning inside . . . like a fury. It won't stop. Won't . . . turn off."

Another silence fell between them.

"I can't believe you managed to sleep in that miserable

Land Rover. And while on that awful road, too. I could actually hear your head occasionally bounce off the window, and yet you never woke up. You've got a real talent there." Micah shook her head and smiled ever so slightly. It was the first smile Gabe could recall in quite a while.

"I suppose I do. What do you make of Afarôt?" he asked.

"Don't know, really. He's not like us; that much is certain. I think he's been here for a very long time."

"In Axum?"

"On Earth. He's clearly mastered his abilities, which means he probably wasn't born when we were, since we're still mostly, you know, clueless. He's probably one of those left behind after the first war between the realms, if what Carlyle said about the only exception to the rule separating the dimensions is right. Also, he acted strange when I told him about Yuri, like it was somehow difficult to believe. If he's as old as I think he is, then he knows more than he's letting on."

"In a way, that's kind of a relief," Gabe said.

"How so?"

"Well, we've had no plan apart from getting here and obtaining a ring that, if we're being honest, might not even exist. And there's no proof that it can do what the legend suggests. We've been running on blind luck since Durham. If Afarôt has any sort of strategy, I'd feel a little better about trying to fulfill our duties. He doesn't even need to tell me about it, just so long as there is one."

"You're worried."

"Worried doesn't even begin to cover it. All these doubts about my part to play—it's not like we've been given an instruction manual. I keep thinking we're going to get to the Emerald City and Toto is going to pull the curtain back to show us that there is no wizard," Gabe said.

"What's scarier is if there is a wizard. And he's pissed."

Gabe laughed, his gaze falling from the stained glass window to meet her eyes. They hid behind fallen strands of hair. She caught his look and smiled but then glanced away, finding refuge in the décor of the church. He discovered in that smile a hope he thought lost.

The hope for something more.

Footsteps echoed behind them at the entrance.

His father entered the sanctuary. "We're being summoned. It's time to see about Solomon's Ring."

CHAPTER SIXTY-ONE

Ine of Afarôt's men held back the reattached curtain for Micah, Gabe, and his father to enter the Temple of the Ark and then retreated to the compound, his weapon slung around his shoulder, clamoring against his utility belt as he joined his regiment. Soldiers surrounded the building but at a distance.

Afarôt again sat on his throne behind the large altar. His young features seemed at odds with his authoritative posture and demeanor. "Thank you for coming. You have traveled far for the secret of the ark, and I apologize if I have been insensitive to the struggles of your journey. The time this world sees in the light is threatened. Our enemy's roots have anchored deep into Earth. Its influence has become long in reach. But their confidence is also where we may find weakness.

"There are weapons, very powerful, which like you the enemy seeks. Weapons more powerful than the enemy realizes. Even against the combined power of the enemy's dark magic and man's wicked nature, these weapons hold to bind and destroy evil." Afarôt's voice echoed off the walls.

"The ark," Micah guessed.

"No. Weapons like that which the ark has carried throughout its existence," Afarôt corrected. "And the one it conceals even now. The ark is and always has been merely a means to transport and protect the treasures and gifts devised unto man by God."

"So it's luggage?" Gabe asked.

"Again, no. It performs a special task meant to keep its contents safe and more importantly, hidden. But the ark is not limited to corporeal design. It is what it needs to be and operates to form a sort of negative force to conceal energies emitted by these items, thereby muting their aura and rendering them impossible to trace or detect."

"A cloaking device, then," Gabe said.

"Very astute," Afarôt said. "Hence the means by which I have kept my presence hidden upon this realm."

"And why Enoch couldn't sense you in the world," his dad said.

Afarôt nodded.

"So then, where is it? Where is the ark?" his father asked.

Afarôt removed the decorative cloth adorned with Watcher symbols to reveal a marble slab underneath. He closed his eyes as if praying and placed his hand atop the altar.

Gabe looked to Micah for an explanation. She shrugged, just as lost.

Light formed under Afarôt's palm. A bright green design, invisible a moment before, glowed inside grooves in the stone. It filled the room and cast shadows of the four observers against the walls. Then another glowed. And another. In total, four came to life, each a symbol of an archangel, glowing side by side.

A seam formed in the altar's stone, illuminated by the same source, burning inside like a furnace.

Gabe's pulse quickened, and he took a step back.

More seams formed in the base of the altar, exposing different sections, and they in turn expanded, moving like a great mechanical puzzle. The room filled with a symphony of light and the grinding sounds of stone sliding against stone.

Afarôt completed his ritual and backed away from the centerpiece, giving it room.

"I can't believe it . . . the Tabernacle of God," his father managed.

The altar split in two and opened like a briefcase. Inside, walls unfolded, lifting upwards from the floor, three sides in total, forming a standing structure that looked to Gabe like a wardrobe rising from the floor. In the center of the space, the fourth side traveled in grooves up the new walls to create a top to the structure while revealing a circular chamber open beneath, big enough for a man to enter.

The light faded as the reconfiguration finished.

"Come. See." Afarôt motioned them over.

Gabe was reminded of the manholes in New York. Colorful tiles lined the stone rim, which encompassed a ladder that descended into the darkness.

"Every Watcher has a purpose. I am the Healer of God and the chosen Sentinel of the Ark. Both of you will also have a purpose in this war. Attributes, unique to each one of you, will shine before the End of Days is upon us.

"You are to descend to the tabernacle, enter the ark, and discover that which waits. One of you will be ordained as the

Heir of Solomon. The ring will choose who is best to wield it and bestow upon you its power and its burden carried by Solomon's line.

"Be wary," Afarôt warned. "Solomon was a powerful man before exploring its wonders. He did so with great success but to the detriment of his life, which ended in madness. As Sentinel, I cannot be the one to whom the heirloom is bequest. Only one of you."

Afarôt paused, distracted by something, his attention drawn beyond the red curtain. The sun faded behind it, and the shadow on the floor disappeared. "You must hurry. We haven't much time. Go. Now!"

He moved them to the opening. Gabe grabbed the ladder first and carefully stepped down into the darkness of the shaft.

CHAPTER SIXTY-TWO

The first rung of the ladder was loose. The old wood bent and creaked. Gabe felt the ladder shake in his hand and didn't know if it was from its age or his nerves.

Above him, Micah followed, careful not to step on his fingers. Afarôt apparently didn't wait until Gabe reached the bottom before sending her. He looked at the dry, brittle wood and questioned the sturdiness.

As they descended, the light reaching from the temple faded away.

Gabe clutched the ladder, momentarily lost in the darkness. "You okay, Micah?"

"Fine. Scared witless but fine."

"Only one way now."

The splintered crosspieces bit into Gabe's hands as he led the way down the chamber. At every step, the ladder objected to their combined weight with a crack or a groan. He thought of a few choice words for Afarôt about the upkeep.

Gabe could hear Micah above, nearly invisible in the darkness, doing well to stay close. His eyes eventually adjusted to the lack of light, though there was little to notice in the shaft other than the granite stonework lining the wall. He looked closer and noticed the tiny crystals in its surface were glittering.

"I think I can see something," Micah called from above. "There's light!"

Gabe looked below his feet, no longer distracted by the rocks. He could see it, too: an iridescent halo at the bottom of the shaft, and he was nearly there. Climbing down to the last rung, he leapt from the ladder and dropped to the floor.

Micah sounded excited. Gabe could hear her breathing quickly in anticipation, but she was descending too fast. He heard the wood under her foot split and then break in two.

"Gabe!" she screamed.

He tried to catch her, but her weight drove him to the floor with a thud. Dust scattered into the air as their bodies tangled together.

"Damn." Gabe moaned under her.

"It's that stupid ladder. I'm so sorry." She laughed. "You okay, then? Anything broken?"

"Just get off, please." He threw her feet out of his face.

She stopped her teasing, her eyes fixed in wonder on something behind him. Sounds echoed from wall to wall like passing whispers, filling the space with an ambiance of movement, but both Micah and Gabe remained still. A shimmering reflection in her eyes caught his attention.

"What is it?" Gabe asked and turned to follow her stare.

The stone walls of the circular room wrapped around to meet the ruins of an arched doorway. Two pillars supported the arch over the doorway, covered in patches of gold leaf eroded by time. Crowning the pillars, brittle statues of angels kneeled toward one another. Their forward-swept wings connected above the entrance.

Strangely, there was no physical door in the doorway—only a gateway shielded by a barrier of liquid that seemed to defy gravity, rippling and flowing vertically like light made from water.

The small statue adorning the arch was one Gabe had seen countless times in his father's academic books that recalled several artists' renditions of the ark.

"*This* room is the Tabernacle of God. And *that*," he said, pointing to the archway, "is the ark."

CHAPTER SIXTY-THREE

nergy, as palpable as the desert heat, came in rolling waves that traveled across the floor like a ghostly mist from the entrance to the Ark of the Covenant. The door to the ark seemed alive, the motion of its liquid gateway rippling to the rhythm of Gabe's beating heart. "Can you feel that?"

The mist moved over their bodies, drifting over their skin, connecting them. He felt fear and excitement, and as Micah looked at him, Gabe felt the spark of all that he'd hoped had not died within her, and these feelings were as real as his own.

"Yes," Micah said and gave him a knowing smile.

"I thought you'd given up."

She shook her head and shrugged. Her gaze drifted toward the ark. "I can hear thoughts in my head. Thoughts that aren't mine."

He could hear them, too. Voices filling him with knowledge and urges and an understanding of everything before him. It was as if he were a child wanting to ride a bike for the first time but being able to do so without anyone showing him how.

"It's like I just know. It wants us to enter," Micah said.

Another wave of warmth rolled out from the liquid, calming and welcoming. It moved over them, hushed whispers filling the air as it passed, and Gabe felt the fear and anxiety leave his body. The ark called to them, beckoning them to step beyond the doorway.

Gabe stood and helped Micah to her feet. "Are you ready?" he asked.

"Together?" She reached out.

"Together." He grabbed her hand.

They took a step in unison toward the arch. The liquid called out, inviting them into its mystery.

Gabe looked at Micah, at her lips, and felt her longing. A question hung in the air between them, and inside he felt the desire to know the answer. But in her eyes, he found a shard of doubt. *Bad timing*, they seemed to say. She drew back, perhaps only a millimeter, but it was enough to steal Gabe's confidence.

Her thumb traced the contours of his knuckle, and she offered a conciliatory smile.

She turned to the undulating barrier of the ark. Together they walked into the liquid.

It embraced them and took them in, but he remained dry.

Deeper into the emptiness of the ark, a path appeared at their feet. It led to something dark but substantive—a room, Gabe thought, but he could not see it clearly through the blur of liquid surrounding him. Then the path seemed to split, forking in another direction toward a bloom of white light. He felt drawn to it.

They continued forward, but where the path became two, Micah's footing failed. She fell, caught in the gravity of the dark room. Her hand slipped from his, and they were torn apart, Micah crying out as she disappeared in the fading room. His path now separate from hers, Gabe struggled against the pull of the light, desperate to go back and save her, but he could not escape the gravity that held him. He reached out again, cursing himself for being too weak.

His body then lifted from the path and tumbled toward the blinding white. There, he felt a presence nearby, surrounding him, too great to be Micah.

The light grew, as did its warmth. Gabe felt as though he were falling into the sun, but instead of heat, he felt embraced in happiness, and all his fears of losing Micah were swept away. His body relaxed, he was no longer able to keep his eyes open, and he felt like he was drifting into sleep.

His body seemed to twist, contorting into a comfortable position. Gabe felt something cradle his legs, and he quickly realized that he was sitting in something. The warmth of the light faded. The sound of voices filled the air, words he recognized. A horn honked somewhere, and a door chimed. He opened his eyes and saw the plush leather chair beneath him, pulled up to a familiar tall table.

Impossible, he thought.

CHAPTER SIXTY-FOUR

The aroma of fresh ground coffee beans. The sounds of milk steaming behind the bar and spoons clanked against the inside of mugs, stirring in sugar and cream.

Not memories but real.

Gabe sat at his favorite table at The Study Habit Café near New York University. Students and customers went about their everyday lives, drinking various beverages and reading magazines or studying for class.

Stacked neatly atop his table was a collection of college textbooks from courses he never had the opportunity to take—sociology, business law, and other literature. Beside them, a notebook and an uncapped pen waited to be used with lessons and outlines scribbled inside the pages in hand-writing he recognized as his own.

Coren approached his table, smiling her unforgettable smile as she held her notepad and tray. "Have you finally figured out what you want? The usual today or something else?"

"Where am I? What's going on?"

She put aside her tray and notepad and sat down at his table. At once, her jovial demeanor evaporated like the steam from the half-drank caramel macchiato beside his books. "Do you not know, Gabriel? You are where everything your heart desires can be found. A life of infinite normalcy. Of infinite possibilities. Education. Career. Here you may become a doctor or a lawyer. Anything you want to be in life. In this world is found the beginning of what you have lived all your life to attain."

Gabe considered the scene around him, and for a moment he felt like he could reach out and grab his dreams.

"Love and happiness—a family in the future, perhaps. Possessions and money—all the things you have ever wanted in life. Is this not what you seek? Your *usual*? Do you not desire this most in your heart?" Coren asked.

These things were in his heart—that much was undeniable. The desires did exist, he realized, but not in a vacuum.

"I do want this," he said. "But I want this in a reality that no longer exists."

"Does it not? Do you not trust that the world will right itself again? That God will not correct that which is out of order? Look around you. Can you not see a future that is attainable?"

Gabe observed the café. Faces on some of the customers began to change. The space around a man in a business suit holding a briefcase shifted, blurred. His face became an older version of Gabe's—grayed and distinguished. Another man, who wore hospital scrubs, sat at a table nearby and chatted with a woman. His face changed as well, also mirroring that of Gabe's—smiling, happy, and older.

"No, this is not what I want."

"Are you certain? Look again."

The front door chimed, and a woman entered. Black hair flowed in her wake, trailing behind her unmistakable beauty. Micah, older now and somehow more refined in her dress suit, approached his business-suited doppelganger and kissed him to begin a conversation. They carried on touching each other, flirting and laughing at unheard jokes.

Gabe stared at the couple, the possibilities swirling in his mind.

"Yes," Coren said, "you know what you want. Do not be afraid. You can have it. All of it. You simply must choose to accept, and it will be yours. I can give you everything you want. A life unencumbered by stress and conflict. A life of peace and serenity. Lust and love wrapped into one. Success of unimaginable proportion, free from the trials of failure. A long life, filled with happiness and satisfaction. All you need to do is ask, and everything will be as you desire."

The temptation was strong, but he thought of Micah's kiss in the tabernacle. The love he felt in the kiss was real. Gabe could still feel her lips on his. But this also felt real.

"Who are you?"

"I am simply a giver of gifts. A provider. You need only ask, and everything as you see it now and as you envision for yourself can be attained. Take control, and all the pain that is done will be undone."

The door chimed again. Richard entered, healthy and alive, followed by Gabe's father. They smiled and laughed as they ordered coffee from the barista. Carlyle soon followed. Micah rushed to embrace him.

Gabe's heart tore apart at the sight of her smile.

"I can restore them," Coren said. "All can be made right in *your* world. All the horrible futures you've seen, all the despair and war can be calmed. All the tragedies for those you love can be erased. Your world will be one of peace and order. Of light and hope, unhindered by the darkness and burdens you have seen. These broken pieces will be mended. Those you love most will be saved and live as they would had all the perils you have come to know been removed from it. No war. No suffering. And you will forget the hate you have come to witness in the world *you know now*. You and your loved ones will be burdened only with happiness. In *your* world the heavens and Earth will finally be at peace. But *you* must make the choice."

Gabe looked around the room, weighing the offer. Thoughts raced through his mind. With one simple choice, he could bring peace to his world.

My world, he thought. Deep inside, he felt a disconnection between her offer and what he'd left behind. "My world *is* the world *I know now*. What you offer is a lie." He motioned to the café. "This isn't real."

"It is not a lie," she said. "It is as real as the chair in which you sit. As real as the books on this table, and it will be real for those you love. Their reality will merge with yours in your world."

"No. I am an archangel. That's real. And if that's my reality, then so be it. I may want these things but not at the expense of my duties. Not at the expense of what I owe *my world* and not at the expense of the truth."

"God will forgive you. That, I can promise."

"Maybe, but I couldn't forgive myself. I choose what has

been destined for me, regardless of whether or not I want it. I choose to fulfill my duty." Gabe stood from the table in defiance of Coren's offer.

Her eyes narrowed, and the airy softness of her demeanor hardened. "Even at the sacrifice of yourself?"

"If that's my destiny, then yes."

"And if the ones you love are sacrificed because you choose not to save them now, would you deny them peace and happiness? You would give them up to a death of unmentionable horror should you fail your duties?"

"We *won't* fail. But even if we do, we'll die knowing that we did everything we could. My decision is made. You can stuff *your* world. All the things you offer would do nothing but ensure victory for our enemy," Gabe said. "And if that is what you intend, then you are also my enemy. I'll do whatever is in my power to stop your darkness from spreading to my world. Whatever it takes."

Coren leaned back in her chair. "A human's understanding of time and space is as predictable as it is simplistic. Yet you never cease to surprise me with the unbound measure of your heart. If only more were like you, my dearest Gabriel. Fortitudo Dei indeed. Truly, there is strength inside you.

"However, I am not your enemy," Coren said, and a smile, warm like the summer, drifted across her lips. "Nor do I wish for darkness on the Earth. I wish for Light."

The room slowed and then stopped. Coren stood, and her skin began to glow. Light brought forth in rays like the sun through clouds. It spilled out, growing brighter, its streams crashing into the walls and knocking them open to the city to reveal an endless white sky above. Tables and chairs, people and cars were struck by her rays and sent into the heavens.

Gabe put his arms up to protect himself, but the floor crumbled away to reveal a glowing white abyss. He plummeted into the void until he felt the embrace of warmth again.

"Go forth, Gabriel," said the echo of Coren's voice. "And have faith that you are that which you are."

Gabe twisted through the light as he fell, then landed on hard ground, knocking the wind out of his lungs. He opened his eyes and lifted his head to see the ladder in the tabernacle. He lay on his side in an awkward position with his right arm caught underneath.

"Gabe!" Micah's voice reassured him. "What happened?"

"I don't know." Gabe struggled to catch his breath. He looked around and no longer saw the mist covering the floor. He also no longer felt Micah's emotions. Whatever psychic connection the ark had built between them had been broken.

"Here, let me help you up. Can you move?"

"I think so."

Micah extended her hand and pulled him up with surprising strength. Then she gasped. "Look at your hand."

He turned his palm out.

On his middle finger was a gold ring, its sheen faded from time. A curved stone set flush with the band and glistened in the light of the arch. In the jewel shined a small, engraved pentalpha.

"The Ring of Solomon," Gabe said. "I am the heir."

CHAPTER SIXTY-FIVE

Septis walked under the streetlamps, making his way toward the distant gate at the end of the road. Humans lined the sidewalk, cowering in their hovels, looking desperate and in need of pity, though he had none to give. One of them approached, his arms held out begging, pleading for help. Disgusted with the creature's presence, Septis grabbed it by the throat and snapped its spine.

The onlookers screamed, running into the night as the corpse fell to the ground, and Septis felt invigorated by the sound and knew the darkness would offer no reprieve from what hell he was about to reap upon this land.

Ahead, soldiers took notice and aimed their pathetic instruments at him, but he paid them little regard. Spotlights towering above the gate came to life, flooding the street below. Septis called to his power. Shadows fed off the night and grew strong, stealing away some of the light surrounding the buildings before flowing across the street to meet him. He reached out, and from the darkness surrounding the distant steps leading to the gates, shadows came alive and attacked the soldiers, like predators lying in wait, pouncing from the ground, their smokelike forms ripping the life from the bodies of the men.

An alarm rang out over the compound, and more humans stormed to the gates.

Septis welcomed the challenge.

They opened fire with their weapons, but the bullets did little but tear through his clothes. Septis laughed, toying with the humans, manipulating the shadows into a weapon of his own, an extension of his arms, their actions synchronized with the gestures of his hands. Through his bidding the formless creatures grabbed the men with their darkness and tossed them into the metal gates or high into the air, only to watch how they broke as they hit the ground.

Red eyes in the shadows glowed bright in anticipation, as if begging to be loosed from a chain. He waved a hand, and his pets flowed through the streets in all directions, like rivers of black water surprising the soldiers with their speed. Becoming more alive with every passing second, animal snouts and clawed legs appeared in the moving flood of darkness, without taking physical form. They roamed like dogs chasing down game, leaping from the ground to grab the fleeing humans.

Cries of death echoed throughout the street as the blood began to spill, and Septis smiled.

Though he enjoyed the sport, his determination remained on what drew him to this place. Fortitudo Dei's presence burned here like a freshly lit candle, stronger now than he had ever felt. The boy's powers were growing inside him, and the opportunity to quell his ability to influence control over this realm was slipping away. Septis knew that now was the time for his redemption. He would kill the boy here, along with all that stood in his way, and ready this world for the Hellgate to open for those that would claim rightful authority over Earth.

He thought of the glory that awaited. Mastema would be pleased by these accomplishments, and Septis knew he would reap a generous reward. But first, he must locate the boy. As the humans repositioned to fire upon his position, Septis animated the shadows once more. They pulled into his body, swirling around his tattered clothes, and funneled into the ground.

He closed his eyes, and the living world appeared to him, dark all around except for the church ahead. The beings swarming over the grounds appeared in his mind as weak embers, their meek glows just visible. Something ahead troubled Septis. There was a void of neither light nor dark beyond the gate, as if energy had been omitted from the world. Worse, he no longer saw Fortitudo Dei's beacon shining.

Escaped. Again, he thought. A fury lit inside, shaking the ground where he stood. A building by the street buckled and fell. Humans screamed as the rubble trapped some. Before he started tearing apart the town with his rage, something drew his attention. A presence, like a beacon of light, just beyond the church in the distance.

Septis opened his eyes, and his anger turned to a renewed determination. "There you are, boy."

CHAPTER SIXTY-SIX

The ladder objected to their hurried pace with every creaking rung climbed. Light grew in the shaft as Micah reached the top of the ladder just ahead of Gabe; however, something was different. The light above seemed muted, softer than it had been before their descent. It flickered in the room as if lit by a candle.

A crackle of noise echoed from above. *Kalashnikovs.* In the distance, he could hear sporadic gunfire mixed with screams of agony.

"Hurry," Afarôt shouted down the round opening. "Do you have it?"

"Gabe does," she said, and he helped lift her from the ladder.

Gabe followed. His body still hurt from the experience in the ark. Before he could protest, his father grabbed him under the arms and hoisted him to his feet. As he was pulled from the shaft, the pathway folded in on itself, and soon the altar reformed, shutting off the way below.

"Are you okay?" his dad asked. "You've been gone hours."

"Hours? What's happening?" Gabe asked, seeing the

black of the windows.

"The enemy has found us," Afarôt said. "We make our stand here. Come with me, Gabriel."

"What about me?" Micah asked.

"You are not yet ready. Stay here. Without your full powers, only the ring will stop the enemy."

Gabe followed Afarôt through the curtain and into the night, leaving Micah and his father behind. On the road below, beyond the gates of the compound, stood the last of the soldiers, running to the aid of their fallen comrades and fighting to their deaths. Most of the refugees had managed to escape, vanished into the hills, but bodies in the compound formed a sort of path leading to the street, some in a grotesque state, contorted beyond recognition.

Gabe felt like he was on autopilot, driven into a situation for which he had no control. Hands shook, his heart beating in triples. He and Afarôt moved past the trees and toward the main gate. Gabe hoped to find some measure of hope that his new friend might enlighten him on how to use the ring, but Afarôt remained silent, wringing his hands as they approached the chaos. One thought prevailed above all others: *This is happening.*

Without guidance from the Ethiopian, Gabe looked to the dull metal of the ring for a sign, anything that might give him a clue. Its jewel only looked lifeless against his finger.

The gunfire ahead began to diminish, reduced now to only a few sporadic bursts, a few flashes of light.

As they walked the short distance from the temple garden to the gate, Gabe watched the body of a soldier fly into the air, launched by an unseen force. It crashed against a building and fell to the ground in a lifeless heap, leaving a distant man standing alone in the street. He wore a black suit and overcoat, which had been torn open. Crimson lines swirled on his chest, and blue eyes fixed on the gate's entrance.

Gabe looked at the remains of the army littering the ground, single-handedly dispatched by this man, and a crippling fear set into his mind.

CHAPTER SIXTY-SEVEN

Septis anticipated the delicious moment of the kill. It hung in the air like the promise of a decadent dessert. *The hunt is over*, he thought.

Two stood at the gates and two more at the small temple beyond the entrance. Besides the boy, he could feel a powerful essence coming from one in particular. The presence had not been felt since the first war between the realms, but there was no real cause for concern.

Afarôt the Healer.

Even together, they would be unable to stand in the way. Gabriel had yet to find his true power, and the healer was a mere inconvenience. Septis felt encouraged, his timing perfect.

Much blood had been let. Pools of it gathered in the street, some flowing in the gutter. This pleased him.

A good place to end the light.

The man who haunted Gabe's visions, as real as the building

storm in the darkened sky, had just stepped out of his nightmares and now waited amongst a scene worse than any of his visions had imagined. The full measure of the carnage was visible in detail. Bloodied, deformed bodies lay in crimson pools on the steps and contorted in broken piles near buildings, blood spray splattered across the walls. Weapons, useless against the enemy, lay smoking on the ground, spent to no avail. Some of the refugees lay facedown in the streets, their backs torn open. Gabe's stomach turned at the sight of the gore. So many innocents had already perished.

I could have prevented this, he thought and reconsidered his choice in the ark. He pushed the feeling aside, knowing that the rampage would have happened anyway.

The visions played in his mind's eye. The burning city of New York. The death of his father. *All shall come to pass. Here and now.*

Afarôt walked to the top of the steps to meet the man in black. "Prepare yourself," he whispered as he passed by Gabe.

"How?" Gabe asked, nearly in shock.

"You will know," Afarôt said and then turned to the street. "It has been a long time, Septis."

"Yes, Afarôt. Much too long," Septis said. "Love what you've done with the place." He motioned to the world around him. "Nothing like a constant state of war with which to decorate your paradise of peace and love."

He approached a body facedown in the street and kicked it over. Blood spilled from the corpse's mouth. Septis snarled as he wiped his dress shoe off on the dead man's clothes. "This . . . meat doesn't want paradise. Or peace. It wants war and destruction.

Death and intolerance. Those rights are *ours* to claim. We now have title to this realm. They have chosen this; they have chosen *us*. You, most of all, should remember! *That* was the agreement."

Gabe didn't understand what was meant by *agreement* or why Septis acted as if he knew Afarôt.

"That was long ago," Afarôt said. "Mankind's mistakes do not grant you claim to this world."

"Oh, Afarôt." Septis laughed. "You'll forgive us if we respectfully disagree."

He raised his arms, hands empty as if lifting a heavy, unseen object from the ground. Suddenly, clouds grew low in the dark sky above Axum, and a buzzing sound filled the air accompanied by a vibration in the earth.

Tremors shook the ground as Gabe watched Septis strain against the unseen weight.

Around him, pockets of dirt burst from the ground, and millions of hornets streamed into the air. Septis lifted his hands high, controlling the insects as they converged into a swarm, then threw his arms forward toward Afarôt.

The hornets took after him like a guided missile.

Gabe watched, trembling as Septis used his power. Stricken with an unbearable fear, he backed away from the gates and ran toward the Temple of the Ark.

Outside the small building, Micah and his dad stood in the garden. Gabe could see terror in his father's eyes.

He motioned to Gabe. "We need to find safety. Quickly!" He stepped toward the curtained entrance, pulling Gabe to the throne room.

But Micah did not move. Nor did her focus stray from

Septis. "No, Joseph. This is our fight. Carlyle always said that if I reached down far enough, I'd discover the power inside me. If there is anyone in the streets left alive, I have to help them. You should seek cover, though. Take the ladder down to the tabernacle and seal the way behind you."

A deep sorrow formed on his father's face. He reached out and hugged Micah but only looked to his son.

Gabe understood. Embracing would mean acknowledging that it might be for the last time.

His dad's eyes suddenly went wide. "Wait. The stone. Damn it. I nearly forgot. You'll need it to complete the sword. It's still inside."

Without another word, Micah followed him through the entrance.

Gabe watched from outside, the red curtain held back.

"Bloody fool I am. Here it is." His father retrieved the two pieces from next to the throne. "If ever there was a time to unite the two . . ."

Micah took the sword from his dad and presented the forked tip to him. He held up the stone tip. The grooves matched one another like lock and key, sliding into place and connecting.

The hilt seemed to pulse in her hands. "The energy," she said. "It's amazing. I can feel it flowing through me."

Gabe took a step closer. The sword responded to its connection with Micah. She held it out from her body, and the blade glowed white-hot, showering the room in light. Even from outside, Gabe could feel the power emanating from inside the temple.

"Oh, my God," his father managed, moving back.

The sword and the stone melded together as if being forged anew. Seams between the two pieces disappeared in a smoldering heat, becoming one. The engravings on the blade burned the color of fire. When it was over, the sword was united into a singular whole. The metal shined so bright it was as if it cast its own light. Engravings in the blade had disappeared to leave behind only one—the symbol of the archangel Michael.

Micah turned to Gabe. "I think I'm ready," she said.

"I'll be waiting for you both when this is over." His dad put his hands on the altar and tried to open the door to the tabernacle. It wouldn't budge. "Micah, I can't get it open."

She laid her hands on it and seemed to concentrate, eyes closed, but nothing happened. Micah turned to Gabe. "We need Afarôt."

He didn't hesitate and ran toward the gate, desperate to figure out a way to get his father to safety.

Afarôt was standing his ground near the steps by the road, holding his hands out to fend off the hornets. A barrier of white energy hung in the air, projected from his hands to create a shield against the attack, but it was not enough. He only managed to repel one wave as the swarm re-formed for another assault.

The hornets moved too quickly and maneuvered around the shield faster than Afarôt could expand its coverage, rendering it useless. He abandoned the tactic and ran to Gabe as the hornets gave chase. He turned and with a parting energy bolt from his hand sent the hornets retreating into the sky.

"Afarôt, it's my father. Please, we can't get him inside the altar. It's the only place he's safe."

The Ethiopian was out of breath, panting hard. "I'll see to him. You have the ring. Have faith in it. Have faith in yourself, and you will know what to do. Now is your time, so do not hesitate," he said and turned toward the temple. "Micah, bring the sword! Bring the sword!"

Gabe was left alone to stare at his hands, hoping for a sign—anything that might help him use his power. Yet he felt nothing inside.

The swarm organized above him. He heard his father's voice yards away, shouting behind the temple's red cloth.

Micah pulled the curtain away from the door, peering outside. "Afarôt, we can't open the ark!"

CHAPTER SIXTY-EIGHT

*N*o, Septis thought. *The ark!* He heard the girl's words and recalled the device's use from an age long ago. It had been the treasure of Solomon, kept in his temple along with what gave him his power—the ring. *If they have found the ark, then they must have also found weapon*, he thought. His confidence wavered, and for the first time, he felt his victory might be in jeopardy.

No longer concerned with healers and fledgling archangels, he maneuvered the hornets and sent them crashing against the domed building, but the effect was in vain. They scattered harmlessly into the air and turned back to dust.

A singular thought rang in his mind like the alarm sounding in the compound. *They have the ring! They have the ring!* No longer, he realized, could he toy with his meal. They had to die before the weapon could be used against him. *But if I can obtain it for myself, I could rule over all, even Mastema.*

Eyes closed as if in prayer, he called upon all the dark energy inside him. Shadows flowed back to him from the bodies of soldiers and the places hidden from the light cast by the towers and streetlamps. They found him where he stood and slithered up his legs and body, absorbing into his skin.

Septis could feel his power threatening to tear him apart as the shadows, fueled by the dark energies flowing inside the world, joined with his being, becoming part of him. Soon they could no longer be contained within his earthly shell. They came to the surface, churning over his skin in waves like an ocean in a storm.

Shock waves of invisible energy pulsated from his body, burning the air as they rolled out, hurling the remains of Afarôt's soldiers into the air.

His rage focused on the building that housed the girl and Afarôt. Only Gabriel stood alone outside, but he looked lost, bewildered, and horrified by the display of power.

Gabe watched the streetlamps burst above the man, showering him with falling sparks. Septis seemed to be engulfed by a spinning darkness, like he stood inside the eye of a hurricane. It whipped around his form, furious and angry.

But what worried Gabe the most was the intensifying rumble in the earth. His enemy no longer looked at him. Instead, all his efforts seemed focused on the temple, where his father and Micah were being helped by Afarôt.

As the shadow continued to build around Septis, the man

lifted his arm and leveled it at the small building housing the ark.

Flashes of Yuri turning on Carlyle by the River Wear ran through Gabe's mind. In an instant he was running toward the gated garden, desperate to reach his father and friends. He screamed in desperation, "Get out! Get out of the temple!"

Septis watched the boy run, laughing as the sensation of the power's release became impossible to hold back.

A jet of dark energy and shadow erupted from his outstretched hands like a cannon and traveled in a continuous trajectory over the ground toward the temple. With a precision hit, it collided with the building, sending a concussive blast rolling out from the impact. The explosion threw brick and wood in every direction. Glass and metal shattered out into the compound, knocking Gabriel from his feet.

With all his power released, Septis felt a sense of euphoria wash over him. He staggered slightly, winded from the effort, and steadied himself to survey the damage of his wrath. Smoke billowed up from a pile of rubble in a clearing where the temple had once stood. Almost certainly, everyone who had been inside was dead and all the dangers of the ark had been quelled.

Septis approached the steps leading to the gate. He mastered control of his growing excitement, remembering his mistake in New York when he'd been too quick to celebrate his victory. The mission, after all, was still incomplete. Gabriel remained alive.

Not for long.

CHAPTER SIXTY-NINE

The ringing in Gabe's ears was real this time, the hurt beyond that of any bruise or kick to the chest. He tasted blood, felt the cold electricity in the nerve endings of torn flesh. Blood trickled into his eye from a gash on his brow.

He lay on the ground amongst the debris of the former building. Gabe tried to sit up, but a knifing sensation in his arm traveled over his body. Then he saw stars and heard a cry of pain—his own. His right arm folded in an unnatural way, and he collapsed back to the ground.

It was broken. Badly.

Yet despite the severity of his injuries, he focused on what remained of the temple. Nearby, amongst the wreckage, he could see his father, thrown from where the temple had stood. He lay unmoving on top of a mangled and twisted part of the temple's steel gate. Memories of the future given to Gabe by the Entheos Genesthai found their way into his mind. Adrenaline surged through his body as he was struck by the realization—the vision had come true. His father was dead.

Gabe pushed his body into action, ignoring the debilitating pain in his arm, and crawled to his dad. As he approached he could see dust and smoke moving away from his father's mouth.

He's breathing, Gabe thought. Tears filled his eyes from the relief.

His dad opened his eyes. He made eye contact but didn't move. *Run*, he mouthed.

From the street, laughter bellowed out into the night from Septis. The sound was getting closer.

Scanning the wreckage, Gabe saw a wisp of black hair dancing amongst a pile of rubble entwined with uprooted plants and flowers in what had been the garden. He used all the strength he had to overcome the pain in his broken body and tried to get to his feet but buckled from the pain. His knees gave out instantly, unable to support his own weight. He managed to catch himself before collapsing and stumbled to Micah. Under a large slab of wall he found her, hair spread out on the ground and matted with blood, her sword gone, likely buried amongst the rock and debris.

She gasped for air, and Gabe could tell she was dying. All the color had drained from her face. She choked and coughed up blood, which trickled down her chin.

Gabe wiped it away. "Hold on, Micah. Please hold on. Everything will be okay," he said.

Her breaths came in short and fading gasps. Her eyes met his and told him everything. She didn't have long.

Gabe bent down and tried in vain to move the slab. It was as big as a person. He grabbed it with both hands and gritted his teeth through the torture of using his lame arm, but it was impossibly heavy and would not budge.

Tears streaked down the dirt on her face. It was a familiar

look, not unlike the one Gabe had seen in Carlyle before Yuri struck him down. The same feeling of helplessness to stop the inevitable consumed Gabe.

She knows.

"No," Gabe said, falling back to her side. Tears flowed uncontrollably down his face. "Please stay with me, Micah."

She reached up and touched his face, as if telling him it was okay.

Micah's eyes widened as the end took hold. In an attempt to draw in one last breath, she opened her mouth, struggling to find air. Then her eyes rolled back. The moment seemed to last a lifetime. Finally, her jaw slacked and her eyes shut.

CHAPTER SEVENTY

Something inside Gabe came alive, coursing through his veins like the warmth from the Entheos Genesthai.

In his refusal to accept what was happening to Micah, he felt himself surge, change. Anger turned to strength and found its way to the muscles in his body. "You're not leaving me," he shouted.

Gabe grabbed the slab again with his one good hand. The concrete crumbled in his grip. With enormous effort, he hurled the slab into the air, freeing Micah's broken body.

He didn't waste a second trying to make sense of anything, and in an instant he was on top of Micah, breathing air into her lungs. Her chest rose and fell with every breath he put inside. After a moment he stopped. Nothing happened. Her eyes were still open, vacant.

He tried breathing into her mouth again. Her chest filled with air once more, rising and falling with his efforts. He pulled away and waited. Still, nothing.

"Damn you, Micah. I can't do this on my own." Gabe's emotions overwhelmed him, and he beat his fist against her chest several times before diving back on top of her and blowing air into her mouth as hard as he could.

Micah's body shuddered, and Gabe felt her cough into his mouth. He pulled back, and her eyes rolled and fluttered shut. Her chest rose and fell, drawing a breath. It was weak, but she was breathing again.

"Poor girl," Septis said, watching from the street. "She is broken, can't you see? Very doubtful that she'll make it. Shame, I suppose. She was quite beautiful."

As Septis approached, Gabe's rage refocused on his enemy. He turned from Micah and pulled himself to his feet and faced him. If those he loved could be saved, he had to end this now. *I have power. Use it*, he told himself.

Gabe lifted his good arm, his hand covered in Micah's blood, and held it high like Yuri had done under the bridge in Durham and like Afarôt had done in the temple. He willed something to happen, but he was met with only silence. No bluish-white energy shot from his hand. Nothing struck Septis but another howling fit of laughter.

"Stupid boy. Do you really believe yourself to be an archangel? What lies have been laid upon you? You are a fraud. Many battles I have witnessed with their kind, and be assured, friend, you are not of their pedigree."

Gabe stood helpless, hearing the demon's words echo his own doubts.

And yet a voice in his head told him to believe. "*Have faith in yourself*," she said.

Septis moved for Gabe so quickly, there was little time to react before he was seized and lifted from the ground by the throat.

"I will eat your souls before the day is done. I'm especially looking forward to hers."

Gabe kicked his legs in the air and fought to breathe as Septis took measure. His other hand opened, palm aimed point-blank at Gabe's chest. Shadows swirled like vapors of smoke around his fingers.

With his good arm, Gabe gripped the wrist of Septis and tried to pry off his hand. He looked to Micah on the ground below and fought to free himself. A tingling sensation came alive on his skin, electrical, and not unlike the feeling he'd experienced when the soldiers had threatened them upon their arrival to the church. His clothes became charged with a building static.

Septis seemed mildly amused. "Is this the extent of your power? Pathetic."

Electrical currents traveled over Gabe's body. Small arcs of light leapt from his clothes to his captor's like tiny bolts of lightning. On his finger, the stone hidden under a swath of blood sparked.

Septis grabbed the wrist and turned it. The ring caught light cast from the gate tower, which had been toppled by the temple's explosion. It glistened through the blood on Gabe's finger. His enemy's eyes narrowed in a moment of confusion from the jewel's sheen.

Gabe also studied the ring, unsure of what was happening. It was warm on his finger, radiating power into his hand, up his arm, and into his body. He felt like he'd received a double shot of adrenaline after an overdose of caffeine. His muscles tightened, and he felt as though he could bend steel if he wanted.

The confusion in the face of Septis turned to something

else. His eyes grew wide as he apparently recognized the weapon on Gabe's hand. The demon gasped, and his mouth fell open in disbelief.

Gabe recognized the look. He'd seen it many times over the past days.

Fear.

All his doubts quieted in his mind. All the promises made by his father and Afarôt were now confirmed in the terrified eyes of his enemy. The engraved pentalpha began to glow. "It seems you are the fool," Gabe said. "I *am* the archangel Gabriel, *friend*."

The power grew inside Gabe, lit by the flame of hatred he felt for his enemy and what he'd done to those Gabe loved. But unlike the restraint he'd attempted with the soldier, Gabe allowed himself to lose control of the power. The electricity dancing over his clothes became a furious swarm of arcing bursts of lightning, his body a live wire. Like his vision before, his skin started to glow. It covered him like a glaze of liquid light and expanded outward, a barrier of humming energy, becoming something more. Something powerful and physical but raw and undeterred.

Dirt and rock were blown away from the ground where Septis stood still grasping Gabe. Winds swirling with debris spun around them like the eye of a hurricane. Its vibrations shattered boulders of rubble on the ground, reducing them to sand.

The feeling built into a crescendo that Gabe could no longer sustain. He felt the earth quake under Septis's feet, and as the light field began to quiver under its own power, Gabe saw the ring glow and knew his abilities were being augmented by the ring. A flare of blinding white ignited around them.

CHAPTER SEVENTY-ONE

The explosion separated Gabe from Septis and threw Gabe into the air. He landed hard on the concrete stairs by the compound gate. The blast carried Septis until he crashed against a building on the street below. The impact took down part of the roof and a wall.

Gabe rolled to his knees, overwhelmed by the pain in his arm and weakened from the release of energy. Exhaustion overcame his body, stripping away the fight inside. He'd hoped the ring did its job and that Septis had been killed by the blast.

However, as he watched the street below, the fallen wall pushed aside. Septis rose from the remains of the building, his clothes tattered. As he stood, Gabe could no longer see any reservation in his enemy's expression. Instead, Gabe was met by the hardened stare of a killer. Septis tore away his shredded shirt, revealing the full extent of the intricate scars on his body.

Gabe glanced at the ring, hoping it would do something, but the stone was once again cold, lifeless. Without help from the ring, Gabe knew he could do no more. He felt defeated, a failure, as he looked to the temple garden where Micah lay unconscious. Nearby, his dad was trying to crawl toward him, but Gabe knew his father could not protect him now.

Gabe watched as shadows flowed from the dark crannies of the surrounding buildings and found their master. They became alive and slithered over the ground like serpents toward the demon, leaping into the air, gnashing and striking out in anger, and Gabe now understood, like Carlyle had by the River Wear, that his last moment was upon him.

As Septis approached, he raised his arm, directing his dark creatures at their target. They raced forward, honing in like a pack of wild dogs let loose for the kill, their dark forms leaping from the flood of darkness that spilled forth over the ground, their excited hisses growing closer and closer to Gabe.

He dragged his mangled body to the bottom of the stairs, away from the view of his father, so as to spare him from having to witness the death of his only son.

The shadows followed. Hundreds of red eyes smoldered in the blackness, and the shadows resumed their animal forms that stretched and grew, clawing over one another to be the first to the prize.

At once they were upon Gabe. He watched as they rose into the air, blotting out the night sky, a wave of darkness that crashed down and engulfed his body.

CHAPTER SEVENTY-TWO

Shadows surrounded Gabe, enveloping him in a sort of spinning cocoon that forced the air out, creating a vacuum. He fought for a breath and felt as though he were drowning as his lungs began to collapse. Red eyes flashed by, and beastly heads opened their smoke-formed mouths to chatter their teeth, hissing in the storm.

A tasty morsel . . .

It looks delicious . . .

Bones to gnaw on . . .

The sphere of formless creatures lifted Gabe from the ground, and he let himself go limp as they held his body, beating against it, clawing and tugging at his legs and arms, as if he were being positioned.

The pain in his broken arm became unbearable as it was struck and manipulated, and he felt his consciousness slipping away. His eyes fluttered, and he started to pass out, but instead of fighting, Gabe welcomed the peace of the coming sleep. Images of the broken and disfigured soldiers in the street filled his head, and he accepted his fate as the same. He let go of all remaining hope and prayed he would die quickly.

He closed his eyes, and the world fell into a black silence. Time slowed, the shadow creatures' presence no longer felt. His mind drifted from the violence, somehow removed from his body. A familiar voice echoed in his mind.

"Why do you still not have faith in yourself, Gabriel? Even now?" Coren asked.

"I do have faith. I just can't win," he answered in thought.

"No, what you call faith is nothing more than acceptance. Faith requires true belief, and you have yet to truly believe in anything. Including yourself. Now you are defeated, and all is lost."

"You've made a mistake. I can't match the demon's strength. He's too strong."

"If that is what you choose to believe, then you are correct. Know that I, too, had a choice. I chose to bestow upon you the ring because I have faith that with it your enemy can be vanquished. Should you choose to believe and have faith in the power within and not just accept your world as it is, you may discover greatness beyond your ordinary dreams. But the choice is still yours to make. It always has been."

Searing pain in his arm shook him awake. He opened his eyes to see the walls of the shadow storm compacting around him, closing in for the final assault. In the blur of the passing shapes he caught glimpses of the street below flashing by between breaks in the sphere's shadow wall. Septis stood, manipulating his creatures with outstretched hands, leading his wretched symphony like a conductor.

Gabe could see that he was now being held several feet from the ground, arms outstretched, his body hung in a cruciform ready for the final strike. He turned toward the compound and saw in the gaps of the swarming beasts flashes of his father. The look of anguish stole Gabe's breath. His dad had raised him as a child of discipline. Taught to try his hardest at school and everything he wanted to do. Now he was a young man, his father's son. Asked to do the impossible. The unimaginable.

Yet his father still pushed him to do well in this, as he would something as trivial as a soccer game or a history test. He still pushed him to succeed, believing that in all Gabe ever set his mind and heart to, he was capable. A father's unconditional faith.

That is faith. Gabe realized he felt the same way about his dad. Even when Gabe doubted his father's intentions, he understood and believed that his father, with every breath he took, would always be at his side and would always love him. That, too, was faith.

Faith. Love.

His dad believed Gabe was special. Faith that he was not ordinary but different. Chosen. An archangel. And Gabe believed in his father. They shared a love that his father would not betray if he didn't truly believe Gabe could accomplish what had been asked of him. He knew because of his faith in his son that Gabe could stop the enemy.

He began to see himself through his father's eyes. It became real. True. And in himself, Gabe found his father's strength inspired by his love and faith. A purpose set into motion.

His purpose.

CHAPTER SEVENTY-THREE

rom a distance, Septis held control over the
shadow sphere that engulfed his hostage, his
hands reaching out before him, as if holding
the thing itself, palms moving to come together.
Responding to his will, the sphere tightened around
Gabriel Adam, spinning faster as it compressed. Across its
surface, shadow beasts swarmed in a fury of anticipation,
caught in a feeding frenzy. Claws and toothy snouts leapt
from its depths only to dive back into the middle, awaiting
the order to begin their feast.

Still recovering from the blast that had separated him
from the boy, Septis struggled to maintain control. Such a
surge could only be contributed to Solomon's Ring, but
Gabriel had not yet mastered the weapon. This pleased Septis,
and the reward he stood to gain filled his imagination. He
would crush his enemy, tear him apart, and let his pets feed.
From the archangel's corpse Septis would seize the ring for
himself, and he would reign over all in this realm. No one, not
even Mastema, would hold position above him.

Septis felt in the winds a new dawn approaching. With
the death of Fortitudo Dei, he would right all the injustice

done to his kind. The humans and their cancerous hold over Earth would be broken, and the pathway to the realm of creation would be shut forever.

The anticipation of the moment caused him to falter. He watched, and for a moment, he thought the sphere seemed to expand. Septis redoubled his efforts, pushing aside thoughts of glory to finish the deed. With all his strength, he tried to collapse the shadows around the boy and at last squeeze the life from him. Responding to the command, his creatures dove inward, forming a tight, smooth surface in the sphere, the shadows tightening, spinning faster.

But the sphere resisted manipulation. He fought to maintain control, but through his disbelief, Septis knew it was slipping away. The sphere had grown, and as it continued to do so, the integrity of its surface started to fail. From inside the center, he saw a flash of white light, and something screeched in pain, but the cry was not human.

On the surface, the shapes of his creatures formed again. They clawed at the sky and the ground as the ball spun, this time to escape.

"What is this?"

His answer came quickly. Shafts of light pierced the shadows of the sphere. One by one, they burst out from within to the sounds of his dying pets. The ground shook under Septis's feet until the sphere could no longer contain what was inside, and he knew now that he had failed.

The eruption struck with an inescapable force. A blinding starburst expanded out from the sphere and devoured the shadow creatures, tearing them apart like shrapnel as the light cut through their forms, extinguishing red eyes.

Septis could only watch as his fears were realized in the boy's newly discovered power. He fed off the ring, its glow pulsing from his outstretched hand, his body electrifying the air into a crackling display of energy. The boy seemed to hang, suspended above the stairs where the epicenter of the explosion had occurred, his back arched to the night sky above. Light took on a fluid form and reached out from his back like the wings of a great bird of prey. They unfolded, and Septis felt the excruciating warmth cast from their terrible magnificence. Once spread to their fullest, they began to dissipate into the air around as the boy descended to the ground. Pieces of light fell away like feathers shed from the wings until they had vanished entirely.

Anger lit within Septis like a torch. He would not concede without a fight.

CHAPTER SEVENTY-FOUR

Gabe breathed in as though his lungs had never known air. His heart beat as if for the first time. The ring in his hand pulsed with a pleasant calm that radiated into his body, masking the pain in his broken arm. He lifted his right arm to Septis, the jewel of the ring pointed at the demon. Gabe knew what to do.

Septis seemed to know as well. He began to change, his body undergoing a metamorphosis. His remaining clothes and human skin stripped away as flesh and bone grew, building new mass and shape. In an instant, he nearly tripled his original size. Hands elongated, transforming into claws. Talons tore through expensive shoes. Wings, skin-like and tethered to exposed bone, ripped from his back. Yellow eyes shone from a beastly head. Teeth filled his mouth as his jaw stretched, adjusting to its new length, until finally his new form was complete.

He looked like a deformed dragon made from human parts, turned inside out, pitiful and grotesque with an exposed bony structure built like an armored exoskeleton. Oozing muscle tissue stretched between the exposed ribs and vertebrae of an elongated neck adorned with a row of spiked scales on each side of the spine. Each fist-sized plate hooked from the beast's winding back to a point like rows of teeth in a shark's mouth.

Septis's ghastly form crouched on the ground, monstrous, breathing heavily and ready to strike.

"Do you think this is the end, boy?" Septis growled. "Do you think this is over?"

"It is for you," Gabe said.

Septis lashed out, his serpentine neck craning to an impossible length, attacking with an open mouth of razor-sharp teeth. "This realm is ours. We have rights."

Gabe didn't move. The ring glowed and seized the demon in midair.

"You are bound, Septis. You are no more."

The ring opened up, and from the jewel ropes of light were thrown at the demon, lassoing his arms and legs. His body ignited into flame where the ropes wrapped around the beast. Septis fought against the tangle of light, and Gabe felt his struggle jerk at the lines like a fish caught in a net.

More ropes of light flung out from the ring, covering and binding the wings and jaws together. Gabe could see them constrict, pulling tight, and the demon's bones cracked. Septis roared in agony as his body folded in on itself, his bones breaking down, yellow eyes disappearing into the threads of light, his body now a pyre of flame.

The ropes of light at last engulfed the demon in a mass of glowing twine. It then imploded, crushing its prisoner to nothing as if Septis had been dissolved by the ring's power.

On Gabe's hand, Solomon's Ring seemed to open a whirl-pool of spinning light that extended beyond his arm's reach. Ropes of light retreated into the jewel, swallowing whatever remained of the demon. Once again, the heirloom grew dark on his finger.

The enemy was gone.

CHAPTER SEVENTY-FIVE

With the ring's power fading, the warmth left Gabe's body. He staggered, suddenly filled with an oppressing exhaustion. Pain returned to his arm so great that he felt he might become sick on the street. His legs struggled to support his weight, and he knew ligaments in his knee had been torn.

He wasted little time thinking about the enemy's demise and turned toward the compound. Dawn was breaking on the horizon. As the sun's first light shone through, the full extent of the devastation was revealed in horrifying detail. Dead soldiers and refugees lay in the streets, their remains clawed open and chewed upon. But Gabe's concern was for the living. His father and Micah.

Gabe limped to where his father had fallen but could not find him.

"Gabriel!" his dad shouted from where the temple once stood. Gabe could see his father on the ground by the mangled red gate of the garden. He was waving frantically.

Relying on what little strength he had left, Gabe tried to ignore the searing cold of the pain in his broken parts and limped to his father's side. During the fight his dad had somehow managed to crawl over to Micah, and now he was attempting to comfort her.

Gabe looked at her, and the sight stole his breath. Tears welled in his eyes. The end was near. With each passing second, Micah's life slipped away. Gabe fell and looked into her half-opened eyes, but they were vacant and unresponsive. He brushed his fingers through her hair, moving the strands from her perfect face. Breathing came in shallow gasps, her skin cold to the touch.

Despite her state, Gabe thought she looked peaceful. He wondered if she even realized what was happening to her. He held her hand, massaging her fingers as tears trickled down his face.

His father reached for Gabe's shoulder. "It's okay. She'll be at peace soon. She'll be with God," he said.

Gabe found no comfort in the words. He didn't care about her being with God. He wanted her to be here with him.

Nearby, Afarôt emerged, digging himself out from under a pile of wreckage. He stood and brushed his clothes off. His shirt had been torn and a large bloodstain covered his hip, but he moved without favoring the leg, giving Gabe the impression he had not been injured.

"Afarôt, quickly!" his father said, his voice hoarse.

Seeing the broken girl, Afarôt ran to them. When he reached Micah, he shoved Gabe out of the way and kneeled beside her. He put a hand on her sternum and then one across her forehead.

"Barely," he said. Afarôt closed his eyes. His palms glowed like they did at the entrance to the tabernacle. Warmth radiated off his body and into Micah. The pools of blood gathered under her skin faded.

Gabe moved back from the growing heat as Micah was covered in a haze of light. Her body shuddered, and her back arched from the ground. Gabe thought of the electric paddles in hospitals used to revive a patient's heart. He could only watch and listen as Afarôt's power flowed into her, amazed by the sounds coming from beneath her skin. It was as if he could hear bones and tendons mending inside her legs and torso. "What are you doing to her?"

Afarôt smiled and in his heavy Ethiopian accent whispered, "I am not called Healer of God for nothing."

Her breathing got deeper and deeper. Gabe stared in disbelief as her dilated pupils shrank, revealing the brown in her eyes. She coughed. Her eyes fluttered for a moment. Finally, they opened, looking full of life.

Gabe's emotions overflowed, and he began to sob uncontrollably.

Micah looked at him, and a smile blossomed on her lips. "What happened?" she asked in a weak voice.

"I thought we'd lost you," Gabe said.

"Luckily we did not." Afarôt removed his hands and bent over her, beaming. "It seems Gabriel has managed to best the enemy."

She turned to Gabe, and her eyes seemed to sparkle in the soft light of dawn. "I never lost faith that you would."

Gabe laughed through the pain in his arm and wiped his eyes. "You could have told me that sooner. Between you and my father, I think I was the last to know."

Afarôt turned his attention to Gabe's dad, laying hands

on the injured leg, the light haze glowing over his body.

"My skin is tingling," his father said. He couldn't suppress his smile as he watched. "It feels like warm water but inside my muscles and bones."

Gabe was next. Afarôt sat beside him and looked at his arm, shaking his head as he did so and said, "Such an injury might have been your undoing. You have shown uncanny strength. Fortitudo Dei indeed. We all are very proud. But perhaps we should consider a less heroic method of dispensing with demons in the future should the enemy be inspired to try again. Perhaps some training, yes?"

"What happened to you?" Gabe asked. "Where were you?"

"I'm sorry, dear Gabriel. My injuries, too, were severe. It took some time for me to heal myself. I do hope you will forgive me."

Gabe nodded as the Ethiopian's hands warmed against his skin. Gabe felt the strange sensation of all the pain and injuries retreat from his body. His arm mended with a popping sound. The gash on his brow sealed. He put his hand to his forehead and felt not so much as a scratch. His knee became hot, and it felt like snakes moved under his skin as ligaments reattached themselves. Strength filled his joints and muscles as the sun began to rise above the distant orange hills.

"We shall be in need of the Vatican's services now, I think," his father said as Afarôt removed his hands from Gabe. "You wouldn't happen to have a phone nearby, would you?"

"In due time. But there is another matter to which we should attend first. You are a priest, are you not?" Afarôt stood along with Gabe's dad, and together they walked past the compound gate and into the streets.

Gabe noticed refugees emerging from where they hid, gathering around their fallen.

Micah sat up and followed Gabe's gaze to the carnage in the city. "I don't think the world will ever be the same after this."

"I don't, either. I think I'm learning to accept that." He stood and helped her to her feet. His father and Afarôt were comforting the people below. "This isn't over," Gabe said, facing Micah. "Septis said they wouldn't stop. Not until they got what was rightfully theirs."

"Maybe that's true, but regardless, at least we've managed to gain some time. When you're trying to stop the End of Days, time is the most valuable commodity there is. Besides, we have Solomon's Ring," she said. "And we have you."

"Maybe I sit the next one out and let you do all the heavy lifting."

Micah laughed and playfully punched his shoulder. "I think I'm going to see if there is anything I can do. Why don't you find someplace quiet and catch your breath?"

"I think that's a very good idea. Thanks."

"Thank you, Gabriel Adam," she said with a smile and left him to join his father and Afarôt.

Gabe turned and walked toward the main building, its white dome bright under the morning sun. As he walked, something glittered in the light, catching his eye. Under a loose pile of debris he found the Gethsemane Sword. Its blade shined through the dirt and dust covering the metal. He picked it up to give to Micah later.

Before he retired to the peaceful silence waiting inside

the main church, Gabe looked once again to the street below. He didn't notice the devastation anymore. He could only see Micah putting her arm around a crying woman, consoling her. He wanted nothing more than to hold Micah in his arms and tell her all the things he felt for her in his heart, but there would be plenty of time for that later.

Gabe cupped the ring in his hands and studied the faded sheen of the band and the dark jewel lit by the clearing blue sky. There was comfort in knowing what he could do with it, but even as powerful as it had been, Solomon's weapon paled next to the strength given to him from those he loved. He knew the future was uncertain, but for now, none of that mattered. Whether the enemy would rise from these ashes and try again to cast the world into darkness was a question that didn't much interest him at the moment. Instead, he watched his father below and the life shining in Micah's face.

All was well, and he could not wish for anything more.